Murder on Tyneside

Murder on Tyneside

Agnes Lockwood Mysteries Book One

Eileen Thornton

Acknowledgement

I would like to thank everyone at Creativia Publishing for their help and support during the writing process.

As always, for my husband Phil.

Chapter One

Agnes Lockwood pulled up her collar. She realised she should have worn her scarf. But with the sun beaming through the window of her hotel room, she had thought it wouldn't be necessary.

It felt good to be back on Tyneside at last. A number of years had passed since she'd last been here. Coming back to visit the place of her birth was something she had wanted to do for a long time. Yet, somehow, there had never been time. Even from the age of twelve, when her family left the area, her life had run in the fast lane. Until now, some forty years later, there had never been time to slow down and reflect on the past.

It all began when her father had been offered an important diplomatic post in France, which resulted in her family making the move away from Tyneside. On their return, her father was offered a job based in London. Therefore it was impractical for them to live too far from his place of work. Looking back, it seemed strange they had never found time to visit Tyneside.

But now, having finally made the decision to visit the north east, Agnes had chosen to stay in a hotel on the quayside – once the very heart of Tyneside.

Agnes moved across the pavement to the edge of the quay and looked down at the River Tyne. It was certainly much cleaner than she remembered. When she was last here, it had seemed more like a mud bath than an imposing river flowing through the city to the North

Sea. Back then, it was said you only had to jump into the Tyne and you would die through the sheer pollution in the water.

Still gazing down at the river, it occurred to her there must have been accidents back then; where men died because they slipped and fell into the murky water. Some may have even taken their own lives by throwing themselves into the river, because they had found life too hard to bear. But worse still, how many might have been brutally murdered; their bodies thrown into the water never to be seen again?

She shuddered at the thought. Thankfully those days were over. Glancing back along the quayside, she realised it wasn't just the river that was clean; the whole place had changed. The heavy industry of Tyneside had long disappeared making way for cafés, restaurants and other more genteel activities.

Even though Agnes hadn't been in the city when the changes were taking place, she had read about what was happening. Yet she still hadn't been prepared for it to be quite so fashionable. She sighed as she turned away from the river and leaned back against the railings. The past was gone; there was no point her dwelling on it. Like the people who still lived here, she needed to change with the times. To move on. But move on where? What did the future hold for a widow of a certain age?

She scolded herself for having such negative thoughts. First of all, she needed to pull herself together and stop dreaming about the past. Life had been good to her.

Jim Lockwood had been a wonderful husband and a devoted father. A smile broke across her lips as she thought about her boys. They were men now. Married and living on the other side of the world. Yet to her, they would always be 'her boys'.

Though there had been a number of years before Jim was due to retire, they had made plans to visit their sons more often when that day came. What would there be to stop them? They would have both the time and the money. Jim had held down a good job with the foreign office and had saved a great deal of money over the years to make sure they had a comfortable retirement. But then, all too soon, an aggressive form of cancer had taken Jim from her and her world had fallen apart. She sniffed and blinked back the tears forming in her eyes. It just wasn't fair.

Her boys had wanted her to sell up and move out there with them when their father had died and, for a short while, she had been sorely tempted. Yet she had decided against the idea, firmly telling them they had their own lives to lead.

Pulling herself together, she glanced at her watch. Very soon she would need to return to her hotel and change for dinner. She looked back towards where her hotel was situated and was surprised to find that she hadn't actually walked very far. Perhaps she had time to continue on to the foot of the Tyne Bridge before turning back. Tomorrow it could be raining and she didn't relish the idea of stomping along here in the rain. If that were the case she would prefer to take a trip into the town centre and do some shopping.

* * *

Back at the hotel, Agnes took a shower before deciding what to wear for the evening; she had brought far too many clothes. In the end, she chose a deep blue dress with matching shoes and bag. Being tall and slim, finding clothes had never been a problem for her. Jim always used to tell her she looked good in whatever she chose and he was proud at having her by his side.

She pulled on her dress and checked in the mirror as she smoothed it down. But then she frowned; were a few grey hairs beginning to show? Moving nearer to the mirror, she took a closer look hoping she was mistaken. However it was no mistake. Her auburn hair was starting to change colour – and it wasn't a colour she favoured. She sighed as she turned away from the mirror. Had they appeared overnight? They weren't there yesterday. She was going to have to visit the hairdresser when she got back home.

She was just about to go down to dinner, when she heard raised voices outside her door. She sat down on the bed, deciding to wait a few minutes until the people had moved on before venturing out into the corridor. They might be embarrassed if she suddenly appeared in the middle of what sounded like a row. However, the voices grew louder and though she didn't mean to pry, she couldn't help hearing most of what was being said.

It seemed that the lady had lost a necklace or more to the point, she believed it had been stolen from her room while she was out shopping that afternoon. The gentleman with her didn't agree. He was trying to calm her down, saying that it couldn't possibly have been stolen. She must have put it down somewhere and forgotten where.

"You are always doing that, my dear," the man told her. He spoke slowly, obviously trying to soothe the woman. "Give it some thought while we have dinner, you'll soon remember where you put it."

However the lady wasn't in the mood to be pacified. "I distinctly remember putting it in the top drawer of the dressing table before we left." She insisted. "Yet when I went to put it on this evening it was missing. Don't you realise that the necklace was the one you gave me for our Wedding Anniversary. It must have cost you the earth."

There was a pause and for one brief moment, Agnes thought they had gone. She was about to open her door when she was suddenly startled by a loud screech from the woman outside.

"Oh my goodness, George; don't you realise? Someone must have been in our room while we were out." Her voice became hysterical. "I could have walked in and found some intruder going through our things; I could have been murdered. Call the police right now!"

"Calm down, Angela. There is no need to call the police. No one came into our room..." George began.

But with the thought of an intruder scouring through her personal belongings, Angela was not about to be silenced. "How the hell would you know?" she yelled. "You weren't even there. You stayed down-stairs in the bar with your so-called, business partners." There was a slight pause. "I want to see the manager – now! Are you coming with me or are you going to sit back and leave everything to me as usual?"

The voices grew faint as the man and woman hurried off down the corridor.

Agnes took the room key out of her bag and stared down at it. It wasn't an old-fashioned conventional key. It looked more like a credit card, which you placed into a slot on the door. When withdrawn, a green light flashed to tell you the door was unlocked. She recalled the first time she had used this type of key. She and Jim had been staying in a hotel in Las Vegas.

He had been amused at her attempts to unlock the door to their room. "It's simple," he'd said. "Slide the card into the slot; remove it and open the door."

Yet when she tried, a red light appeared and the door had refused to open. Only when Jim explained she was being too hasty in removing the card and needed to slow down, was she able to gain access to the room.

Now she was fine with this new-fangled idea and thought it was probably a lot safer than a standard lock. They could be picked by some unscrupulous guest staying at a hotel.

She looked towards the door and screwed up her eyes as she gathered her thoughts together. So, if there was no lock to pick, how could someone have managed to get into the woman's hotel room without one of these magic key cards? It wasn't possible. Unless one of the staff, having seen the lady wearing the necklace sometime during the day, had decided that it might be worth stealing.

Some members of staff had access to what was called a master key card, which opened all the doors to the guest rooms. These were only meant to be used by domestic staff when they serviced the rooms. Was it possible they were kept in a place where they could be accessed by other staff?

Agnes shook her head. For goodness sake, she needed to get a grip. Jim had often said she had read far too many *Agatha Christie* novels and was always trying to solve a crime when there was no crime to solve.

Perhaps George was right. This Angela, whoever she was, might be the sort of woman who put things down and then forgot about them. He should know. He was probably her husband. If not, then he must know her well enough for them to be sharing a room. Agnes thrust her key back into her bag and hurried down to dinner.

Chapter Two

The smell of food wafting from the kitchen as Agnes entered the Dining Room made her realise how hungry she was. She enjoyed her meal so much it was only now, as she ordered coffee and a liqueur, that she really noticed the other people in the dining room.

Everyone looked smartly turned out. No one was wearing jeans. But then, being fairly new on the scene, the hotel was rather up-market. There were a few of the diners wearing more elaborate outfits. Agnes assumed they were going somewhere else after dinner. She knew there were a number of theatres and concert halls in the city.

Though she wasn't the only person sitting at a table set for one, she noted that most of the tables had at least two diners. There were even a few tables with six or more people enjoying dinner together. She suddenly felt conspicuous at being alone.

She heaved a sigh. Jim had been gone for almost a year. She should be getting used to it by now. And she was – normally. But there were times when she felt it would be nice to have someone with whom to have dinner now and then or even the occasional drink.

It was while she was sipping her coffee that she became aware of loud voices coming from somewhere in the corridors outside the dining room. Some of the guests sitting nearest to the door leaned back and forth, trying to see out into the reception area. But judging from the shaking of heads, Agnes guessed they couldn't see who was doing all the talking.

As the voices grew louder, Agnes realised that they were the same people she had heard in the corridor outside her room. Until now, she had completely forgotten about the incident.

"I'm telling you that you have a thief on your staff! I suggest you start searching their belongings before someone leaves the building with my necklace." There was no mistaking Angela's high-pitched voice.

"Madam, I can assure you that we will speak to all the members of our staff. But I am certain no one working at this hotel stole your necklace."

Agnes didn't recognize the man's voice, but she guessed he must be the manager. He sounded as though he was trying to stay calm, yet his tone told her he was becoming very exasperated with this particular guest.

"Don't give me all that rubbish. I want the police informed this minute." By now Angela was in full flow. Nothing was going to stop her from having her say. "I refuse to be fobbed off any longer! The necklace was a surprise gift from my husband. Tell him, George."

"My dear, it…" George didn't get any further as his wife continued her rant.

"If you don't get on the phone right now, I will speak to your Head Office."

"Very well, I will call the police," the manager said. "Can we please go into my office while we sort this out? I have no wish to continue this discussion in the hotel reception."

"Yes, a good idea, Mr Jenkins. Thank you. Come along my dear, the manager's office is just across the hall. It will be more private. We can talk about it there. I'm sure we don't need to involve the police." George sounded as though he would like to be a thousand miles away.

"Very well. We shall go to your office, Mr Jenkins." Angela retorted. "But, be aware, I have far from finished this conversation. And, George, what are you talking about? Of course the police must be called."

There were a few more words spoken and then there was silence in reception.

Agnes glanced around the dining room as everyone resumed their own conversations. It had gone very quiet during the row in the reception area. It seemed she hadn't been the only one eavesdropping.

* * *

After dinner, Agnes went through to the Drawing Room. She hadn't wanted to go straight back to her room where she would be on her own. At least being here she was among lively people and, even if she wasn't part of their group, their enthusiasm added a spark of life to her otherwise quiet world.

Agnes gazed around the room, taking in her surroundings. The hotel had been newly built during the renovation of the quayside. At first she thought that perhaps it might have been better if they had kept the façade of whatever had stood here previously and added a new interior. Some of the cafés and restaurants seemed to have done that. But maybe that wouldn't have worked in this case. She recalled that the Court House, a short distance from the hotel, was also a brand new building.

Everything about the hotel was modern, including this room. The sofas were comfortable, the walls were decorated with expensive draperies and to top it all, there were large ornate mirrors reflecting different aspects of the room. But then she noticed a couple of the mirrors were placed at such an angle, areas of the reception and the entrance to the hotel could be seen from where she was sitting.

How creepy is that? she thought. *If we, sitting in here can see who is entering the hotel, does that mean that anyone standing at the entrance can peer inside and see people sitting in here?*

Agnes deliberated as to whether to change her seat, but decided to stay where she was. Other guests in the Drawing Room might think she was crazy if she suddenly started moving from one sofa to another. Instead, she turned away from the mirror and began to think about what she might do the following day.

A trip to the shopping centre seemed a good idea. She simply adored shopping. But she also wanted to visit the places of her childhood in the hope she would meet someone from her past; though she did wonder if she would recognize anyone. Many years had passed since she had lived here. People changed as they grew older. For goodness sake, even she had changed over the years. She looked nothing like she did on her old school photos.

She glanced around at the people in the room. There could be people here whom she had met all those years ago, but couldn't recognize now. What was she doing here? Why was she trying to rake up her past? There wasn't anything she could identify herself with any more. It had seemed such a good idea at the time, but now she realised it was a big mistake – for more reasons than one…

She was just about to go back to her room, when she heard more raised voices in reception. It seemed the police had arrived. At least Angela would be happy now. Though for everyone else it could mean the hotel would be in turmoil while guests and their rooms were searched.

Instead of being upset at such disorder, Agnes hid a smile. It would be different from the usual mundane ritual she was becoming used to. It would be exciting to be considered a suspect in a police enquiry.

Of all the wonderful, crazy things she and her husband had done in the past, they had never been under suspicion of theft and had their room searched. She clapped her hands together. This was a first. How Jim would have loved it. Perhaps things were beginning to look up.

Chapter Three

By now Agnes had joined the crowd gathering in the Reception. They were told that once the police questioned all the staff who was still on duty, they would need to speak to the guests. Meanwhile no one could leave the hotel.

The manager was horrified at the thought. He said he could not allow it; insisting no one could enter any of the hotel rooms without a key card. "It is absolutely impossible."

Agnes felt a little sorry for him. This was certainly not good news for the hotel. She looked at the people standing near the manager, wondering whether Angela was one of them. Her eyes rested on a woman who seemed to be bursting to say something. Surely that had to be Angela.

She was about forty-five or thereabouts. It was hard to tell as her face was layered with make-up. She was wearing a closely-fitted, dark red dress. But, at the moment, Agnes's eyes were fixed on her necklace. It looked very expensive. If the one she'd had stolen was similar, it was little wonder she was making such a fuss.

Agnes was proved to be right when the woman finally got the chance to butt in.

"That's rubbish!" Angela said, wagging her finger at him. "We read about people hacking into computers all the time. I'm sure such a scoundrel could devise a master key card to every hotel room as simple as that." She snapped her fingers. "I absolutely insist that every room be thoroughly searched right now." She was so enraged her face had almost turned as red as her dress and her long dangling earrings shook violently as she spoke. "Someone here has stolen my valuable necklace given to me by my lovely husband. I want it found and the thief prosecuted."

Agnes looked at the men standing nearby, wondering which one was the 'lovely George'. He hadn't said a word during the whole episode in reception. However, for some reason after Angela's last remark, one of the men opened his mouth to say something. But he didn't get the chance, as Angela held up her hand to interrupt him.

"George, I am dealing with this. Leave it to me."

Without another word, George pushed his way through the crowd and headed towards the bar.

Agnes watched him disappear into the bar. She thought he looked relieved to be out of the spotlight. Summing him up, she thought he appeared to be slightly older than his wife, quite tall, and rather slimly built. Probably a very attractive man in his youth, but at the moment he looked as though he was carrying the world on his shoulders.

Agnes understood how upset Angela must be at having a gift from her husband stolen while they were out enjoying themselves, however the woman did seem to be a bit of a dragon where he was concerned. Did she really have to act so – dominant?

She placed her hand over her mouth to suppress a giggle. Dominant! Where did that come from? But somehow it seemed to fit nicely with Angela's personality. It was possible George enjoyed his wife being dominant in the boudoir. He did look like the tall, silent type. Maybe Angela just carried it a little too far when they were in the real world.

"I am so terribly sorry for the inconvenience." The voice of Mr Jenkins interrupted Agnes's thoughts. He had disappeared into his office for a few minutes, but now he was back trying to soothe the throng of guests who had gathered to see what all the fuss was about. He took out his handkerchief and mopped his forehead. "I have spoken with a police superintendent and it seems that I have little choice, but to allow a complete search of all the rooms at the hotel. However," he held up his hand when the people standing in front of him began to protest. "However," he repeated. "I insisted that a senior police officer is placed in charge of the investigation – someone who will respect the privacy of our guests. I am pleased to say the superintendent has agreed." He paused. "Meanwhile, I have been asked to inform you that no one will be allowed to leave the hotel until the search has been made. But I am assured it will be carried out as soon as possible."

By now, the reception area was buzzing with activity. Agnes looked around at her fellow guests. There was some making a fuss – most especially the ones she had previously thought might be spending the evening at a concert. Others were calling friends and relatives on their mobile phones to pass on the news of them being held inside the hotel.

"No June, we're not being held at gunpoint," Agnes heard one woman yell down her phone. But, the way the woman went on to describe the scene, they might well have been. However, most were making their way to the bar. To them, it seemed a stiff drink was called for.

"Does that mean we won't be able to check out this evening?" said a man to one of the police officers.

"Yes it does," replied the officer. "Is that a problem for you?" he added narrowing his eyes. Could this man be the culprit anxious to get out of the hotel?

"Heck, no," said the man, his American accent showing through. "We're on our honeymoon and would love an extra night here. That's great, man – err, I mean, officer."

Agnes left the reception area and went back into the Drawing Room. Despite her previous thoughts on the strategically placed mirrors, she chose a sofa where she could see most of what was going on outside in reception. For a while it was quite calm. A few people checked in at the desk, most of the new guests had already arrived earlier in the day. But, she noticed that after being given the keycard to their room, they were shown across to the Drawing Room, where complimentary drinks were offered for the inconvenience.

However, the calmness was about to be broken as Mr Jenkins, accompanied by another man, appeared from his office. They both walked across to the reception desk, where Mr Jenkins spoke to one of the staff on duty. She nodded and rang the small bell on the desk.

Some of the people sitting in the bar and the Drawing Room went out to see what was going on.

"Chief Inspector Johnson would like to speak to you all," called out the manager, once he had their attention. "I'm sure the chief inspector won't detain you any longer than necessary." He nodded towards the detective, indicating he could begin his inquiry.

"I understand how inconvenient this must be to everyone staying at the hotel. However, it seems that one of the guests has had a rather valuable necklace stolen and..." the chief inspector was interrupted.

"She's simply mislaid it." The voice came from the back of the reception area. "She does this sort of thing all the time."

Agnes recognised George's voice, even though his words were very slurred. Obviously he'd had too much to drink.

"Will you stop saying that? I have not mislaid my necklace," Angela hissed. "It has been stolen!" She paused when she realised all eyes were now pinned on her. "I'm sorry, inspector, do please carry on."

"Chief Inspector," he corrected her before continuing. "As I was saying we need to search each guest and also their rooms before anyone is allowed to leave the hotel. We'll begin with those guests who need to check out this evening." He paused when one of the officers whispered something in his ear. "I have been reminded that some people are going to the concert being held in The Sage this evening. Therefore we will try to check your rooms first." He nodded towards his sergeant, before continuing. "I'm sure we can do this in an orderly manner and get it over with as quickly as possible. My sergeant will take the names of all those who need to leave the hotel this evening for whatever reason."

The moment the chief inspector stopped speaking, everyone started talking, Agnes stood there wondering what to do next. Should she go into the Drawing Room and wait until she was called. She was booked into the hotel for another five days and hadn't any plans for the evening, which meant there was no rush for her or her room to be searched right away.

She glanced across at the chief inspector. He looked rather tired. Perhaps he had just been about to go off duty when this call came through to his office. Or was it simply because he saw this as another case where some over-rich woman had hidden her necklace in a safe place in her room, but then forgot where she had put it.

Agnes couldn't help thinking Chief Inspector Johnson was a rather attractive man, despite the lines of tiredness etched on his face. Placing her head on one side, she peered at him inquisitively and made a guess that he was about her age. He was rather tall, clean shaven and his dark hair was showing a hint of grey at the sides. Something she thought made him look rather distinguished. He was wearing a dark grey suit, white shirt and a dark grey tie. She noted that his shoes were so polished, he would be able to see his face in them should he ever be caught without a mirror.

But then she realised that all police detectives wore suits these days; it was their badge of office so to speak. She guessed that the character in the TV show, *Morse* probably had a lot to do with that. But this particular detective's suit looked a cut above regular suits. Could it be handmade? She wondered whether the wages of the police force stretched to hand made suits.

Agnes blushed slightly and looked away quickly when the chief inspector glanced over in her direction. She casually walked across to the window, but, out of the corner of her eye, she could see that he was still watching her. Did he think she looked guilty? She really had to stop trying to analyze people. Jim always said it would get her into trouble one day. But she couldn't help herself. It was simply a habit she couldn't break.

Agnes was staring out of the window at the bright coloured lights on the quayside, when the Chief Inspector spoke to her.

"Excuse me," said the detective.

Agnes caught her breath; she hadn't heard him approach. Rather surprising, she thought, policemen were known for their big feet. Pushing the thought from her mind, she turned around to face him.

"Yes," she said, giving a broad smile.

"I'm sorry to bother you, but are you Agnes Harrison by any chance?"

Agnes peered at the detective. It had been some years since anyone had called her by her maiden name.

"No – yes – no," she sighed and shook her head. Now she was beginning to sound like an idiot. "Can I start again?"

The detective grinned. His brown eyes twinkled and he nodded for her to continue.

"I was Agnes Harrison before I was married. I am Agnes Lockwood now." She peered at him. "Should I know you?"

"My name is Alan Johnson. I think we were in the same class at school."

"Alan Johnson," Agnes repeated the name twice to herself before she made the connection. "Yes! I think I remember you. You were always talking about joining the army. Or was it the air force?"

"The army," he confirmed. "Yes that was me."

"And did you? Join the army, I mean."

"Yes, I did."

Agnes gave a slight grin. *That would account for his smart suit and polished shoes,* she thought. "But now you are with the police force?"

"Yes – long story." He hesitated. "Look, you will have gathered that I'm rather tied up at the moment," he said, glancing back at the commotion going on behind him. The quiet atmosphere of earlier had quickly changed into chaos as people realised that the search was really going to happen. "But would you care to meet up with me later for a drink in the bar? We could catch up with what has happened to us over the years. Ask your husband to join us," he added, suddenly noticing the wedding ring on her finger.

"Thank you," Agnes replied. "That would be nice. However, I'm afraid it will just be me. My husband died a year ago."

"I'm sorry to hear that. I best get back to the investigation," he added, changing the subject. "I'll meet you in the bar in about an hour or so."

Agnes watched until he disappeared into the crowd by the reception desk. His sergeant looked relieved to see him return; the guests were becoming a little more agitated. The sergeant then glanced in her direction and frowned. He was probably wondering who she was. Or, might he be thinking she was a suspect?

She turned back to the window. It seemed she had a date. It would make a nice change having someone to sit with in the bar or the lounge. She had felt the odd one out since she had arrived at the hotel. It would be fun talking about all their old friends at school and as Alan still lived in this area it was possible he was still be in touch with a few of them. If that was the case, she would ask him to make arrangements for a re-union. After all, that was the reason for her visit to Tyneside in the first place.

She glanced at her watch. There was time for her to pop up to her room and freshen up. She almost skipped up the stairs and very nearly bumped into Angela at the top. Angela was wearing her glum face and didn't even try to smile when Agnes apologized.

But, at that moment, Agnes couldn't care less. Tonight, at fifty five years old, she had a date!

Chapter Four

Alan was already in the bar when Agnes arrived. Though she had given him a little longer than an hour, she was rather surprised he had found the time to change from his suit into something a little less formal. Though she had to admit, he still looked very smart in his jacket and casual trousers.

"I explained to my sergeant what I wanted him to do and left him to it," he said, as Agnes sat down.

"Are you allowed to do that?" Agnes asked. "I mean, is he okay with you shooting off on a date at the beginning of an investigation. According to Angela her stolen necklace is worth a great deal of money."

"Allegedly stolen, there is a difference."

"Don't you believe her? Angela seems very sure it has been stolen." She thought back to the angry voices earlier that evening. "Yet you think she might simply have mislaid it after all." Agnes leaned forward, rested her chin on the palm of her hand and screwed up her eyes. It was something she always did when she thought hard about a problem.

Alan shrugged. "That's what we have to find out."

Agnes's eyes widened. "So you think there may be another possibility?"

He shrugged again and then smiled. "But we haven't met up after all these years simply to talk about Mrs Hargreaves' necklace."

"Yes, you're right. Sorry." Agnes sat back in her chair. She was slightly disappointed they weren't going to discuss the case any further. This was the first real life investigation she had been caught up in. It was exciting. It was different. For goodness sake, it was so very different from the dull day to day life she now had to get used to. "Okay, do you remember anyone else from way back yonder – and, are you still in touch with any of them?

"Yes and yes quite a few of them actually. There was a get-together organized by a couple of old class mates just over a year ago." replied Alan, slowly. "But I gather from your tone, you are more interested in the case I'm working on than talking about the past." He raised his hand to catch the eye of passing waiter.

"Yes, I am, simply because I enjoy mysteries – *Miss Marple* and *Hercule Poirot* that sort of thing. I…" She broke off. Alan was staring at her. Did he think she had something to do with the missing necklace? "Oh my goodness, you don't think I took the necklace, do you?"

"Good heavens no. Of course not."

They both laughed and Agnes noticed that, for an instant, the tired lines on his face disappeared.

"I was just a little surprised at your interest," he added. "But I can't discuss an ongoing case with anyone, you should know that."

"Yes, you're right of course. So how did the reunion go?" Agnes asked, changing the subject.

The waiter took their order and disappeared back to the bar.

"It went very well indeed," said Alan, catching up on their conversation. "There were far more people than I thought there would be. Several had made the trip up from different parts of the country. It was just as well they had booked a fairly large venue."

"I would love to have been there," said Agnes. "But I'm afraid I lost touch with everyone after we moved away." She paused; allowing her thoughts to travel back over the years. "A few of us promised to write to each other, and we did for a while," she continued. "But you know how it is…"

The waiter brought the drinks and Alan paid him, telling him to keep the change.

Agnes was enjoying the evening so much, she didn't realise how late it was until the barman called for last orders. She was feeling rather sorry it was all about to end very soon.

"How long are you staying at the hotel?" Alan asked. "It's just I thought we might get together again before you have to rush off back to – where did you say you were living now?"

"I don't think I said," Agnes laughed. "Can you believe it? We have chatted about everything and everybody in our past, but I don't think we actually said much about ourselves – what either of us did after leaving school."

Alan took a sip of his drink and set his glass down. He cocked his head to one side.

"I take that to mean you want me to go first." Agnes grinned. "Okay, briefly, as I can see the guy behind the bar is getting agitated. I used to be a Personal Secretary with a large firm in London, until we had the boys. After that I became a full time mum. I did get a part time job when they went to school and carried on working until a couple of years ago. Now I am a lady of leisure, living in Essex at the moment. My two sons live on the other side of the world, in Australia to be exact!"

"You say you're living in Essex at the moment, does that mean you are planning to move somewhere else? Perhaps even to Australia, to join your sons?"

"No, not Australia," said Agnes thoughtfully, "though my boys asked me to join them out there after Jim died. They were worried about how I would cope on my own. But I decided against it. I told them that I didn't want them to feel they had to look out for me all the time. I wanted them to get on with their lives, just the way Jim and I did."

"But they wouldn't have always been looking out for you," ventured Alan. "I mean with you there, not far from where they were living, they would have been able to pop in to see you or vice versa."

"Yes, you're right," Agnes agreed, "but not all the time. Like I said, they have their own lives to lead. There was a long pause before she continued. "They need to do their own thing without them having to

watch out for their mother all the time. Jim and I did our own thing."
For a moment her eyes sparkled as she spoke of Jim. "We both worked
hard and we played hard. Together we saw the world." By now her face
was flushed with excitement. "We did the most wonderfully stupid
things and we enjoyed every minute of it because, let's face it, you
only get one crack at life. We wouldn't have listened to our parents.
They knew that, so they never interfered."

She looked down to the floor and sighed heavily.

"But that's not the reason you didn't go out there, is it? Alan spoke
quietly. "You wouldn't have interfered in their lives. You would have
given them your blessing on whatever they wanted to do."

Agnes looked up at him and blinked back the tears welling in her
eyes.

"No," she said. "The truth is I was scared. I was scared of moving to
a new country and I was scared at having to make new friends.

At last she was admitting, even to herself, why she hadn't gone out
there to join them. All this time she had told everyone it was because
she was worried she would be stopping the boys from getting on with
their lives.

"That's the reason I didn't take up their offer. I was terrified of taking
such a big step alone. If Jim had put forward the idea that we went out
there to live, I would have gone with him without a second thought.
He was my rock. But to go on my own, that is different." She looked
Alan in the eye. "Can you even begin to understand what I'm talking
about?"

Suddenly feeling uncomfortable, she turned away. How could she
have poured out her emotions to a relative stranger? She glanced towards the bar and held up her glass. She needed another drink.

"They called last orders ten minutes ago," said Alan, quietly.

"That doesn't apply to me. I'm staying here at the hotel. The bar is
still open for residents. Do you want another drink or will your wife
be expecting you back?"

Chapter Five

Agnes awoke the next morning with a dreadful headache. She'd had far too much to drink the previous evening. But her outburst had left her feeling rather embarrassed and the alcohol had helped hide her discomfort. Alan had been very kind. Changing the subject, he had told her a few things about himself.

He had been married, but he and his wife were divorced. For some strange reason, once he and his fiancée had tied the knot everything had gone wrong. "Everything was perfect before the ceremony. We were so happy together we both thought it was the real deal. Yet the moment we were married, everything changed." He had paused at that point as he thought back to the divorce. "It was so strange," he said picking up the story. "Once we were back from our honeymoon, we couldn't agree on anything." He shrugged. "I suppose some would say the magic was over."

Alan had gone on to tell her that he had never thought about remarrying. "Footloose and fancy-free – that's me." Yet there was something in his voice that told her he would give marriage another whirl if the right lady came along.

Agnes showered and dressed before heading down to breakfast. Alan had said he would be calling at the hotel again to carry on with the enquiries. Perhaps she would bump into him and learn a little more about the case. She frowned; he wasn't really allowed to talk about ongoing enquiries. But surely it wouldn't hurt if she just happened to be around when he made some startling discovery.

The Dining Room was almost empty when she walked in. Some of the guests would have checked out by now, while others probably wanted to get an early start on a full day of sightseeing.

Agnes was still making her way across to her table, when she noticed a young woman sitting alone at a table in a corner of the room. She was focused on something in the newspaper she was reading. But quite suddenly she folded the paper and stood up to leave.

Agnes was a little intrigued as she watched the woman walk across the Dining Room. It was almost as though she had read something upsetting. But Agnes shrugged it off. Why did she have this thing about construing more into what people did? Perhaps the woman had simply finished breakfast and had decided to leave. Or maybe she suddenly realised the time and was late for an important appointment. She was very smartly dressed. Her skirt and blouse were perfectly matched.

The woman didn't look in Agnes's direction as she made her way to the door. However she did manage to give the waiter a thin smile as he rushed forward to clear her table.

Agnes promptly forgot about the woman when she noticed a couple of policemen hanging around the reception area, though there wasn't any sign of the chief inspector.

A waiter brought her the menu and after glancing at it briefly, she decided to have the full English breakfast. "To hell with the diet," she laughed as the waiter wrote it down. He told her she didn't need to diet, as he headed off towards the kitchen. It was true. She had never had a weight problem. Most of her friends had always envied her slim figure.

She had almost finished breakfast when she saw Alan passing the entrance of the Dining Room. When he saw her, he gave some instructions to his sergeant, before strolling in to join her. The sergeant nodded and made his way over to the lift.

"Good morning, Alan. Do sit down and have some coffee." She gestured to the chair opposite her, before attracting the waiter's attention making signs that she needed another cup. "Are you any further forward in finding the missing necklace?"

"No, I'm afraid not," he said, as he sat down. He paused as the waiter placed a cup and saucer in front of him. "The rooms we have checked so far have all been cleared," he continued. He looked down at a piece of toast in the toast rack. "Is that going spare? I missed breakfast this morning."

"Yes, help yourself. I have had more than enough to eat." She leaned forward as she poured some coffee into Alan's cup. "I saw the lovely Angela this morning. She seemed rather subdued. Certainly nothing like the woman we heard ranting yesterday. Her husband was with her; he looked even more fed up than ever."

Alan turned and looked around to make sure no one could hear him. "Well she doesn't need to rant about it anymore. It seems she has friends in high places."

"What do you mean," asked Agnes.

"She's got the Chief Constable involved. He's asked me to do everything necessary to find the necklace as quickly as possible." Alan gave the hint of a smile. "I suppose he wants her off his back and I can't say I blame him."

Before Agnes could reply, Alan's sergeant hurried into the room.

"You had better come upstairs, there's been another robbery." He looked rather agitated. "It's a bracelet this time and ... " He broke off and shook his head.

"And..." The chief inspector prompted.

"It belongs to someone in the room next door to Mr and Mrs Hargreaves."

"No! I can't believe it." Alan turned to Agnes and made his apologies before hurrying out of the Dining Room and over towards the lift.

"Don't forget you promised you would check my room this morning," she called out after him. "I don't want to be stuck in the hotel all day." But she wasn't sure he heard her.

Agnes sat back in her chair and pushed her cup and saucer away from her. Why did all this have to happen while she was staying here?

All the guests, including her, would now have to have their rooms checked all over again.

Peering through to the reception, Agnes could see the manager of the hotel trying desperately to pacify his irate guests. She had to agree, it certainly wasn't good for the hotel.

She wandered idly from the Dining Room into the Drawing Room. She was just about to sit down, when the detective sergeant burst into the room.

"The chief inspector wanted you to know that your room has been searched and you are free to leave the hotel." He coughed and looked towards the bag she was clutching. "Once I search your handbag."

"Yes! Yes of course." She thrust the bag towards him. "Help yourself."

She watched him empty the contents of her bag onto the coffee table. This was the first time she had actually seen the sergeant properly. Other times he had been on the other side of the room. He looked quite young to be a sergeant, but then she found it difficult to judge the age of young people these days. Like his boss, the sergeant was clean shaven and was wearing a suit, though it didn't look as well made as Alan's; this one was more, off the peg.

"Everything seems to be in order," he said, handing the bag back to her. "Enjoy your day."

"Thank you." She was about to ask him about the latest missing necklace, but he rushed back out into the reception area before she got the chance.

Later, outside the hotel, she made her way to the taxi rank. She had decided to take a trip up to the shopping centre and treat herself to something new. Not that she needed anything; her wardrobes back home were all full to bursting point. But Agnes could never resist the urge to shop.

* * *

The shopping trip was a success. There were so many shops to explore she couldn't get around them all in one day. Another trip into the city centre was definitely a must before she returned to her home in Essex. But that didn't stop her from buying two new dresses and a pair of shoes on this visit.

Carrying two bags of new skirts, dresses or whatever else had caught her eye, she was heading towards the taxi rank when she caught sight of Angela and her husband.

Angela was pointing towards a jeweller's. However, from what Agnes could see, George didn't appear to be very keen. He opened his mouth to say something, but Angela didn't wait to hear. She simply flounced off into the shop, leaving him standing there on the pavement.

For a moment he didn't seem to know what to do. He stood there with his hands in his pockets and looked around at the other shoppers, all going about their business. But then he suddenly caught a glimpse of Agnes watching him. She gave him a smile of encouragement, but it seemed to make matters worse. Looking embarrassed, George turned and hurried after his wife.

Agnes sighed as she continued towards the taxi rank. *Poor George*, she thought. *Nothing the poor man did seemed to be right.*

Back at the hotel, she paid the taxi fare and walked up the steps into the hotel. She loved this hotel; the views were brilliant and it had up to the minute facilities. Yet she still couldn't help thinking it stood out from the rest of the buildings along the quayside. Not because it was impressive, which it was, but because it looked too new and didn't fit in with some of the other buildings.

Perhaps it would have blended in better if the architect had designed the outside to look a little more like the older buildings along the quayside. Though, on the other hand, it didn't look so out of character as the new Law Court building further along the quay. She sniffed as she stepped into the lift. That was only her opinion. It was obvious by the number of people staying here that the hotel was appreciated by lots of people.

Agnes only had time to remove her coat before she heard a tap on her door. Believing it to be one of the staff, she hurried across to open it and was rather surprised to see Alan standing there.

"Is there a problem," she asked. She glanced up and down the hall half expecting to see his sergeant. But he was alone.

"I was just passing and I wondered whether you might like to have dinner with me this evening." He grinned. "Actually I am still here looking into the case of the missing necklace. Or I should say the case of the missing necklace and bracelet."

"Come in," Agnes grinned. "How did you know which was my room," she asked as she closed the door.

"I'm a detective – remember," he replied, tapping his nose. "Anyway, would you like to join me for dinner? There's a nice little restaurant further along the quay you might enjoy."

"Thank you, Alan. That's very kind of you."

"Not at all! We can continue the conversation about old times, without the thought of any interruptions from my sergeant regarding the ongoing case."

"How is it going?" Agnes enquired. "Are you any further forward in recovering the jewellery?"

"No! Unfortunately not. They both seem to have disappeared without trace."

"Cheer up, Alan. I'm sure everything will work out in the end." Agnes wasn't really sure about that. If the necklace and bracelet had been stolen and not simply mislaid, they could be in some back street second hand jewellery shop in another town by now.

"I'll pick you up at about seven, if that's alright with you," said Alan, starting to walk back towards the door.

"Lovely, I'll look forward to it."

She walked across to where her afternoon's shopping lay unopened. Perhaps she would wear one of her new dresses this evening.

Chapter Six

The rest of the afternoon seemed to pass rather quickly. Agnes had decided to pop out to the nearby café for coffee rather than sit in her room. She enjoyed watching people coming and going. It was certainly better than being alone upstairs. After finishing her coffee, she had taken a short stroll along the quayside.

On her way back to the hotel, she saw someone leaning out of one of the hotel windows. For a moment she thought the person was waving to someone across the river, but glancing over to the other side of the Tyne, she couldn't see anyone responding. A few moments later, the person disappeared back inside the room. She turned away; the person had probably been admiring the view.

* * *

Now, showered and dressed, Agnes pondered on whether to go downstairs to wait for Alan. But in the end she decided to wait in her room. Perhaps she would look too keen if she was almost standing at the hotel entrance waiting for him to appear.

There was a tap on the door. Alan was standing there when she opened it.

"All set?" he asked.

"I just need to get my bag and I'll be right with you," she replied.

It was beginning to rain when they emerged from the hotel. However, Alan had a taxi waiting at the entrance and a short while later they pulled up outside the restaurant. By now the rain was falling heavily, so they hurried inside. The restaurant was rather full. It seemed it was popular with the locals.

A waiter led them to their table and asked if they would like to order drinks while they chose from the extensive menu. Agnes took a few moments to look at their surroundings. She found the atmosphere to be warm and comfortable – quite cosy, really. The walls were covered with photographs. Some showed the quayside from the past to the present, while others displayed various areas of the city centre. Above the bar area hung models of the large ships, which had visited the Tyne in the past and in one corner of the restaurant stood a large dresser filled with local memorabilia.

Looking at the various items, Agnes's memories were stirred as she recalled seeing similar things in her grandmother's house. She had been very young so her Grandma had only allowed her to look at the precious treasures through the glass doors of the cabinet in her front room. "When you are older, I will let you hold them."

But it never happened. Her grandmother died shortly after they had moved abroad. Until now, she had forgotten all about the ornaments in the old house. Though, thinking about it now, she wondered what had happened to them. She glanced back at the dresser. Perhaps some of them had ended up here. How proud her Grandma would be if she knew her possessions were still on show.

The evening passed very quickly. Agnes was interested to know what Alan had done since he left school and he was happy to tell her. He had enjoyed his days as a soldier, but once he finished his service, he had headed straight back to Tyneside.

"I really missed the place," he told her. "It was good to be home. Though it had changed a great deal during the time I was away, and it's been changing ever since!" He went on to tell her about his work as a policeman and how he had climbed the ladder to the rank of Detective Chief Inspector.

"Now then, what about you," he asked, "what did you do after you left the country?"

Agnes told him about her life abroad with her parents. "I found it daunting going to a new school and making new friends. It was even more difficult as I couldn't speak their language. But they were all so kind and helped me. Some of them even tried to learn English from me." She laughed. "Can you imagine it? They were teaching me French, while they were trying to learn English. I must say we had some fun over that."

She paused. "After a few years my parents came back to England and settled in London."

"You never thought of visiting the north?" he enquired. "You know, just for old time's sake."

"No," Agnes said. "There never seemed to be time. But looking back, I wish I had made time to bring Jim up here. He would have loved it." She paused for a moment, but then continued. "But that's life, isn't it. You do everything you can, yet there is still always something you wish you had done and then find it is too late."

It was quite late when they left the restaurant. The rain had stopped and the dark clouds had rolled away making way for the full moon to shine down onto the quayside.

"Shall we walk back to the hotel?" Agnes suggested. "It's rather pleasant now." In the distance she could see the coloured lights glowing from the Millennium Bridge. "I did so want to see the lights, but I was a little anxious about coming out on my own after dark."

Alan agreed.

They were just about to set off when they heard a loud thud. It came from somewhere on the opposite side of the street. At first they couldn't see anything, but crossing the road, they were able to make out something lying on edge of the pavement.

"You wait here, I'll see what it is," said Alan.

"Not on your life," Agnes replied and began to hurry towards the object. Alan caught up with her and they arrived together to find a woman lying at their feet. Her body was stretched across the edge of the pavement and onto the road.

At first they thought the woman might be drunk and had fallen over. However, when Alan leant over the woman to take a closer look, he saw there was no sign of any movement. He felt for a pulse, but there was none.

Agnes gasped and took a step backwards when he looked up at her and shook his head. She glanced up and down the street, half expecting to see someone lurking somewhere in the shadows, but there was no one to be seen. It was at that moment she heard something and looked up in time to see a window closing somewhere above her head.

"Alan," she said, pointing upwards. "Someone has just closed a window up there."

By now, he was on his phone calling for back-up.

"Do you think she could have been pushed from up there?" Agnes asked when he had finished his call.

"She could well have been, but she was shot first." Alan pointed down towards the woman.

Agnes stepped a little closer and looked down at the body. She was horrified to see the woman's legs twisted under her. One of her arms was stretched out to one side, while the other was lying across her chest. But what really sent her reeling was the sight of blood surrounding a hole in the woman's forehead. When she had first looked down at the body, the women's hair had been covering half of her face. Alan must have brushed it aside while checking to see whether she was drunk and had simply fallen over.

Agnes clasped her hand over her mouth and quickly looked away. But there was something familiar about what the woman was wearing and after a moment's thought, she turned back and looked again. She swallowed hard and forced herself to look at the woman's face for a second time.

"I've seen her before," she uttered, swiftly turning away again. "She's staying at the hotel. I saw her this morning in the Dining Room.

She didn't speak to me. I don't think she even noticed I was there. She had finished breakfast and was pouring over her newspaper."

"Well, that's a start," said Alan. "We'll make some enquiries at the hotel; they should have her home phone number at the very least." He stood up. "I better get you back to the hotel. Once my officers arrive I'll ask someone to take you back."

Agnes pulled a face. "No. I would like to stay. Besides, aren't I a witness or something?"

"Well yes, technically," he sounded doubtful, "but you didn't see any more than I did. We arrived on the scene together – remember?"

"Ah, yes, but it was me who saw the window close – remember?" Agnes had no intention of being shunted off in some police car, not when there was a possible murder enquiry on the cards. "You wouldn't have known about that if I hadn't told you. Also," she added before Alan could get a word in. "It was me who recognised the victim as someone staying at the hotel."

Alan held up his hands. "Okay, but..."

Before he could say anymore, a police car swung around the corner, followed by a van carrying the pathologist.

Chapter Seven

The police officers spoke to the Chief Inspector, leaving the Pathologist to see to the body. Alan quickly filled them in with what he knew, though it was precious little.

"And who is this?" one of them asked, pointing towards Agnes.

"This is Mrs Lockwood," replied Alan. "We discovered the body together. While I was bending over the body, she saw a window close up above." He pointed upwards.

"Did you see which window it was?" The police officer was now addressing Agnes.

"Yes, it was that one on the first floor." She pointed towards the window she meant. "There, just above that plaque on the wall." She placed her hand in front of her mouth and looked at Alan. "Oh my goodness, this is Bessie Surtees House." She paused. "And the window I saw being pulled shut, was the one Bessie climbed out of all those years ago when she eloped with her young man."

The name of Bessie Surtees was well known on Tyneside. However, the story of the plucky young woman, who edged her way through the tiny window to run off with a man called John Scott, was now known worldwide.

Her father disapproved of his daughter marrying the penniless young man and had forbidden her to see him. But Bessie disobeyed her father and, despite wearing a crinoline dress, she managed to squeeze through the window and run off with her young man. There was a happy ending to the story as John proved his worth by becoming 1st Earl of Eldon and Chancellor of England.

"But that room is a museum now." The officer took off his hat and scratched his head. "Why would anyone be in there at this time of night?"

"I don't know," said Agnes. "But that is the window I saw being closed after we found the body."

"Did you see the face of the person closing the window?" asked the officer. He held his pen over his notebook ready to take down any useful notes.

"No," said Agnes thoughtfully. "The window was almost closed when I looked up. I wasn't able to see anyone's face."

"I see," said the officer, lowering the notebook. "Not much to go on, is it?"

Agnes picked up the note of sarcasm in his voice.

"I suppose not. But on the other hand, you wouldn't have known anyone was up there and that there is the possibility the woman was shot inside the house and thrown out of the window," she retorted. "You would have simply assumed she was shot right here on the spot where she lies and begun your investigation in the wrong place."

"The lady is right," said Alan. He had been about to intervene when the officer made his curt remark. But Agnes had beaten him to it. "Therefore we now know we need to begin our investigation by checking out this old house." He paused. "I suggest you get on with it, constable."

"Yes sir." The officer gave Agnes a sweeping glance before striding across to the door and tugging on the handle. "It's locked," he said with a shrug.

Alan stared at him. "Of course it's locked. This is a museum. You need to find out who has the keys and get that person here tonight. Then you will have to check out all the other key holders. Find out where they were this evening – do I really need to spell it out for you?" He paused. "And you," he said looking towards the other officer, "take a look around the back; see if any of the windows are open or broken. Meanwhile, I am going to commandeer your car and take Mrs Lockwood back to her hotel. I will return in a few minutes."

"Right, sir." The officer glanced at Agnes and mumbled something under his breath, before pulling out his phone.

The other officer had already disappeared to check out the rear of the building.

"I heard that," Agnes said, as she strode past him towards the police car.

"Sorry, ma'am," he said. He looked towards the senior officer hoping he hadn't heard. Alan continued to walk to the car without as much as a glance at him. It seemed he hadn't picked up his tetchy remark.

* * *

Alan pulled up at the hotel to find another police car parked outside. Looking further up the road, he was surprised to see his sergeant's car.

"Now, what?" he mumbled under his breath as he opened the car door and stepped out onto the pavement.

Agnes didn't wait for Alan to come around to open the passenger door; she quickly heaved the door open and clambered out. This evening was becoming more thrilling as the hours passed by.

"Gosh," she uttered, excitedly. "I wonder what has been going on here."

"I think we are about to find out," Alan hissed as he saw his sergeant waiting for him at the entrance to the hotel.

"There's been another theft. I put in a call for you, but I got a routed message saying you were on your way." He paused, when he suddenly saw Agnes hurrying around from the other side of the car. "Good evening, Mrs Lockwood. I'm sure you don't want to be caught up in another robbery. You must be very tired."

"No, I'm fine," she replied. "I think I need a drink. What about you," she added looking at Alan, hinting that there was no way she was going to go anywhere without hearing all the details.

Alan shook his head. "Nothing for me," he said. "But, yes, you go ahead." He knew there was no way Agnes was going to disappear upstairs like a good little girl. "You say there's been another robbery here at the hotel?" he added, turning back to Sergeant Andrews.

"Yes sir."

"The woman is dreadfully upset." He paused for a moment. "The manager is in his office. He's in a bit of a state about all this."

"I'm sure he is and what I have to tell him isn't going to help."

"Why, what's happened?" Andrews asked.

"One of the guests has been murdered. Mrs Lockwood and I discovered the body about half-an-hour ago. Mrs Lockwood recognised her as a guest at the hotel."

"Murdered! How? Where?"

"We found the body outside Bessie Surtees House. She had been shot in the head. We assume she had been thrown out of a window. Mrs Lockwood saw someone closing the window while I was examining the body. I left a couple of officers at the scene. I said I would only be a few minutes."

"Please call me Agnes. Mrs Lockwood sounds so formal."

Alan turned around in surprise. "I thought you had gone for a drink."

"I did. I have it here." Agnes held up her glass. "Have I missed anything?"

Alan shook his head. "No I was just telling Sergeant Andrews about the murder." He turned back to his sergeant. "I think I better have a word with the manager. Is he in his office?"

Andrews nodded.

"Okay, I'll just be a few minutes, and then you can bring me up to speed on the robbery before I go back to the murder scene." Alan called out as he strode off through the reception.

* * *

Back at Bessie Surtees House, the chief inspector found more officers had arrived and the area had been cordoned off. Dr. Nichols, the pathologist, and his assistant loaded the body into the van. At this point, he was unable to tell Alan any more than he already knew. The woman had been shot within the last three hours. The bruises to her head had occurred after death. He explained that any further information would only be found once he had carried out a post mortem.

At that moment a man, escorted by a police officer, headed towards them. He was brandishing the key to the museum and didn't look too happy at being dragged from his bed at such an unearthly hour.

"This is Mr Donaldson," said the officer. "He is the museum curator."

Mr Donaldson glanced briefly at the pathologist still dressed in white coveralls, before turning his attention to the chief inspector. "Your officer told me that you believe the victim was killed in the museum and the body was pushed through a window."

Alan nodded. "Yes, that one." He pointed to the window Agnes had seen being closed. He held his hand out for the key.

"That's impossible. No one can get into the building without a key, the curator mumbled. He dropped the key into Alan's hand.

"Well, it appears someone managed to do it," replied the chief inspector. He handed the key to one of the police officers and nodded towards the door. "Unless of course one of the keys was stolen or..." he broke off and peered at the curator.

"Or," Mr Donaldson prompted.

"Or one of the key holders is responsible," Alan continued. "We need a list of everyone who carries a key to the building."

"Isn't it possible someone could have got in through a window at the back of the house – where they wouldn't be seen?"

"Mm, now there's a thought." Alan folded his arms. "Why didn't we think of that? So, are you saying the windows at the back of the building are usually left unlocked?"

"No! Of course not, I simply meant that it might have been forced or even broken," Mr Donaldson snapped.

"Do you think we didn't check the back of the house while we were waiting for you to turn up? None of the windows appear to have been forced or broken." Alan was trying to stay calm, but this man was beginning to grate on his nerves. "We'll take a better look once we are inside."

While they had been talking, two police officers, followed by two forensic experts, had gone inside to check out the building. One of the officers now arrived back at the front door and told the chief inspector that there was no one inside. "Whoever did this has gone," he said, gesturing towards where the body had been found. "Officers are checking for any evidence the perpetrators might have left behind. My colleague is making sure the windows haven't been tampered with." He paused and looked at the curator. "But this is starting to look like an inside job."

The chief inspector nodded. It was certainly beginning to look that way. Or else, they were dealing with one very clever individual.

The pathologist had gone through the dead woman's pockets before the body was moved, hoping to find something the chief inspector could work on. But there was nothing. Not even a driving license. Someone had removed all forms of identification before throwing the body from the window.

Alan had taken a photograph of the woman's face earlier. He had shown it to the manager of the hotel when he had taken Agnes back. However, without a room number, the manager couldn't name her. Yet he felt sure his reception staff would recognize her, once they saw the photo. "They deal with the guests on a one to one basis every day," he'd said.

Alan had already forwarded the photo to his sergeant's phone; instructing him to show it to all the night staff. If no one recognised her he was to have a copy printed off ready for the day staff coming on duty. For goodness sake, someone must know who the woman was.

* * *

Back at the hotel, Agnes was far from sleepy.

Once DCI Johnson went back to the murder scene, Sergeant Andrews tried again to persuade her to retire for the night. "Why not go to upstairs to your room? There is nothing you can do here."

Are you kidding me? No way! Agnes thought. "I am a witness to the murder – well, a witness to seeing a window close after the body was found," she told him. "What if Alan comes back and needs to speak to me? Anyway, what's all this about another robbery? I mean that's why you are here isn't it?"

"Yes it is," Andrews replied. "But I can't discuss the case with you."

Agnes eyed him as she took another sip of her wine. "Was it Mrs Hargreaves again?"

"No it was..." The sergeant stopped mid-sentence and frowned. "You know I can't tell you who it was."

"Well, shouldn't you be up there now questioning the woman about her missing jewellery?" She paused. "Asking all those questions about when she last saw it."

"I have already tried to speak to..." He stopped short and frowned at her. "Look, I'm sorry, but I must go back upstairs. I left a constable with her until she calmed down a little." Andrews started walking towards the door. "She was quite upset about the robbery."

"Is the constable a man or a woman," Agnes asked, catching up with him.

"It's a man." The sergeant stopped and looked at her. "I didn't have any women constables with me."

"Then perhaps I could be of help," Agnes insisted. "I mean, as a woman, I could comfort her while you ask the necessary questions."

Andrews looked at her. Perhaps she was right. When he had tried to question the woman earlier, she had been too distraught. It seemed the missing item was the last gift her husband had given her before he died.

"Okay," he said after a long pause. "But if she is unhappy at you being in the room, you must leave immediately." He sighed. This wasn't supposed to be how it was done. But there seemed to be no alternative.

"Understood," Agnes nodded. She placed her glass on a nearby table and followed the sergeant across the reception area.

Chapter Eight

At breakfast the next morning, Agnes couldn't help scrutinizing each guest as they entered the Dining Room. Anyone of them could be the person stealing the jewellery. But then another, more frightening, thought struck her. The murderer could also be staying at this hotel. Therefore, anyone of them could be the murderer.

Last night, aware that someone seemed to have access to all the hotel rooms, she had taken the precaution of carefully placing her jewellery into her pillowcase for the night. They had been gifts from Jim, and were very precious to her.

But a thief was one thing, a murderer was something else altogether. Tonight she would place a chair in front of her door.

As she buttered her toast, her mind flew back to the woman she had spoken with the evening before. To be honest, Sergeant Andrews had done most of the talking, while trying to find out exactly what items were missing and when she had last seen them. However, Agnes had been able to comfort the woman, whose name was Brenda Arrowsmith, as she had tried to answer the detective's questions.

Like Agnes, she was staying at the hotel alone. Her husband had died a couple of months ago and she had simply come to the hotel to get away from the empty house for a few days. "I miss Peter so much."

Through hers sobs, she told the sergeant how she had brought these particular pieces of jewellery with her as she'd had the dreadful thought that her house might be burgled while she was away. "The gold necklace was the last thing Peter bought for me. It was a gift for my birthday, two weeks before he died." She paused. "I can't believe it. I never thought for one moment it would be stolen from my hotel room."

Agnes had held Brenda's hand throughout the interview. She hadn't said very much at all. Not because Sergeant Andrews had told her not to interfere with his questioning, but because the lump in her throat wouldn't allow her say anything. She had felt so sorry for Brenda, but it had made her all the more determined to keep her own jewellery safe.

When Sergeant Andrews was satisfied he had all the necessary information he took his leave, promising Brenda the police would do their utmost to find out who had stolen her jewellery and have it returned as soon as possible. But Agnes had detected a note in the sergeant's voice that said he didn't really hold out much hope of that happening. The stolen jewellery was probably well away from the hotel by now. Taking a sip of her coffee, Agnes recalled how she had stayed with Brenda for almost an hour before returning to her room. The poor woman had been so upset; she hadn't wanted to be left on her own.

Agnes was about to replace her cup on the saucer when she saw a man entering the dining room. She had seen him last night when she accompanied Sergeant Andrews to Brenda's room. The man had smiled briefly and nodded towards Andrews as they passed in the corridor. But for some reason she had the impression the man looked a little startled when he saw her by the sergeant's side. She had no idea why that should be. She couldn't recall seeing him anywhere before. But there hadn't been time to ask Sergeant Andrews about him, as a few seconds later they had approached Brenda's room.

Agnes was still watching him as he hovered in the doorway. It was as though he couldn't make his mind up whether to come in or not. After some moments, he made the decision and walked across to a table by the wall. He looked fairly young, quite tall and slightly built, all of which she had noticed the previous evening. But, while last night he had been wearing a casual outfit as though he had been to a club or even a party, this morning he was dressed in a very smart suit and carrying a briefcase. She wondered whether he was a businessman preparing to go to some important corporate meeting. He sat down and unfolded the newspaper he had been carrying under his arm. But as he began to open it he shifted his gaze to the people in the room.

Agnes looked away and hastily returned the cup, which she had held poised in mid air for several minutes, back onto the saucer. She hoped he hadn't seen her peering at him. Attracting the attention of a passing waiter, she ordered more coffee. Perhaps the man would simply believe she had been looking around the room for a waiter.

The smartly-dressed young man continued to look at his fellow guests. Agnes watched his reflection through a mirror on the wall at the other end of the room; his eyes darted from one table to another. It was almost as though he was looking for someone. Maybe he was. He could well have been expecting someone to join him for breakfast. But then his gaze rested on Agnes. Even if she hadn't been able to see him looking at her, she would have known he was watching her; she could feel his eyes boring into her back.

* * *

Agnes finished her coffee and left the Dining Room. As she turned into the reception area, she caught a brief glimpse of the man sitting at his table. He was still finishing his breakfast with his newspaper propped up in front of him. She wished Alan would arrive. Or even Sergeant Andrews. She really wanted to know who this man was and why he seemed to be taking such an interest in her.

Sergeant Andrews might recall seeing him the evening before. He may have even interviewed him regarding the stolen jewellery. However it was likely that both Alan and his sergeant would be caught up with the murder investigation now. No doubt the thefts would have been handed on to another officer.

Agnes decided to sit in the Drawing Room while she made up her mind what to do with herself for the rest of the day. When she had arrived, there were countless places she wanted to visit. In fact there had been so many on her itinerary, she had wondered how she might fit them all in. But at the moment, there were only two things on her mind: the body pushed from the window at Bessie Surtees House and the robberies here at the hotel. Well, there were three things, if she included the strange man in the dining room. She had only been sitting there for what a seemed like a few minutes when she saw Alan enter the hotel. She had chosen an armchair with a clear view of the main entrance, just incase he should call in. She waved and he strode straight across to join her.

"I understand you assisted my sergeant last night," he said, pulling another chair closer to hers.

"I didn't do much. I think I felt as sad as the poor woman."

"Still, Andrews thought Mrs Arrowsmith was a little calmer with you there. At least she was able to answer his questions."

Agnes saw the man from the dining room making his way across to the reception desk. "Don't look now, but a man at the desk seems to know me from somewhere."

She went on to explain how she had seen him the evening before and again in the dining room at breakfast this morning. "I just don't understand. He was peering at me as though he was surprised to see me here at the hotel, yet at the same time he looked angry that I am here, if you see what I mean. I wondered whether you might have some idea who he is."

Alan made a big thing of reaching into his back pocket so that he could turn his head without the man realizing he was looking at him. He glanced at the man standing at the desk and then back at Agnes. "No I don't recall interviewing him. Andrews might have spoken with him. Did you mention it to him?"

"I didn't get the chance. We arrived at Brenda's room a few seconds after we saw him in the corridor. Anyway, how are you getting on with the murder enquiry," Agnes changed the subject. She guessed Alan wouldn't be able to stay long and she was curious as to what he had found out.

"We haven't really got very far at all. That's one of the reasons I'm here. I need to speak to the day shift. Last night, no one recognised her from the photograph, so we gather she didn't ask for room service during the evenings. Andrews left a copy of the photo here, but so far, no one has come forward to say they recognize her." Alan paused. "I could have left that to my sergeant, but the second reason is I wanted to let you to know I hadn't forgotten you. I thought we could have dinner again somewhere and hope that, this time, we don't find any bodies lying around the streets."

"Yes, that would be lovely. But quite honestly, finding the body didn't spoil the evening." She coughed. "That didn't come out how I meant it. Naturally I am sorry for the poor lady who was murdered, but before that happened I was having a very nice evening."

Alan grinned. "It's okay, I know what you mean. I enjoyed it, too." He paused and glanced across towards the desk. The man Agnes had pointed out had finished his business with the receptionist and was now heading towards the lift. But then he stopped and looked around him. Alan turned his head away slightly so he could only see the man out of the corner of his eye. But he did see the guy stop in his tracks when he caught a glimpse of Agnes sitting there with him.

Fortunately, Agnes was looking the other way otherwise she would have seen the man glaring at her.

Alan was rather alarmed. Agnes was right; this man did seem to have a grudge against her. When she had first mentioned it, he had thought she might have been imagining things. But now he had seen it for himself. He decided there and then, that she needed some sort of protection. It crossed his mind that a constable should be allocated to watch out for her well-being. But what with cut backs and everything else going on in the force that would be too much to ask. No, he was going to have to call in a few favours. Meanwhile, he would check out this man's credentials at Reception.

* * *

As he drove along the quayside to Bessie Surtees House, Chief Inspector Johnson thought back to what he had learned at the hotel. The lady who had been murdered the evening before was called Mary Swinburne. She had been staying at the hotel for the last week and was due to stay another four days. But during her stay, it seemed she kept herself very much to herself.

Apart from having most of her meals at the hotel no one had really seen much of her. She had either gone out for the day or spent much of the time in her room. It was one of the Dining Room waiters who had eventually put a name to the face and that was only because she had signed a receipt for the wine she ordered to have with her evening meal.

Once Alan had a name to go on, the reception was able to check the records and give him some of the information he needed. At least he now had a home address; it was somewhere to start.

His thoughts then drifted to the man Agnes had mentioned. The lady on the desk had told him his name was David Drummond and he had been at the hotel for about three days. "His details show that he is here on business," she had said. "Though he did tell us he is also going to a friend's stag party. I believe it's someone he hadn't seen for a while."

Apart from that, no one knew much more about him. But then why should they? People who stay at a hotel don't usually tell everyone their life's history when they check in. Still, his attitude to Agnes was very strange. He seemed to have taken an instant dislike to her. Why was that? Agnes was a rather nice woman – correction, a very nice woman. What did this man have against her? Was there something Drummond knew about Agnes that he didn't?

Alan rounded the corner and drove into Sandhill. Bessie Surtees House was on the left hand side and he could see a few people standing around the tape that marked off where the body had been found. Some were carrying cameras and were taking shots of the fading chalk outline on the ground where the body had lain. "Reporters," Alan mumbled to himself, as he parked the car. He climbed out and walked across to the museum.

A police officer standing by the door nodded as he approached.

"Any problems here," Alan asked.

"No sir," the officer replied. "The reporters haven't been here very long." He pointed across the road to where a few lads were standing. "I'm not sure what they want; unless they're just being curious. But they've been hanging around for about twenty minutes."

Alan turned and looked across the street to where the officer was pointing. "Probably nothing," he said. "But I'll have a word."

The lads shifted their feet uneasily as the chief inspector approached. "We haven't done anything," said one of them, stubbing out a cigarette.

"No one said you had," said Alan, calmly. "My officer was simply wondering why you are all hanging around only a few feet from a murder scene."

"We don't know nothing about any murder," another lad chirped in. "We're here looking for work." He pointed to the building behind them. "Job Centre sent us here. They said the foreman wanted some labourers. But he ain't here yet."

Alan looked at the building where large signs told the public that they were sorry for the inconvenience, but a new vibrant nightclub would be opening very soon. He nodded at the lads. "Okay. Good luck with the jobs."

Back across the road, he told the officer there seemed to be nothing to worry about. "Nevertheless, keep an eye on them to make sure they weren't just screwing me around. I'm going to take a look upstairs."

Inside the museum, Alan went straight up to the room where the body had been thrown from the previous evening. The scene of crime officers had confirmed that all the windows had been tightly shut.

Sergeant Andrews was going to speak to all the key holders that morning. But quite honestly, Alan realised that no one was going to admit to being here last night or to having loaned the key to anyone.

He looked out of the window and down onto the street. The reporters were still milling around outside. They were probably waiting for him to come back to give them all the information they needed to satisfy their readers. Shifting his gaze to across the street, he could see the four lads talking to someone. It was probably the foreman. He was holding up three fingers. If that meant there were only had three jobs going, then one lad was going to be very unlucky. Perhaps, they would be able to work out a deal where the building site employed four labourers for the price of three.

Alan sighed, as he turned back to face into the room. He had a case to solve. But where did they start with this one? Using his fingers, he counted off what the police knew. One: there was a body. Two: the victim had been shot and thrown from this window. He and Agnes had seen that happen last night – well almost. Three: there was no blood found in the room. Four: the Scene of Crime Officers team had found no trace of blood in the entire building. Five: According to the curator, the windows and doors were all locked before he went home that evening. Yet the murder must have taken place here. Why would anyone carry a dead body up here only to throw it from this window back down onto the street? It just didn't make any sense. And then there was the question of how they got in.

The chief inspector paused realizing that he had come full circle and was back at the beginning. Until Andrews had spoken to the key holders and they had accounted for their whereabouts the evening before or Forensics could match any of the fingerprints taken last night, there wasn't anywhere to start working the case.

Chapter Nine

After Alan had left the hotel, Agnes sat for a while deciding what to do with herself. She was meeting Alan again this evening for dinner, but that seemed a long way away. She had made a list of places she wanted to see during her stay in the northeast. Recalling her past had been the whole purpose of this visit. Yet all that seemed to have gone out of the window since the robberies at the hotel followed by the murder at the museum further along the quayside.

She smiled to herself at her pun. Her plans had gone out of the window, just like the body last night. Perhaps she would take another walk along the quayside while the weather was clement. She could even stroll across the Millennium Bridge and go inside the Sage Building and the Baltic Art Gallery on the Gateshead side of the Tyne. The Sage was a new building, but way back in the past the Baltic had been a flour mill.

The cool air on her cheeks helped to refresh her as she stepped outside the hotel and slowly made her way along the quay. It was quite busy. Many people looked like tourists enjoying the late summer sun. She was just about to step onto the bridge, when she had the strange feeling she was being watched.

Ordinarily, she would have shrugged it off. With so many people milling around, anyone of them could be looking at her for no other reason than because she was in their line of sight. However, this felt very different to someone giving her a casual glance. She had a strong feeling she was being studied. She shivered. Maybe she was overreacting. But since the episode with the man in the hotel, she didn't want to take any chances. Halfway across the bridge, she stopped to take in the scenery. Or at least that's what she wanted the person watching her to think. She glanced back and forth, as though taking a mental picture of both sides of the quay. Then she turned around to look in the opposite direction. All the time she tried to give the impression she was actually looking in the direction she was facing. But in reality, her eyes were darting from side to side trying to see who was peering at her.

Suddenly she saw the man from the hotel. He was wearing an overcoat with the collar turned up. Whether it was to shield him from the cool breeze or an effort to disguise himself from her, she wasn't sure. But if it was for the latter it didn't work, she recognised him instantly. Comforted that she had at least spotted him, she turned and continued on her way across the bridge towards the art gallery.

Agnes paused at the end of the bridge for a few moments before making her way across to the gallery. As she drew nearer to the large building, she was able to see the reflection of people walking behind her through the large windows of the café. At first she didn't see the man and wondered if he had decided to go back. But then she caught a glimpse of him. He was tucked behind a group of people, all heading her way.

If this were after dark with not many people around, she would have been terrified. But on this bright sunny morning, with people everywhere, she felt quite safe. Besides, Alan had given her his mobile number. If she felt threatened in any way, she wouldn't hesitate to call him. Meanwhile, she would have a little fun and lead this guy on a wild goose chase.

The sudden thought of the chief inspector, caused her to wonder how he was getting on at the museum.

* * *

Before leaving the Bessie Surtees Museum, Alan decided he would take a look around. You never know, the SOCO team might have missed something in one of the other rooms. Though he knew that wasn't usually the case. They were very thorough.

He wandered around the rooms hoping to find something that would give him a lead to work on. Yet he found nothing. It was as the team had said, no evidence of any blood being spilled. In fact there was no sign that anyone had even been in here since the curator went home. Truthfully he was beginning to wonder whether a murder had even taken place. Could he have imagined the whole thing? But then he thought of the body lying in the morgue and how Agnes had been with him when he found it. No! It was true enough.

Despite the seriousness of the inquiry, he couldn't help but stop to admire his surroundings. The city could well be bustling outside, but in here it was almost as though the world had stood still since the house was built in the eighteenth century. The carved oak paneling above the fireplace and the magnificent ceiling had all stood the test of time.

He shook his head. What he doing? He was supposed to be investigating a murder and here he was, standing around as though he were an awestruck tourist. Satisfied that there was nothing further to glean from the old house, he made his way down the stairs and out of the building.

The officer was still standing by the door when Alan arrived downstairs. As he had predicted, the reporters rushed towards him as he stepped out onto the pavement.

"Any further forward in solving the murder?"

"Can you give us any more information?" called out another.

"Who was the victim?"

The questions came at him from all sides. Alan could only repeat that he had no further news for them. "As for the identity of the victim, I'm afraid you will have to wait until we are able contact the next of kin."

There were a few muttering from the frustrated reporters and several more photos taken by the photographers before they all moved off towards their parked cars.

The lads across the road had disappeared. For a moment Alan wondered what had happened to them. Had they all managed to get jobs or was one of them having to trundle back to the Job Centre. It seemed rather insensitive to send four people to a building site when there were only three jobs available. He shrugged. It wasn't really any of his business. Except that in a way it usually ended up being his business. If the young men in the city didn't have work, they could turn to crime.

The chief inspector had a few words with the officer standing guard before he got into his car and headed towards the police station.

Sergeant Andrews was on the phone when Alan stepped into the office. He raised his eyebrows at his sergeant, silently asking if there were any further developments. But the slight shake of his head told him there was nothing new.

The sergeant finished his call and shrugged at his boss. "Nothing," he said. "No one seems to know anything and SOCO insist there is no trace of any blood in the room."

"Not even by the window?" Alan raised his eyebrows. "It would have been difficult to drag the body across the floor, and then heave it out of the window without leaving even a drop of blood."

Andrews shook his head. "No, absolutely nothing, the guys who were at the scene are as baffled as we are."

"What about fingerprints?" Alan asked. "Surely they must have picked up some fingerprints?" He was clutching at straws now.

"There are too many fingerprints to be of any use. The house had been open to the public yesterday as usual and it had been rather busy. I gather there were two coach trips during the day. A number of prints were smudged. Any prints found could belong to various people who might not even be in Newcastle today."

"Can this get any worse?" Alan threw his hands in the air in despair. "When is the room cleaned?" he added, more to himself than the sergeant.

"Sorry sir." Andrews enquired. He hadn't quite caught his boss's last remark.

"I was thinking aloud," Alan explained. "I was simply wondering whether they had a regular cleaner and, if so, when the room was last cleaned."

"Good point, sir. Shall I check that out?"

Alan nodded. "Meanwhile, I'll see whether there is any further news from the pathologist. We've got to find a lead from somewhere. At the moment we have nothing whatsoever to go on."

* * *

Agnes was enjoying a coffee and a lovely cake in the rather nice café on the ground floor inside the Baltic Art Gallery. She had chosen a seat by the window, which meant she had a clear view of this side of the quay. The man hadn't followed her into the café. However, she couldn't see him kicking his heels outside either. Therefore, he must be lolling around somewhere in the entrance hall. She would need to be careful when she left the café.

She sighed. Of course he might not really be following her. She could be imagining the whole thing. At this very moment, he could be upstairs admiring the artwork on display in the gallery. Or even in the gift shop across the hall.

Thinking of the gift shop, she thought she would make that her next port of call. She might find one or two gifts for the children who lived next door to her home in Essex.

She paid the bill and made her way out of the café; careful not to give away the fact that she was scanning the area. She tried to give the impression to any passersby that she hadn't quite made up her mind what to do next.

At first there was no sign of the man who had been following her. But then she caught a glimpse of him just before he concealed himself behind a large billboard.

"Hmm," Agnes mumbled to herself. "So much for thinking that he might not actually be following me." She heaved a sigh and a few minutes later she was inside the shop, browsing the well-stocked shelves.

Almost an hour had passed before she left the shop. She dithered on whether to go upstairs into the gallery or leave that for another day. In the end she decided to visit the Sage building, which is what she had intended to do when she first left the hotel.

On the way up the steps leading to the Sage, Agnes paused when she saw the Millennium Bridge was being raised to allow a vessel to float underneath. She pulled out her mobile phone and took a video. She also took the opportunity to scan the quayside, hoping to capture the strange man who had been following her. Then she saw him. He wasn't actually looking at her at that point. Instead, he was watching the bridge being raised. But then he moved his attention to the vessel passing underneath.

Agnes quickly focused her camera on the bridge again when the man looked towards her. Let him continue to believe she was merely another tourist interested in the workings of this impressive bridge. Yet, she knew she had caught him on her camera phone.

Once the bridge was back in place, Agnes turned and continued up the steps towards the Sage Building at the top. A brief glance back down towards the quay told her the man was no longer following her. In fact, he appeared to have lost interest in her altogether. Instead, his eyes were glued on the yacht as it moored alongside the Jetty.

Agnes's mind was in a whirl as she continued towards the Sage. At first, she had thought of hanging around at the top of the steps to see what happened next, but swiftly changed her mind. What if the man was simply waiting for her to disappear from sight before following her up the steps? It wouldn't help if he found her watching him. Best let him believe she had no idea of his presence. That way, she could keep an eye on him and, in due course, she might even learn what this was all about.

She didn't see the man any more during the afternoon. Yet she still couldn't relax. She kept taking sly glances behind her, half expecting him to pop up at any moment.

Chapter Ten

As previously arranged, Alan called at the hotel for Agnes at seven o'clock. She had thought he might be a little late due to the murder enquiry, but he was spot on time. He had chosen another restaurant on the quayside. This one was set between the Tyne Bridge and the Millennium Bridge giving an excellent view of both.

"I had planned on taking you to a restaurant away from the quayside after last night," Alan apologized. "But with things being the way they are I thought I had better stay close to both the hotel and the museum."

"This is perfect." Agnes replied, as the waiter lead them to a table by the large bay window. Though this restaurant didn't have the same warm, friendly atmosphere of the one they had used the previous evening, the view more than made up for it. Even as she spoke, the coloured lights on the bridges were switched on. "So," she added when they were seated. How are things going with your murder investigation?"

"What investigation?" Alan replied glumly. "We haven't any leads. No finger prints. No blood. In fact, there is nothing to say there was even a murder in the first place."

"Apart from a body," said Agnes.

"Yes, apart from a body," he repeated her words. "Anyway, let's forget about all that for this evening. What would like to drink?"

The evening passed quickly. Again, Agnes found Alan fun company. Despite having entirely different backgrounds, they seemed to have so much in common.

"I was sad when your family moved abroad. I realised I wasn't going to see you again."

"Really?" Agnes was rather surprised. "I didn't think you even knew me – well, not properly. You never seemed particularly interested in me."

"I was shy back then. I wanted to ask you to the Christmas Party; you remember? It would have been the last one before you left the area. But I was afraid you would say no."

"You don't seem to be shy anymore." Agnes laughed.

"Well, I can put that down to life in the army. It was not in anyone's best interest to let the other lads see you were shy, timid or whatever. They would play such pranks." Alan fell silent as his mind drifted back to the days when he first joined the service.

Agnes gave him a nudge with her elbow and smiled to cheer him up. "Hey, where are you, remember me?"

Alan smiled back at her. "Sorry, I got a little carried away."

"Well you're back now." Agnes grinned. "So, tell me a little more about the case."

"Like I said, there's nothing to tell. We have absolutely nothing to go on. I mean, if we hadn't seen the body pushed out of the window I wouldn't have believed it."

Agnes nodded. "I agree; it is so very strange. There was no blood on the pavement so it's obvious the room upstairs was where the murder took place. There should have been blood where the body fell. Yet..." She suddenly fell silent and screwed up her eyes; she was thinking back to the previous evening and working out what she and Alan had actually seen.

"Yet?" Alan prompted.

"Shh, I'm thinking." Agnes flapped her hands telling him to shut up.

Alan looked around the room while Agnes sorted out her thoughts. Catching the eye of a passing waiter he ordered more drinks.

A few moments later, Agnes grabbed his arm. "I've just realised something really important," she said excitedly.

Alan stared at her. "You mean about the case?"

"Yes, of course about the case! What do you think I mean – the school Christmas Party?"

"Well, are you going to tell me or not?" Alan said, impatiently. He couldn't think of anything they had missed the previous evening.

Agnes took a deep breath. "We didn't actually see the body being pushed out of the window." She sat back in her chair, giving him a moment to think about what she had said.

"But we heard the thump, which was why we hurried across to see what it was."

"Yet we still didn't see it fall from the window," she replied.

"Well where else could it have come from?" Alan shook his head.

"A passing car or van," she replied, triumphantly.

"But we didn't hear any passing car or van." Alan wasn't convinced.

"We weren't actually listening for a car, van, lorry or whatever. Were we?" she replied. "Think about it, Alan. All we heard was a thump. The body could have been thrown from a car and the dull thump we heard could have been someone closing the vehicle door as quietly as possible."

"But you said you saw the window being pulled shut." Alan was still doubtful.

"Yes, I did. But that doesn't mean to say that whoever was closing it, killed the woman and pushed her out. They might just as easily have heard a noise and then looked out to see what was going on in the street."

Alan thought about it for a moment and realised Agnes could be right. The woman might have been murdered in another part of the city and the body dumped on the quayside in the hope no one would see it until the murderer and his or her accomplices were well away.

Why the hell hadn't he thought of that? This put a whole new slant on the case. They were looking in the wrong place. But he had been convinced the woman's body had been thrown from the window. More especially when Agnes told him she had seen someone closing it while he was examining the body. Now it was imperative the police found out who had been in the museum last night. This mysterious person might have seen the number plate of the vehicle.

"Well?" Agnes interrupted his thoughts. "What do you think?"

"I think you could be right. We need to start looking elsewhere. And, we really need to find out who was in the room last night. They might have seen or heard a vehicle. But they could have panicked when they saw us, shortly followed by the police, most likely because they shouldn't have been up there in the room in the first place."

"Now we're getting somewhere." Agnes clapped her hands together.

"We?" asked the chief inspector.

"Yes! We!" retorted Agnes. "I am involved in this now and I don't want you to leave me out. And," Agnes continued before Alan could get a word in, "I know you aren't supposed to discuss a crime, case, investigation or whatever it is you want to call it with a member of the public. But I'm not just any old member of the public. I was there with you when the body was found! And, tonight it's me who came up with notion that the body might have been dropped from a van rather than from the window."

"Okay, okay." Alan held up his hands in mock surrender. "But this is between you and me. Understand? You mustn't talk to anyone else regarding the case."

"Absolutely," said Agnes, firmly. Though she had her fingers crossed under the table at the time.

Strolling back towards the hotel, Alan suddenly remembered David Drummond, the man who had been watching Agnes earlier that morning in the dining room. He asked whether she had seen him again that day.

"Gosh! Yes. I meant to mention him to you earlier, but then we got to talking about the murder." She paused for a second. "I saw him again after I left the hotel this morning." She went on to tell Alan how he had followed her across the bridge and hung around until she came out of the Baltic Art Gallery.

"It was only after the bridge was lifted to allow a yacht to pass through that he lost interest in me. I carried on up the steps to the Sage, but he didn't follow me. He was too interested in the yacht."

"I asked about him at reception after I left you," said Alan. "His name is David Drummond. Does that mean anything to you?"

Agnes shook her head. "No. Not a thing."

"According to his details at the hotel, he is here on business."

"Well, he certainly looks the part," Agnes replied. "His suit and brief-case make him look very business-like. I just don't understand why he has taken such a dislike to me. I certainly don't know him and to the best of my knowledge he doesn't know me. If he believes otherwise, wouldn't you think he'd come and say hello or something?"

Alan nodded, thoughtfully. It really was very strange. Sinister, more like. He hadn't forgotten the look of disgust on Drummond's face that morning. Or was it fear? Could it be that this man believed Agnes had witnessed something she shouldn't have? He was quite concerned for Agnes's safety and wanted to warn her to keep away from him. But at the same time he didn't want to alarm her. "I don't think you have anything to worry about," he said at last. "After all, at the hotel there are always people drifting in and out of the reception rooms."

"Yes, you're right," Agnes replied. She tried to sound casual, but, though she might have been mistaken, she thought she heard a note of caution in Alan's tone. Was he suggesting that she should keep in full view of other people?

"Would you like me to see you up to your room," Alan asked when they reached the hotel. He had taken a quick glance to see whether David Drummond was hanging around, but hadn't seen him. Nevertheless, the man could be sitting in the bar or any one of the rooms leading off the reception.

"No, I'll be fine. They have a man working the lift, so I won't be alone on my way up to my floor. It's a quaint old custom they have kept on despite all the cutbacks." She paused and smiled. "Thank you for another lovely evening."

"It's been my pleasure," Alan replied. He was just about to turn away when Agnes caught his arm.

"And don't forget to keep me in the loop about you know what." Agnes grinned and tapped her nose.

"As if you would let me," was his swift reply.

After he left Agnes, Alan was about to flag down a passing cab. But then he changed his mind. A walk would do him good, besides he really needed to clear his head of everything he and his sergeant had been working on. They would be starting a new line of inquiry the following morning.

Chapter Eleven

The late night receptionist looked up as Agnes walked towards the lift. She would be going off duty shortly and a security officer would be taking over until morning.

"I hope you had a pleasant evening," she said.

"Yes, I did, thank you," Agnes replied, as she passed the desk.

The lift attendant smiled at Agnes as she approached. He was also about to go off duty, but he told her he would be happy to escort her to her floor.

Agnes smiled her thanks as she stepped into the lift.

But just as the doors were about to close the man, who she now knew to be called David Drummond, suddenly appeared from nowhere, and called out for them to wait for him.

Where the hell did he spring from? Agnes's heart skipped a beat. Surely she or Alan would have seen him if he had been in the reception area. Now she was beginning to panic. Was it possible he had been waiting for her to appear? But if that was the case, how did he know she was out? Was he watching her every move?

She needed to get a grip; pull herself together or whatever it was they called it these days. There was no way she wanted David Drummond to know what floor she was on. She stepped back, allowing him to give his floor number first. But, like a gentleman, he gestured towards her.

"You were here first," he said, giving her a brief smile, but it wasn't a warm and friendly smile. It was cold and forced.

"Thank you. Tenth floor, please." Agnes hoped the lift attendant wouldn't remember that she had come down from the fourth floor earlier that evening. If he did, he didn't say anything. He simply turned his attention to the man. "I believe you are on the eighth aren't you?"

"Good memory." Drummond mumbled.

Agnes could tell he didn't look too happy with how things were panning out. If he had been planning to follow her to her room, then it had been thwarted.

At the eighth floor the lift stopped and the doors slid open. David Drummond left the lift, but he didn't move away. He was still standing there when the doors closed.

"You're on the fourth floor, aren't you?" The lift attendant said, once the doors were tight shut.

"Yes," said Agnes. "But I didn't want him to know that."

"I sort of picked that up." He pressed the button for the tenth floor. "Best continue the charade. He could be hanging around down there; checking where the lift stops. Once we reach the tenth floor, I will take you back down to the fifth. You could take the stairs from there."

"Good thinking. Thank you." Agnes paused. "How did you know I was anxious about him?"

"I just picked up your vibes." He shrugged. "I guess it comes with the job."

By now they had reached the tenth floor. The lift stopped and the doors opened. A quick touch on the button sent the lift back down to the fifth floor.

Agnes smiled. "Thank you for your help," she added as she stepped from the lift. She was about to open her purse to tip the young man, but he stopped her.

"No. I'm happy to be of help. Besides, it all adds a little mystery to my otherwise boring job."

In her room Agnes poured herself a glass of wine from a complimentary bottle supplied by the hotel and sat down on a chair by the window. What on earth was going on? Who was this David Drummond and why was he so interested in her? Even in the lift, where she had been really close to him, she hadn't recognised him as someone she had met before.

As she sipped her wine, she had thoughts of him touring the tenth floor tomorrow looking for her. Well, he would be unlucky. But how long would it take for him to realise he had been conned? At least she knew what floor his room was on. She had the lift attendant to thank for that.

Tomorrow, she would pass on this latest snippet of information to Alan and see what he made of it. She yawned. But now, it was time for bed.

Agnes had just dozed off when she heard some loud voices from the room next door. Glancing at the clock, she saw it was only two o'clock. It was probably someone arriving back from one of the many nightclubs in the city. They would most likely settle down in a few minutes.

But the voices didn't stop. They grew louder. It seemed the woman had come back to find a piece of jewellery was missing. "Get on the phone to the manager," she screeched.

Her husband sounded furious when Agnes heard him on the phone asking for the manager. "I don't give a damn where he is. My wife has been robbed. Get him up here right now. And while you are about it, call the police!"

Agnes shivered, though she didn't know why. It wasn't her jewellery that had been stolen. She had taken it all with her when she went out last night. What she hadn't worn, she'd carried in her handbag. Therefore no one had been prowling around in her room.

At that thought, she sat up quickly. Or had they? A burglar wouldn't have known there was nothing in the room worth taking. She reached out and switched on the bedside light and looked around the room. Everything seemed to be as she left it when she went out last evening.

Still sitting in bed she drew her knees up to her chest and clasped her arms around them. It was becoming rather worrying to think that someone was able to gain access to the rooms while the guests were out enjoying themselves. It certainly wasn't doing anything for the hotel's reputation.

She heard a tap at the room next door. That would be Mr Jenkins, the manager. But before he could say a word, the man started shouting at him.

"What kind of hotel are you running here? We went out for the day only to come back to find my wife's necklace has been stolen, not to mention two pairs of my gold cufflinks." He paused for a second. "It's an absolute disgrace. I hope you have called the police as I requested!"

"Yes, the police are on their way. Might I suggest we all sit down and talk this through quietly?"

The manager's voice wasn't quite as loud as that of the angry guest, but Agnes could still hear every word of what was being said.

"I can only apologize for what has happened. But I am sure the staff is not to blame." Mr Jenkins continued.

"Who the hell else can get into the rooms? It has got to be a member of staff. Whoever is doing this must have a master keycard."

"Please keep your voices down. People are trying to sleep." Agnes heard the manager appealing to the guests to calm down. "I assure you none of the staff are to blame. The hotel checks out all applicants thoroughly before employing anyone." Mr Jenkins paused when there was another tap on the door. "That will be the police." He sounded rather relieved that someone else would have to deal with this man.

The shouting subsided once the police arrived and Agnes was unable to hear much more of what was being said. She lay back down and tried to go to sleep, but by now she was wide awake and her mind churned over everything she had heard.

So it seemed the couple next door was out all day yesterday. Probably having a lovely time taking in the sights and sounds of the city only to come back to find they had been robbed.

But if it wasn't a member of staff, who could it be? A key card was needed to get into any of the rooms. The manager had told Alan that all the master keys were locked in the safe every morning once the rooms had been cleaned, bedding changed or whatever else needed to be done. Only he and his deputy manager knew the combination to the safe. Therefore it was impossible for anyone to retrieve the keys from the safe, unless it was the manager or his deputy. But why would they risk their jobs and their reputation simply to rob the guests at the place of their employment? It didn't make sense.

Then there was the mysterious David Drummond. Where did he fit into the picture? Was he part of the robberies? Or could he be involved in the murder? And why was he taking such an avid interest in her? Agnes was still trying to puzzle it out when she fell into a deep and troubled sleep.

Chapter Twelve

The chief inspector was already at his desk when Sergeant Andrews arrived the next morning.

"Have you been here all night?"

"Not quite." Alan looked up. "But I wanted to get a head start."

"Does this mean you have some new evidence?"

"Sit down," said Alan. He went on to tell him about what Agnes had said the night before. "She could be right. We were so convinced that the body was thrown from the window, we didn't look for anything else. And that could be where we went wrong." He paused to allow Andrews to think about what he had told him.

"Well, it would account for the lack of blood in the room upstairs and on the pavement." Sergeant Andrews stroked his chin thoughtfully.

"Exactly!" Alan thumped his fist on the desk. "I should have thought about it at the time. Now I have allowed the real culprit time to get away."

"We still need to find out who was in the house at that time of night. But so far everyone is keeping quiet. No one will admit to having been in the room, nor lending the keys to anyone." Andrews sighed. "Do you want me to try again today?"

"Yes," Alan replied, "and make sure they all know that they are hindering a murder investigation. Accuse them with perverting the course of justice or threaten to bring them in for questioning. Do whatever it takes to get them to open up. This nonsense has gone on long enough."

Andrews was just about to leave the office, when Alan called him back. "I'm a little concerned about a man who seems to be following Agnes." He coughed and corrected himself. "I mean Mrs Lockwood. This man is staying at the hotel and is registered under the name of David Drummond. She doesn't recall ever having met him before, yet he seems to think she has. I'm just mentioning this now in case his name should come up while you are questioning the museum staff."

"Where will you be, should I have any information."

"I'm going to the hotel. It seems another robbery took place sometime yesterday. The theft was only discovered late last night. I have been instructed to look into it." The chief inspector raised his eyes to the ceiling. "I gather Mrs Hargreaves has been speaking to the chief constable again. Anyway," he added brushing his last remark aside, "I'll catch up with you later."

* * *

At the hotel, Agnes was just finishing her breakfast when the chief inspector arrived. Despite her late night, she had awoken early. She had rather hoped to catch a glimpse of the couple next door as they left their room, but it was not to be. They must have made an early start to their day; a member of staff was already in the room making the bed as Agnes made her way towards the lift.

"I gather there was a bit of excitement on your floor last night," the lift attendant had said on the way down to the ground floor. "The police were called in."

However Agnes, not wanting to say she had heard anything, tried to sound surprised by telling him that she had been so tired she had slept like a log. "So what happened?"

Unfortunately, he had been unable to tell her anything more than she already knew. She rather got the impression he was looking to her for more information on the incident. No doubt everything that happened in the hotel was filtered and passed on below stairs, so to speak. Perhaps it would be a good idea if Alan were to start his robbery investigation down there.

Alan saw her leaving the Dining Room as he stepped out of the manager's office. He smiled warmly as he strode over to her. "There's been another robbery," he said.

Agnes looked around her to make sure no one was listening. "Yes, I know. It took place in the room next to mine." She led him across to the Drawing Room and sat down. "The commotion woke me up. It seemed the couple had just come back to find some jewellery had disappeared. I assume the night security guy came up first. But then the manager was called. I guess Mr Jenkins must have an apartment here at the hotel as it didn't take him long. Then the police arrived." She paused. "It really is bad, isn't it? I mean no one will feel safe in this hotel, what with their belongings going missing, a guest being murdered and a man following guests around – well, following me anyway."

She hesitated, wondering whether to tell Alan about last night in the lift, but then thought it would be best to be upfront about everything. "He got in the lift with me last night." She went on to tell him how the lift attendant had outfoxed him. "Anyway, his room is on the eighth floor, which means if he is in the lift with me, then I'll have to go to the tenth floor and scoot down the stairs."

"I knew I should have seen you to your room last night," said Alan. "In future I shall see you to you room and there will be no arguments."

"Does this mean we are going out together again?"

"I certainly hope you will allow me to take you out again during your stay," he replied, sheepishly. "Actually, I rather hoped we could go out again this evening or we could even have dinner here if you'd prefer." He grinned. "Unless you're fed up with me hanging around all the time; you must have plans of your own."

"Not during the evening," she told him. "I do have a few things to do during the day. I wanted to look at some of the old places I used to haunt. But enough of that, how are you getting on with the case?"

"Which one?" Alan asked.

"Both."

"Well, as for the robberies, we don't have a clue about the missing jewellery. The robbery yesterday could have taken place at any time during the day as the couple went out straight after breakfast and didn't arrive back until very late. So far, we haven't been able to nail the thefts down to any special time of day. All the people who have been robbed seem to have spent a great deal of time away from the hotel on that particular day."

"And the murder?" Agnes prompted.

Alan glanced behind him to make sure no one around. "You do know that I shouldn't be discussing any of this with you?"

"But," Agnes cocked her head on one side.

"Truthfully, we don't have any information on that either, "Last night, after I left you, I walked along the quayside trying to get a clearer picture of the whole episode. Nothing makes any sense." Alan could tell she was about to interrupt, so he held up his hand and quickly continued. "Yes, I agree with what you said regarding a car or small van being in the area when we heard the thump. But that's only a starting point. There are still a great number of things unanswered. Why drop the body there? Why not drive a few more yards and throw it in the river? Or maybe the killer shot the woman where we found her and used a silencer?"

He paused for a moment to allow Agnes to throw her thoughts into the pool. However, she remained silent. He didn't know whether it was because she had none or she was still pondering on what he had said.

"The restaurant we were at on the night in question is across the road from the museum," he continued. "But it is also just out of sight of where we found the body due to the curve in the road. So yes, we heard a thump and when you saw a window close, we assumed the body had been dropped from there. Everything we, by that I mean the police, did afterwards was based on the understanding that the body had been thrown from the window. But there is absolutely no evidence that is the case. There is no blood in the room. In fact there is no blood anywhere in the house, which indicates the shooting did not take place there."

By now, Alan was tossing thoughts from one side of his head to the other in a battle to outwit the opposition, rather than actually reciting the facts to Agnes.

"Yet the shooting didn't take place outside the museum either or else we would have heard the gun shot and your team would have found blood on the pavement," said Agnes thoughtfully. She heaved a sigh. "Therefore, the whole murder must have taken place in another street in another part of the city. Somewhere in the centre of Newcastle; somewhere where the sound of a gun being fired would have been muffled by the voices of the people coming and going from the night clubs. I have heard it can be very noisy..."

"I could kiss you!" Alan interrupted, sharply. "You are so right. Of course! Anywhere in the city is noisy at night, but none more so than the streets in and around the Bigg Market."

Alan pulled out his phone and called his sergeant. "Andrews, as soon as you have finished with the staff at the museum, get up to the Bigg Market. Take some of the lads with you and start looking for blood." There was a pause while Andrews said something back to him. "Anywhere, Andrews you need to check out the whole of the Bigg Market area. If you don't find anything, move on to another part of the city where there's loud music and throngs of people late at night." There was another pause, while Andrews quibbled. "For goodness sake, Andrews, I know the whole city is heaving at night. Just get on with it. You're wasting time! I'll join you as soon as I can."

Alan shut his phone with a snap. What had he been thinking? He had got this case so wrong. Normally, if no blood had been found at the scene of a crime he would have widened the search. He would never have stuck to that one area. This wasn't like him at all.

But since meeting Agnes, his mind hadn't really been focused on the job. He was enjoying their friendship – perhaps he was enjoying it a little more than he should. She would be going back to Essex shortly and he probably wouldn't see her again. He needed to pull himself together and concentrate on his job.

"Are you alright," Agnes asked. Since Alan had given his instructions to his sergeant, he had gone very quiet.

"Yes. Sorry, Agnes, I was thinking about the case. I seem to have totally messed this one up. I'm normally so absorbed when working on an inquiry, but my attention seems to be slipping on this one." He looked across towards the reception. "And then there are these damn burglaries. It seems that someone staying at the hotel is incredibly clever."

Alan looked down at the floor. For the first time in a long while he felt despondent. Usually he picked up on some detail that didn't seem right and he would focus on it until the case was solved. He recalled how Andrews had often likened him to *Sherlock Holmes*; a fictional detective that, once having found even a shred of evidence, wouldn't let it go until the case was solved. Yet in these two cases, he was totally lost.

"So, what are you doing today?" Alan raised his head as he asked the question.

"I'm going to take a taxi across through Gateshead to Low Fell. I want to have a look around the area where I was brought up and then walk down to the school we used to go to – if it's still there. It could be pulled down for all I know."

Alan smiled. "Yes. It's still standing and going strong. That was where I first met you."

"Indeed it was," said Agnes.

Her mind drifted back to all those years ago. What if she had picked up on Alan's keenness to know her better? Would she have kept in touch? Would she have found her way back to Tyneside, to meet up with him again? Her life could have taken a completely different path. She closed her eyes for a second before snapping them back open. The past was long gone.

"It would be wonderful to go inside and look around," she said, putting on a cheerful smile. "But I doubt they would allow it. There are lots of rules and regulations where children are concerned."

"I best be getting on," said Alan rising to his feet. He knew he had spent too long talking to Agnes. But he was reluctant to leave her. "So, would you like to join me for dinner again this evening?"

"Yes, thank you," said Agnes. She smiled. "I'll leave you to choose the restaurant."

"Okay. I'll pick you up at seven."

Agnes watched him walk across to the reception where he had a few words with one of the staff before leaving the hotel.

Chapter Thirteen

Back in her room, Agnes put on her coat and after making sure she had put all her jewellery safely in the bottom of her large handbag she left the room and headed for the lift.

There were already a group of people in the lift when she stepped inside. Thankfully David Drummond wasn't one of them. No one said a word while the lift was in motion, but when they reached the ground floor she did hear one of the women passengers tell her friend that she was wearing all her jewellery today.

"What, all of it?" the friend, gasped.

"There was no way I was going to leave anything in my room while I was out."

"You could have left it in the hotel safe," the friend ventured.

"I don't trust the hotel safe. Whoever is taking the jewellery could have access to the safe. How else are they getting into the rooms?"

Agnes wondered how many other women staying at the hotel would be doing the same thing.

Outside on the pavement, Agnes headed for the taxi rank. She would have loved to look around to see whether she was being followed, but thought it best not to draw attention to herself. If David Drummond was hovering somewhere in the background, it was far better he didn't know she was on to him.

Climbing into the taxi, she allowed herself one brief glance over her shoulder, but she didn't see him. She told the driver where she wanted to go and he moved away from the kerb. Only then did she breathe a sigh of relief. Perhaps Drummond had finally realised she wasn't the person he thought she was.

Agnes enjoyed her trip through Gateshead on the way to Low Fell. How it had changed since she was last here. It was almost another world. Busy roads seemed to run in all directions. She could only ever remember there being one road, which ran straight down the high street and over the Tyne Bridge.

It didn't seem long before the taxi pulled up in the street where she was born. She stepped out of the cab and looked around. At first glance, it seemed nothing had changed at all. But then she noticed that a large detached house now stood on what had once been a piece of spare ground. At the other end of the street, the allotments, once so carefully tended by their owners, had all disappeared. In their place was a block of retirement flats. However apart from that it was almost as though she had been transported back in time.

It was the same at the school. Yes, there were a few new extensions, yet, in her mind's eye, nothing had really changed over the years.

It was then she noticed a car driving slowly along the road. She had already seen that car when she was walking down towards the school. Was it following her?

The car passed her and stopped a short way ahead, but no one got out. She told herself to stop panicking. After all there could be a reasonable explanation.

She decided to walk back towards the shops; at least she could go inside one of them if the person really was following her. It took a great deal of effort to walk slowly along the road. She wanted to run to the nearest shop. When Agnes reached the group of shops on the corner, she stood outside one and looked in the window. From where she was standing, she could see the car. It was still parked. But then it suddenly began to move forward and then turn right.

Agnes breathed a sigh of relief. The driver must have just stopped to take a phone call. However, she was just about to move away when she saw the car pull out of the turning and make its way towards her. For a moment she was rooted to the spot. But the car continued; drawing a little closer with every passing second. She had to do something. She had to get inside the shop. There were a few customers inside. He wouldn't follow her in there.

Once inside the shop, she placed herself at the end of the queue. She half turned, trying to see whether the car was outside. At first there was no sign of it, but then it pulled up near the door. Agnes couldn't see the driver's face, but then he leaned to one side and began to wave at someone. Was he waving at her? She certainly didn't recognize him. At least it wasn't David Drummond.

Agnes watched anxiously for a few seconds more, but then heaved a sigh of relief when she saw a woman hurry up to the car and climb into the seat next to the driver. The woman seemed pleased to see him and leant over to kiss his cheek. The man started the engine and they drove off.

Agnes suddenly felt stupid. Now she was being paranoid; believing everyone was following her. Thankfully she hadn't run into the shop making a fuss about being followed. She waited her turn in the queue and bought some chocolate. Chocolate was a favourite of hers and she knew it would calm her down a little.

Back outside, she couldn't make her mind up what to do next. She had planned on visiting Saltwell Park. She had loved playing on the various swings and roundabouts before feeding the ducks in the enormous lake.

But since her scare, which had actually turned out to be nothing, she had rather gone off the boil about continuing her trip down memory lane. Perhaps she could come back another day and, if Alan had a day off duty, he might even accompany her.

With that thought in mind, she headed off to find a bus or a taxi to take her back to her hotel.

* * *

Chief Inspector Alan Johnson's day had gone a little better. When he left the hotel he headed up to the Bigg Market to meet up with his sergeant. He found Andrews scouring the area with the help of several police officers. So far they hadn't found anything. But shortly after Alan arrived on the scene, one of the officers some distance down Grainger Street radioed to say he had found what looked like blood near the Church.

Alan hurried down the road to find the officer urging pedestrians to keep clear of the red marking. Though it was well and truly dried now, Alan desperately hoped that forensics would be able to match the blood to the victim lying in the morgue. Thankfully, despite some rain, it was still quite vivid.

He looked around at the nearby shops. None of them sold meat, which meant the blood hadn't come from a delivery of fresh meat to a butcher's shop. A few minutes later, the area on the pavement had been taped off.

"Well done, sir," Andrews had arrived on the scene. "Good idea to start looking further afield. I've asked forensics to get here as soon as possible." He looked at the sky. "The last thing we need is for it to start to rain."

Alan nodded towards the nearby shops. "Thank goodness none of them decided to swill the pavement. Otherwise we might not have found anything." It was true. Some of the shops had taken to giving the pavement outside their premises a quick wash before they opened each morning, to keep up appearances. Now we can only hope that if it is blood, it is from the victim in the morgue, otherwise we could have another murder on our hands.

When forensics arrived they confirmed the red mark on the pavement was blood. They took scrapings and several other tests before they went back to the lab.

"I want the results as soon as you have them," Alan called out to the last man as he climbed back into the van. The man nodded as he closed the door and the van took off.

Alan turned back to Andrews. "I don't want this pavement cleaned until we have some results from the tests."

By now, a crowd had gathered around the taped off area. Some were carrying mobile phones and were taking photographs of both him and Andrews, not to mention the blood on the pavement. Alan guessed they would probably end up on social media.

"Pity none of them were here when the murder took place," mumbled Alan. He looked across at the crowd for a moment before wandering over to meet them.

"I don't suppose any of you were flashing your cameras here a couple of nights ago when this took place." Alan gestured towards the blood on the pavement.

As Alan expected, a few of the people mumbled something before moving off. But he couldn't help noticing that one young woman looked a little awkward, as though she was trying to avoid his gaze. She was smartly dressed; not the sort of person you would usually associate with criminal activities. Though, on reflection, it was difficult to tell the difference these days.

Alan really felt the need to speak to her. However he didn't want everyone to know he was focusing his attention on this one woman. She was obviously being cautious for a reason. Had she seen something a few days ago; had she filmed something, but not realised at the time how important it might be? On the other hand, had she simply felt guilty at videoing the scene of a crime?

He knew he would have to tread carefully. The last thing he wanted to do was to frighten her off. He looked behind him to see whether there was a plain-clothed woman constable at the scene, but unfortunately they were all in uniform. The woman might have felt more comfortable speaking with another woman. Someone she didn't actually associate with the police. It was then that he caught a glimpse of Agnes climbing out of a taxi.

The taxi drove off in search of the next fare. Agnes was about to cross the road when she heard a familiar voice.

"What about you, Madam, did you see anything strange going on here a couple of nights ago?"

Agnes glanced from side to side, expecting to see someone alongside her. But there was no one. Was Alan talking to her? What was with this 'Madam' business? "Who, me?" she asked, placing her hand on her chest.

"Yes, you, Madam, I thought you were looking as though you might have something you would like to say." Alan was flashing his eyes from side to side, hoping she would pick up on the signal he needed her help.

"About what?" she asked, walking towards him. "I have no idea what you are talking about. I have just alighted from a taxi. Is there something you think I might be able to help you with?" She paused. "Who are you, by the way?"

"I am Detective Chief Inspector Johnson and I'm investigating a possible crime here." He pointed towards the blood. "I was asking whether anyone here might have seen anything a couple of nights ago. I simply thought you were about to say something."

"No," said Agnes, slowly. She was watching Alan's eyes darting to and from the lady he was standing next to. She moved towards him, guessing there was something he wanted her to do. "As I said, I had just stepped out of a taxi. Though to be honest, I was a little curious about what was going on here." She turned to the lady Alan had been indicating. "Have I missed something?"

Alan moved away, allowing Agnes to have a one to one chat with the woman.

"Not really," said the lady. "I think the detective was hoping someone might have caught something on their camera the other night." She pointed towards her mobile phone.

"Oh, I see." Agnes exclaimed. "How exciting." She looked around at the crowd. "And has anyone come forward."

"No, I'm afraid not."

"That's a shame. I guess the police need all the help they can get." Agnes looked at the woman's phone. "I don't suppose you were in the area, were you? I mean, it would be quite thrilling for you if you were able to help the police with their enquiries."

The woman looked down at the ground for a few moments.

Agnes got the impression the woman knew something, but was reluctant to get involved.

"Well, I was near here a couple of night ago." The woman said at last. She pointed to the corner of the road. "I was waiting for my friends to show up. We were going to go to one of the clubs, but we hadn't decided which one. Anyway, I heard something. I thought it might be a car backfiring, so I wasn't too worried. But then a man pushed past me, almost knocking me over. I had my phone in my hand as I had been about to ring someone to ask if they were on their way, so I quickly took a picture of him. I have no idea why. As far as I knew, he hadn't done anything. He might simply have been in a hurry because he was late for a date or something."

"Have you still got the photo?" Agnes asked, slowly. She smiled warmly trying not to upset the one person who just might have the only clue to the murder.

"Yes." She switched her camera on and found the picture she had taken the other night. "It's not very clear. The man was hurrying up the road at the time; though he did glance to one side just as I took the photo. He might have seen the flash."

"May I see?" Agnes said patiently. Though she really wanted to snatch the camera from the woman and take a look for herself.

The woman nodded and handed over the camera. Agnes gasped when she saw the photo. It was as the woman had said; it was blurred and the man was some feet away when the picture had been taken. Nevertheless Agnes recognised him in an instant. It was David Drummond, the man who had followed her across the Millennium Bridge the other day.

"Do you know him?" The woman asked. "It's just you seemed to recognize him."

"No, I don't know him," Agnes replied. She felt guilty, though she had actually told the truth. She didn't really know the man. "But I think you should show this picture to the detective. He will know what to do. Like you said, it might be nothing at all. But it could ease your mind to think you had done your bit to help the police with their investigation."

"Yes, I suppose you're right." The woman looked across to Alan and waved for him to come over.

Alan, accompanied by his sergeant, walked across to where the woman and Agnes were standing.

"I'll explain later, but for the moment pretend Mrs Lockwood is a stranger to us," Alan mumbled as they drew closer to the two women.

"I took this photo the other night," the woman said, handing the camera to Alan. "I hasten to add that I didn't see anything to do with the blood..." She gestured to where the pavement was sealed off. "But just after I heard what sounded like a car backfiring, this man came rushing around the corner. He almost knocked me over." She paused and looked at Agnes. "Like I said to this lady, that's all I know."

Alan took the camera and looked at the picture before showing it to Andrews. "What made you take the picture?" he asked.

The woman told him what she had already explained to Agnes. "It was a spur of the moment thing. If the phone hadn't already been in my hand, then I wouldn't have bothered." She hesitated. "Look, can I go now?"

"Will you allow me to transfer a copy of the photo onto my phone?" said Alan, taking his mobile phone from his pocket. "While I'm doing that, perhaps you could give your name and contact address to Sergeant Andrews in case we should need to speak to you further."

Alan sent a copy of the photo to his mobile phone and gave the lady, her phone back. "Thank you very much for your help, Miss Thurgood," he said, peering at the name Andrews had written in his notebook. "We'll check this man out."

Miss Thurgood took her phone. "I'm going to delete this photo, if you have no objections."

The detective glanced at his phone to make sure the picture was safely stored. "No, I haven't any objections."

He would rather the woman left the photo on her phone as back-up. But as things stood, he could not insist upon it. She could have deleted the photo at any time and they wouldn't have been any the wiser. Though, on second thoughts, it was possible it could be retrieved from the memory card, if absolutely necessary.

"So I can go now?"

Alan nodded and after giving Agnes a brief smile, Alice Thurgood hurried off up the road.

Agnes was thoughtful as she watched Alice Thurgood turn and wave to her before disappearing around the corner at the bottom of the road. She hadn't noticed it when she was speaking to her, but from a distance, Alice bore a striking resemblance to herself. Was it possible that when David Drummond saw her at the hotel, he had mistakenly believed it was she who had taken the photo that night and not Alice? A chill ran through her at the thought.

"Are you alright?" Alan noticed that Agnes had suddenly turned pale.

"Would you like to sit in my car?" It was Andrews who was speaking now.

"I'll be fine in a minute. I think seeing David Drummond's face in that photo shocked me." Agnes tried to make light of it. Nevertheless she allowed Andrews to lead her to his car. "If I could just sit here for a few minutes, I'm sure I'll be fine."

Alan hadn't taken his eyes off Agnes as she stepped into the sergeant's car. Yes, he agreed, it must have been a shock for Agnes to see Drummond's face suddenly pop up like that. But he felt there was more to it than just the photograph. Agnes had seen the photo a few minutes before he did. She'd had time to get used to it, while she persuaded Alice Thurgood to show it to him. Something had happened in the last few minutes after Alice left them and strode off down Grainger Street. Had Alice Thurgood given Agnes some parting comment, which had weighed heavily on her? He hadn't heard anything pass between them. Alice had simply smiled and moved on. But had there been something beneath that smile, something he had missed?

He was meeting Agnes again that evening. There wasn't anything he could do or say until they were alone. It was obvious she wasn't going to say a word while Andrews was around.

"It's a stroke of luck Mrs Lockwood should turn up at the right moment." Andrews had rejoined his boss.

"Yes. I couldn't believe it when she stepped out of that taxi just as Miss Thurgood was about to move off."

"Quick thinking on your part, sir"

"Quick thinking on Mrs Lockwood's part, I would say," said Alan.

He was still admiring how Agnes had picked up on his signs to question the woman next to her. He looked across to the police car.

"Is she okay? Perhaps I shouldn't have involved her. But I felt it was the only way to get Miss Thurgood to open up."

"She'll be fine once she gets back to the hotel and is able to freshen up," said Andrews. He glanced back at the car. "Women are like that. They want to be involved, but then find it's all too much for them."

Alan glared at his sergeant. How he would love to tell him what an ass he was. But he decided to leave that to April, Andrews' latest girlfriend, who, from what Andrews had told him, stood for no nonsense where equality of the sexes was concerned.

"Hmm, I wonder what April would say to that."

* * *

Alan walked across to the car where Agnes was sitting and opened the door. "Would you like me to take you back to the hotel?" he glanced back at where the police had cordoned off the area. "There's nothing more to be done here." He hesitated, before adding. "I might be wrong here, but I think there's something else I need to know."

Agnes closed her eyes for a few seconds before opening them again. "Yes there is."

Without a moment's hesitation, Alan turned back to his sergeant. "I'm taking Mrs Lockwood back to her hotel. I'll send the car back for you." Without waiting for a reply he beckoned a police officer to get into the driving seat. He jumped into the car beside Agnes and told the driver where to take them.

Not one word was spoken in the car as the driver headed towards the hotel on the quayside.

At the hotel, Alan told the officer to take the car back to where Andrews would be waiting. "Tell someone to take my car back to the station. I'll make my own way back."

Inside the hotel, Agnes told Alan to accompany her to her room. "We need to talk quietly."

At her request, they took the stairs rather than the lift. Agnes was concerned that a different lift attendant might be on duty. She didn't want the floor she was on to be noted by someone else.

In her room she sat down on the large sofa and stared at Alan for a few minutes before looking down at the floor. "I know you are going to think I am crazy, but I have been thinking this through ever since I saw Alice march off down the street and I know I am right." She paused.

"You're right about what?" Alan prompted, after what seemed like a long silence.

"Okay." Agnes clenched her hands together and slapped them down onto her lap. "Today, when I watched Alice walk off down Grainger Street, it suddenly occurred to me how she and I look so much alike." She paused. "I mean, we look alike from a distance."

Alan stared at her.

"Yes, I know Alice Thurgood is a great deal younger than me. But when I watched her walking down the street this afternoon, I realised we could have been mistaken for each other."

Alan still didn't say anything.

"For goodness sake, think about it, Alan. We have, albeit roughly," she shrugged and pointed to her recently cut hair, "the same hairstyle – even similar in colour. We're certainly the same height. We were wearing comparable coats, both almost the same colour. She seems to lean slightly to one side as she walks – as I do."

Alan raised his eyebrows. She pointed to her hip.

"In my case, it's because of some stupid thing I did years ago. I have absolutely no idea why Alice does it. However, in my mind, what it leads to is that, one evening, David Drummond has the need to run up the street. We don't yet know why. He quickly turns around when he sees a camera flash, but he only catches a glimpse of the person taking the picture, before hurrying on. Then, quite out of the blue, he sees me at the hotel and his mind flashes back to the night when someone took a photo of him." She shook her head. "Don't you see, Alan? I believe he thinks that person was me!"

Alan rose to his feet and walked across to the window. His mind was flitting back to earlier in the afternoon when he had been talking to Alice Thurgood. He hadn't noticed it before, but Agnes was right. There *was* a slight resemblance between them. He turned back to face her. "I think you need to pack and leave the hotel as soon as possible. If Drummond is mixed up in something and he thinks you have a photo of him fleeing the scene, then he'll see you as a threat."

Agnes knew the detective was right. In her head she could almost hear Jim telling her the same thing. It was true. The right thing for her to do now would be to go back to Essex pack a case and visit her sons in Australia.

Yet she had never been one for doing the right thing. Even Jim had never stood in her way once she had made her mind up about something. Though quite honestly, things had never been quite as serious as this. Her life could be at stake here.

She looked up at Alan and took a deep breath. "No. I'm going to stay here and see it through. And before you say a word," she could tell he was about to intervene, "there's nothing you can do to stop me." She stood up and stared him in the eye. "So, what's next?"

Chapter Fourteen

Back at the police station, Alan explained to his sergeant why Agnes had been so upset. "I do think she has a point. While she was telling me all this, I kept thinking back to Alice Thurgood. I can't say I noticed any resemblance between her and Agnes at the time, but on reflection, she could be right."

Alan took out his phone and looked at the photo again. "I want copies of this picture printed out and given to every police officer working this case. They need to be aware that this man is a suspect. However, be sure they understand they mustn't do anything to alert him to the fact we are on to him. We need positive proof he is involved before we bring him in. In the meantime we need to keep a close eye on him." He paused. "I want to know his every move."

Andrews transferred the photo to his computer and began printing off some copies.

"Why don't we just go to the hotel and question him?"

"For goodness sake, Sergeant, at the moment we have absolutely nothing on him. Even the photograph is nothing without something to back it up. For the time being, we'll continue to let him believe he has got away with whatever it is he has done and hope he does something to trip an alarm."

Andrews pulled the photos from the printer. "I'll get these spread around the office."

Alan nodded. "And remember. We keep a low profile, watch and listen; make sure everyone understands that. Hopefully we'll get something more solid to go on."

When Andrews disappeared down the corridor, Alan sat back in his chair. If only Agnes wasn't caught up in all this. On one side of the coin, he was pleased she had refused to leave the hotel. It would have been disappointing if she had packed up and left. But, on the other side, he was very concerned about her safety. If Drummond had been involved in the murder it meant he was an extremely dangerous man. More especially if he thought Agnes had evidence, which might incriminate him.

Was there something they could do to make Drummond realise he was watching the wrong woman? What if Agnes was to leave her phone lying around when Drummond was nearby? Maybe if he picked it up and looked at the stored photographs and found nothing to incriminate him he would leave her alone.

Alan looked down at the floor and shook his head. Surely he could come up with something not so damn obvious. Yet, despite giving it more thought, nothing else came to mind. Perhaps they could talk about it over dinner that evening.

The thought of dinner reminded him he needed to book a table somewhere. He pondered for a moment over where to take Agnes this evening. There were still a couple of rather nice restaurants on the quayside, which she might enjoy. But would she rather go up into the city? He should have insisted she made the decision this time. Yet he had the feeling she would still have left it to him.

He would like to have had time to linger on those thoughts for a while longer, but someone popped their head around the door informing him the superintendent would like to see him right away.

* * *

Agnes sat quietly in her room after Alan had left. She had been surprised when she saw David Drummond's picture on Alice's phone. She certainly hadn't expected to see anyone she would recognize. It had left her quite shaken when she realised why he might be tailing her. Even now, she felt uncomfortable knowing he was actually staying in this very hotel. At the moment, he didn't know which room she was in – or even what floor she was on, thanks to the lift attendant. But he could find out easily enough. All he had to do was to point her out to one of the receptionists and they could fill him in on all her details.

There was the option of moving to another hotel. But it was possible Drummond would find her. He could telephone various hotels in the city and ask whether she was staying there; giving some excuse for needing to contact her urgently. To avoid that, she would need to check in under a different name.

Alan hadn't answered her question before he left. When she had asked him 'what's next', he simply told her he was heading back to the station. "I want some copies of this photo printed out."

That wasn't what she had meant at all. Though she guessed he knew that already. He probably didn't want her to get any further involved. She sighed. Yet, for goodness sake, she was already involved and she wanted to continue to help find out what was going on at the hotel.

She ticked off the events on her fingers. First there were robberies. Then a woman, who happened to be staying at the hotel, was murdered, though her body was not found here. Third, today they find that another guest could possibly be involved in one – or even both of the crimes. So what would be next?

She sighed. This was as close as she had ever come to investigating a real crime and she wasn't going be to put off by the detective working the case, even if he was trying to keep her out of harm's way. But where did she go from here? What would be number four on the list?

Agnes took a deep breath. She needed to start at the beginning; when the first robbery took place. But what if that hadn't been the first theft! Something could have happened before she arrived. Perhaps, back then, whatever went missing hadn't been noticed until the people left the hotel.

She shook her head. No. There was no way she could go down that road. She could only dwell on what had happened since she arrived at the hotel a few days ago. Gosh! Was it only a few days ago? So much had happened, it seemed as though she had been here for a couple of weeks.

* * *

Alan knocked on the superintendent's door and walked in. "You wanted to see me, sir?"

"Yes, sit down." The superintendent gestured towards a chair on the other side of his desk.

"How can I help you?" Alan asked once he was seated.

"It's about these robberies at the hotel. I have had the chief constable on the phone asking me what is being done and couldn't tell him a damn thing." The superintendent sat back in his chair. "Are you any further forward with the investigation?"

"There's been a murder since I first started to investigate the robbery. A woman staying at the hotel was found dead outside The Bessie Surtees Museum a couple of nights ago. I thought that would take priority." Alan noticed the superintendent fidget in his chair.

"Yes, of course," the superintendent replied. He coughed. "I think the chief constable wants to be kept in the loop and looks to me for answers."

"We think the murder and the robberies could be connected," Alan suggested. He hoped he wasn't going to be asked to explain why he had come to that conclusion, because at that moment he had no real evidence.

"I see." The superintendent paused for a moment before leaning forward. "Yes, I see how there could be a connection. This poor woman might have seen something and had to be silenced before she reported it. Very good, Johnson, I'll pass that on to the chief constable."

Very little else was said before Alan was dismissed. He heaved a sigh of relief as he stepped out into the corridor. He had come out of that unscathed. It had surprised him that the chief constable could put a robbery before a murder. But he supposed with Mrs Hargreaves on his back he would have to look for something to appease her.

Back in the office, Andrews was on the phone. He looked up as Alan entered and placed his hand over the mouthpiece. "There's been another robbery at the hotel, sir."

"Not another one," Alan murmured as he slumped into his chair to wait until Andrews had finished the call.

"A diamond necklace and a pair of diamanté earrings have gone missing this time," said the sergeant, reading from his notes. "It seems the couple had only been out of the hotel for two hours. They were meeting some friends in the Sage. When they got back the wife went to put her jewellery in a box by the bed and she found some pieces were missing. Before calling the manager, they both searched all the drawers to make sure she hadn't put them somewhere else by mistake. But they weren't there."

"This is ridiculous." Alan thumped his fist on his desk. This whole case was beginning to irritate him. "How is the thief gaining access to the rooms without a key card?" Now he was talking more to himself than to Andrews. "The manager tells us that only trusted staff is allowed to use these cards for cleaning, etc. At all other times the keycards are locked away. Yet somehow, someone is able to get hold of one of these cards, get into the rooms and steal expensive jewellery." He looked across at Andrews. "Despite what the manager says, this has got to be an inside job. One of the staff must know something. Hopefully, when we find out who it is, we will find our killer."

Chapter Fifteen

Agnes felt the need to get out of her room. Alan had suggested she should stay inside the hotel until he picked her up that evening. But she was beginning to feel trapped. Peering out of the window, she saw there were several people milling around on the quayside below. Surely, with so many people about, it would be safe for her to venture out. Even a walk around the outside of the hotel would be better than being a virtual prisoner in her room.

She was enjoying a glass of wine at one of the tables outside a café close to the Millennium Bridge when something above caught her eye. Looking up, she smiled when she saw a bird flying above the café. It was most likely looking for food dropped by people having lunch outside. But as she was about to turn away, she noticed someone leaning out of one of the hotel windows. *Another person enjoying the scenery*, she thought. However, she suddenly realised the person wasn't admiring the view of the Tyne. They were looking down at the pavement beneath the window.

From her position, Agnes wasn't able to see who or what the person was looking at; the café building blocked out the lower part of the hotel. At first, she was tempted to slide off her chair and move to the side of the café to see what this person was looking at. But she noticed the tables outside the café were filling up rather quickly. The chances were her wine would be whisked away by a passing waiter and she would lose her seat. With that discouraging thought in mind, she decided to stay where she was.

A few minutes later her attention had turned to the people streaming towards the Millennium Bridge. Some were wearing casual clothes, obviously tourists, but there were people dressed as though they were going to business meetings. From her brief visit to The Baltic, she had picked up the fact there were rooms available, for such meetings.

She picked up her glass and took a sip of wine, but almost choked when she unexpectedly saw a face she recognised. Setting her glass down on the table, she looked again to make sure. Nevertheless, she had been right the first time. It was David Drummond.

Her eyes followed him as he approached the bridge. At first, he seemed focused on wherever he was going. However, as he was about to step onto the bridge, he stopped abruptly and looked towards where she was sitting. It was almost as though he knew someone was watching him.

She swiftly turned her head in the direction of the café, hoping he hadn't seen her observing him. However, as it turned out, she could see his reflection in the café windows. He stood there for a moment, as though he was considering whether he should come across to speak with her. But when the people gathering behind him urged him to move on, he swiftly continued across the bridge.

Agnes breathed a sigh of relief. Yet she wondered whether it might have been better if he had actually confronted her with whatever was bothering him. If it was the wretched photograph he was concerned about, then she could have honestly told him she had no such picture on her phone. She could even have shown him her phone as proof.

He was halfway across the bridge before she dared to turn to look back at him. She picked him out easily, but then, quite suddenly he disappeared into a crowd of people

Her eyes flashed from one person to another as numerous people crossed the bridge, but she didn't see Drummond again. Part of her wanted to rush across the bridge to see whether she could pick up his trail. He might have gone to the yacht, which was still moored on the other side of the Tyne. If he was meeting up with someone from the yacht, it was possible she could take a photograph of them talking together. The police might be very interested to see it.

But then her cautious side took over. If she was right, and Drummond believed she had photographed him that night, she would only be adding fuel to the fire if he caught her spying on him. Therefore, after further thought she decided to play it safe and stay where she was.

Nevertheless, she couldn't help wondering whether it was Jim, her late husband, or her friend, Chief Inspector Alan Johnson, she could hear shouting in her ear to play it safe and leave it alone.

* * *

David Drummond continued to walk across the bridge. He wanted to turn around to see if the woman was watching him, but he forced himself to keep going. There was no point in making himself even more conspicuous. Besides, there was no need. He could feel her eyes following his every step. That wretched woman seemed to be everywhere he went.

As he drew nearer to the end of the bridge, he quickened his pace slightly and mingled with a group of people in front of him. He had seen them leaving a coach parked on the other side of the river. From their raised voices, he learned that some of them were visiting Tyneside for the first time. The tour guide was explaining all the changes, which had taken place in recent years. If he left the bridge safely tucked in with them, he might have a chance of slipping off to meet his partners without being seen by the busybody on the other side.

Everything had been going according to plan until Mary had overhead him on the phone one evening. How could he have been so careless? Why hadn't he waited until he was safely in his room before making the call? Instead he had used his mobile outside the hotel. Mary had been around the corner smoking a cigarette. Even now he could kick himself. That one stupid mistake had cost the woman her life.

* * *

Agnes heard a tap on her door close to seven o'clock. "Who is it?" she called out cautiously. She had made the decision to be extra careful if anyone knocked on her door, especially if she hadn't ordered room service. Recognizing Alan's voice, she opened the door.

"I'm pleased to see you have taken my advice about being wary who you open the door to," Alan said, as he walked into the room.

"Yes and you are going to be proud of me when I tell you my latest piece of news."

Alan raised his eyebrows, inviting her to continue. But Agnes wasn't prepared to say another word until they were seated in the restaurant and able to exchange information. Never be rushed, Jim had always said. Give a little, take a little. There was no way she was going to allow that to change, no matter who she was dealing with.

"You first," Agnes said, once they were seated in the restaurant.

"Actually," Alan looked down at his clenched hands. "I don't have any further information. And on top of that, the superintendent called me into his office wanting to know why we haven't found who is stealing the jewellery at the hotel."

"Oh, Alan, I am so sorry." Agnes leaned forward across the table. "Surely he must realise a murder must come before some stupid theft."

"Yes, I'm sure he does." Alan sighed. "But, at the same time, he has the chief constable on his back because Mrs Hargreaves has called in a favour. It seems she knows him personally and has put it to him to find the culprit and get her jewellery back. Of course it starts with him, but then it gets passed down the chain until it reaches the likes of me. Then I'm supposed to drop everything until people like Mrs Hargreaves are satisfied." He shrugged. "So what have you got to tell me?" He paused. "I thought you weren't going out anywhere until I called for you."

"For goodness sake, Alan, I'm here on holiday. I am trying to trace my past life. I can't do it by sitting in my room all day. If I have to do that, then I might as well forget the whole thing and go back home."

Alan nodded. What she said was true. But he would be very sad to see her leave. The evenings he had spent with her over the last few days had been a far cry from the weeks and months he had spent alone. Occasionally he would invite someone out for a meal. But no one had met up to his expectations – not like Agnes.

Agnes was different. There was something about her which excited him. She was a woman with a mind of her own. She did what she wanted to do and thought about it after the event.

When he had been in the army, he'd been much the same. He'd enjoyed not knowing what was ahead. Back then, every day had been an adventure. Yes, the sergeant or sergeant major had chirped in with what they'd thought he should be doing or how they believed he should be doing it. Yet, in the end, they had accepted his decision and stood by him. But here in the police force, even if you were a fair way up the scale of promotion, you had to adhere to whatever the top brass said.

"Okay," Agnes felt sorry for Alan. Even without him saying anything further, she'd picked up on his problem. "Let me tell you about my day." She began at the beginning, telling how she had seen someone leaning out of one of the windows of the hotel. "It wasn't the first time I'd seen someone admiring the view. I have to say, the view from the windows of the hotel are really..."

"Okay, I get it," Alan interrupted. He threw his hands in the air. "The view is good; so what?"

"If you are in that sort of mood, then I'm going back to the hotel." Agnes picked up her handbag as though she was about to leave.

Alan reached across the table and grabbed her hand. "Agnes, I am so sorry. I really didn't mean to upset you. I guess I'm frustrated at how this case is going. Please tell me about the face at the window."

Agnes placed her bag back on the floor. She could understand his frustration. His case seemed to be going backwards. Nevertheless, that was no reason to take it out on her.

"Very well," she said after a long pause. "Like I said, I have seen people leaning out the windows of the hotel several times. I thought they were trying to get a better view of the bridges along the River Tyne." She shrugged. "Perhaps they were. But giving it some thought, I realised that all the windows looking towards the Tyne have a slight bay. It's possible to see up and down the river without actually leaning out and maybe falling down to the pavement below."

While she was talking, Agnes was gesturing with her hands. Demonstrating how easily anyone could fall from the window.

"I see," said Alan. "Well, no, I don't really. Yes I agree that someone could lose their balance and fall if they were too enthusiastic about how far they could see. But I'm not sure where you are leading with this."

"I'm coming to that," said Agnes excitedly. "Today, when I was sitting outside the café, I saw someone hanging out of the window again. I couldn't see who it was. But the person wasn't looking up and down the river. They were staring straight down at the pavement beneath the window."

"So?" Alan questioned. He still couldn't see why she was making such a big deal of someone looking out of the window. Surely people did it all the time when they stayed at a hotel.

"Well, while I was sitting there, I got to thinking. What if he wasn't simply admiring the view? What if there was another reason why he or she was hanging out of the window. What if it was all pre-arranged? What if he or she was at the open window for some ulterior motive?"

"Hang on a minute. There are a lot of ifs there. What ulterior motive?" Alan frowned. "I really do think you have read too many *Miss Marple* books. What could anyone be doing wrong simply by leaning out of the window." He looked up as the waiter handed them each a menu. He nodded and ordered a bottle of wine, before looking back at Agnes.

Agnes held up her menu and peered inside. But then she lowered it and looked across at Alan. "What if...?"

"Please Agnes," Alan interrupted, "no more what ifs."

Agnes smiled. "What if," she continued, ignoring his comment, "whoever is stealing the jewellery is getting it out of the hotel by dropping it from the open window into the hands of an accomplice? An accomplice, who just happens to be waiting on the pavement below?" She slowly raised the menu to her eyes again and began to look through the tempting meals on offer.

* * *

Alan stared across the table, as he thought over what Agnes had just said. Was it possible she could be right? Back at the police station the big question had been, how had the thief managed to smuggle the jewellery out of the hotel? No one had been allowed to leave the hotel until they, their luggage and their rooms had been searched. Of course there were occasions when the theft hadn't been noticed until later in the day. Then the thief could have walked out with it in his pocket. On the other hand, how did the thief know when the victims would return to the hotel? They could have simply popped out for a few minutes and returned to find their jewellery missing. In that event, they would have called the manager and the police without further ado. Anyone wanting to leave the hotel would have been stopped until there had been a full search.

The waiter returned with the wine and poured them each a glass.

* * *

"What do you think?" Agnes asked. She took a sip of her wine.

"I think you could be onto something," Alan replied.

"No, silly," Agnes laughed. "I meant what were you going to have from the menu?"

"I haven't even looked. I've been too busy thinking about what you said."

"Well, I have something else for you to think about." Agnes closed the menu and leaned across the table. "When I saw the person leaning out of the window this afternoon, I was tempted to creep up to the corner of the café to see whether there was anyone waiting below.

But I didn't. I stayed where I was because I didn't want to lose my table. Anyway, it was only a few minutes afterwards that I saw David Drummond appear in my line of sight. He was heading towards the Millennium Bridge. He caught me watching him, so I looked away until he was halfway over the bridge. When I looked back, I caught a brief glimpse of him before I lost him in the crowd." She paused. "But it set me thinking. What if..." she held up her hand as Alan was about to interrupt. "Please, Alan, hear me out. What if he had been standing on the pavement beneath the window waiting to catch the stolen jewellery when it was dropped to the ground?"

Alan thought about what she had said. It was feasible. Nevertheless, it was a long shot. There were people wandering past the hotel all the time. Wouldn't someone have noticed and thought it strange that something was being thrown down to a man waiting below?

"I know what you are thinking," Agnes interrupted his thoughts. "The quayside is busy; people walking past would have seen it happening. But what if these two individuals have some sort of an arrangement?"

"What arrangement?"

"I don't know." Agnes flapped her hands in frustration. "I can't think of everything..." She paused. "Wait! I have an idea. What if the guy upstairs, rings the guy on the ground to tell him he's ready to drop the loot? Anyone nearby might think the guy on the ground has left something in his room and can't be bothered to go all the way back up to get it and is asking his pal to drop it down for him; especially if he is standing with his phone to his ear. Does that work for you?"

Before Alan could say anything, the waiter appeared to take their order. With so much talking going on, neither had really taken a lot of notice of what was on offer. They both looked at the menu and ordered the first thing they saw, before getting back to the conversation.

"It's possible," Alan said slowly, once the waiter had disappeared. "But don't you think it is too easy?"

"That's what makes it so probable," Agnes replied. "Why make something longwinded and complicated, when there is a perfectly simple way to smuggle stolen goods out of the hotel. Jewellery is very light, so it wouldn't be a problem for someone to catch it."

Alan still wasn't sure he agreed. However, he was prepared to give it more thought. Meanwhile, he changed tack. "There is still the question of how someone is getting into the rooms to steal the items."

Agnes shook her head. "I've thought about that, too. But I haven't come up with an answer. Unless someone has managed to invent a master keycard, it looks like one of the staff is involved." She paused. "But I don't like to think one of them is a thief. They are all so polite and helpful to the guests."

"Let's change the subject." Alan nodded towards the waiter as he approached them. He was carrying their meals.

"Let's not," Agnes replied. "We haven't mentioned the murder of Mary Swinburne yet. Have you had any results from your lab? Do you think it's possible that the murder and the thefts are connected? Could she have been involved? Or might she have just been in the wrong place at the wrong time?"

"Whoa, slow down!" Alan held up his hands as though shielding himself from the barrage of questions. "At this precise moment, we are no further forward. Hopefully we will hear from the lab tomorrow. But if the blood on the pavement doesn't turn out to be from Mary Swinburne, then it could mean we have a second murder on our hands." He thought for a moment. "Unless there was some sort of an accident there. In which case, we would need to check the hospitals to find out whether anyone had been admitted over the last couple of days." He looked at Agnes and sighed. "Now, can we simply enjoy our meal without all this talk of murder and theft?"

Chapter Sixteen

The sun was shining brightly through the window when Agnes awoke the next morning. How lucky she had been with the weather so far. It could be rather cold and damp in October. However, it seemed summer was reluctant to step back and make way for autumn this year.

She lay for a few minutes, reflecting on the evening before. Alan had insisted on escorting her up to her room. It had been rather late when they got back to the hotel and he had suggested that the lift attendant might have gone off duty. She hadn't argued with him. There was no way that she wanted to be alone in the lift with David Drummond.

As it turned out, the lift attendant had still been on duty and there was no sign of Drummond. But it was better to be safe than sorry.

She wondered whether she should mention any of this to her sons in Australia. She felt a little guilty at keeping them in the dark. They knew she was spending a week or two on Tyneside. But though she had given them each a call on the day she arrived, she hadn't got back to them since. *Best to keep it to myself,* she thought, as she dragged herself from beneath the duvet. They would only worry and no doubt tell her to go back home. Not that she would do as she was told. But if she resisted, there was the possibility one of them might make the long trip to England to talk her into it.

Pulling back the curtains, she looked down onto the quayside. The view was rather striking from up here. It was then she noticed a small chain at the top of the window that opened. The other end of it was fixed to a stationary window, probably to stop the window opening too far. If that was the case, how was the person able to open the window far enough to lean out and drop the booty?

Moving closer, she reached up and took hold of the chain. She moved it around a little, but it held firm. She sniffed. There had to be a way of releasing it. She took a step back and looked at it for a few moments. Then she realised one of the links was slightly larger than the others. It was where it was fastened to the stationary window. She took hold of the chain again and found that, with a little maneuvering, the link could be slid over the bolt holding it in place.

Satisfied that she had solved the puzzle, Agnes set about getting dressed.

* * *

Over breakfast, she deliberated over what to do that day. Should she hang around the hotel in the hope of finding out who was behind the robberies and how the thief was getting into the rooms? But, on reflection, how would she do that? She couldn't wander around the corridors all day expecting to find someone fiddling with a lock. That would only draw attention to herself. She might even be suspected of being the thief! Neither would she learn anything by sitting in the Drawing Room watching people as they come and go about their business. Besides, that would be terribly boring.

In the end, she decided to go for stroll along the quay to Bessie Surtees house; to the spot where she and Alan had found the body a few nights ago. She wasn't really expecting to find any new clues. The police, forensics and goodness knows who else had been over the area with a fine tooth comb on the evening of the murder and the morning after.

Nevertheless, the walk would do her good and she might even go inside the house, if the police had allowed it to reopen.

* * *

Alan's morning hadn't gone well. The blood found on the pavement was not that of Mary Swinburne. "So we are back to square one!" Alan thumped his fist on his desk. "So what the hell was David Drummond doing skirting around Grainger Street the other evening? And if it wasn't Mary Swinburne's blood, whose was it?"

"Sir, do you think we need to start this investigation from the beginning," Sergeant Andrews spoke quietly.

The sergeant was aware that going back and starting from the beginning of a case was something DCI Johnson hated. He was a man who liked to get things right from the outset. Yet that wasn't always possible. There were times when the clues all led to a dead end and there was nothing else for it, but to begin again. It was annoying, but it was something that went with the job.

"And where would that be?" Alan retorted. "Do we go back to the thefts, as the chief constable would have us do? Or do we start with the murder of Mary Swinburne? Or even begin by investigating the cagey David Drummond?"

Alan shook his head. He hadn't meant to jump down his sergeant's throat; it wasn't his fault the investigation was falling apart. Yet at the moment, Alan knew his concentration wasn't entirely on the case. For one thing, he couldn't get Agnes out of his mind. He wasn't looking forward to the day she would return to her life in Essex. But, at the same time, he was very concerned for her safety.

Already, Mary Swinburne, who had been a guest at the hotel, was lying dead in the mortuary at this very moment and no one knew why. Was it possible she had seen or overheard something incriminating and was murdered to keep her from passing on information to the police? If that was the case, then Agnes could be next. She was poking around everywhere, trying to find more and more evidence. Even now, she could be out there keeping watch on David Drummond.

That last thought filled Alan with utmost horror. He had to get to the hotel to make sure she was alright.

"Get onto the pathologist and ask him to take another look at the body; there might be something he's missed." Alan barked out instructions, as he reached for his coat. "After that, start trying to find out a little more about David Drummond. For goodness sake, someone must know who the hell he is."

"Okay, sir." Andrews reached for his phone. "Where will you be?"

"I'm going back to the hotel to do a little more probing around. I suddenly get the feeling that there is more going on there than jewel thefts."

"Such as?" Andrews asked.

"I don't know," the DCI replied, impatiently.

It was true, he didn't know. But thinking about Mary Swinburne, the thefts and now the possibility of another murder in the city centre all being linked, made him wonder why Drummond hadn't simply disappeared when he believed Agnes was watching him. There had to be something else, some greater reason for him to hang around the hotel. But at the moment, his main concern was for Agnes.

"Keep me informed with anything you find. And check the hospitals again. We need to be absolutely sure someone wasn't picked up on Grainger Street and dumped outside an Accident and Emergency department in the city."

* * *

Agnes was enjoying her walk along the quayside. She was going to miss this when she went back to Essex. She lived in a quiet village and though it was very pleasant, she missed having more people around her. True, she had lots of friends in the village. But being here was different. Even though she didn't know the people she passed on the street, they all nodded and smiled as though she met up with them every morning. This was one part of Tyneside she remembered well, the friendliness of the people.

It wasn't long before she found herself opposite Bessie Surtees House. She looked up at the window she had seen being pulled shut that fateful night. There was someone gazing out of the window; obviously the house was open to visitors again. She crossed the road and stood on the very spot where she and Alan had found the body. There was nothing to see. It was as though she had dreamed the whole thing. She wasn't sure what she had expected to find. Alan had told her that no blood had been found either on the pavement or in the house itself. Nor had the police discovered who had been in the house at the time they found the body.

Why had Mary Swinburne been murdered? What had the poor woman done to upset someone enough for them to kill her? Why had her body been dumped here? Agnes looked towards the River Tyne. Could they have meant to throw the body into the river? If so why had they found it necessary stop and dump it on the pavement? And did David Drummond have anything to do with any of this? All these questions and more ran through her mind as she stood there gazing down at the ground.

"You alright, pet?"

Agnes looked up to see an elderly woman staring at her. "Yes, thank you."

"It's just you looked a little lost standing there. I thought you might not be feeling well."

"I'm fine, thank you." Agnes smiled at the woman.

The woman nodded, and was about to turn away, when Agnes quickly caught her arm. "It's just that a friend and I found a body here a few nights ago and I understand the police still don't know why the poor woman was killed." Agnes let go of the woman's arm. She was surprised at herself. Why on earth had she said that?

"Yes, that was a shame. Poor woman, I read about it in the papers. Nasty shock for you and your friend, though, coming across a body like that."

"Yes, yes it was." Agnes nodded. "There are some terrible people in the world. I'm sorry to have troubled you. Thank you for your concern."

The woman started to walk off, but then changed her mind and turned back to face Agnes.

"I did see her one day." The woman nodded down towards the pavement. "Her. The lady who got herself killed. I saw her one day here on the quayside. I recognised her when I saw her photo in the papers. It wasn't a good photo, you understand, 'cos she was lying dead in the mortuary when the picture was taken. But it was the same woman."

"When did you see her," Agnes asked, excitedly.

"It was a few days before she was found dead. I told my Alf that I'd seen the murdered woman here on the quayside. But he said I was off my rocker. Yet I know what I saw."

"Was she with anyone?" Agnes prompted.

"Yes, she was with a man." The woman stared ahead of her as she tried to remember what she'd seen. "They were talking, but I couldn't hear what was being said. I do remember the man seemed to be trying to get her to go with him. At one point, he grabbed her arm, but she was having none of it. She just pulled away and left him standing there on his own."

"She ran away?"

"No. She just walked off looking a bit huffed; exactly like I do with my Alf, when we've had words!"

"Did you tell the police about what you had seen?" Agnes asked.

"No, My Alf said it was best to stay out of it." She shrugged. "He said I'd probably got it all wrong anyway."

"One more thing," Agnes said pulling her phone out of her handbag. "Was this the man you saw talking with the murdered woman." She showed her the video she had taken of David Drummond on the quayside a few days ago.

"Yes, that's him." The woman looked up sharply. "Here, you're not a copper, are you?"

"No, I'm not the police," said Agnes.

The woman looked relieved. "I'll be on my way, then. Nice talking to you." She hurried off before Agnes could say another word.

Agnes stood outside Bessie Surtees House for a few minutes, pondering on what the woman had told her.

It appeared that Mary Swinburne had been talking to David Drummond shortly before she was murdered. What had they been discussing? The woman didn't seem to think that Mary had run away from him. It was more like she had disagreed with him about something and had stalked off. So, now the big question was, what was that something? Had it been enough to get her murdered?

The woman had now disappeared from sight. Agnes was annoyed that, during the conversation, she hadn't asked for her name. But it was too late now.

Agnes was just about to walk towards the entrance of the house, when she got a feeling someone was watching her. She decided against turning around to take a look. Instead, she continued on her way to the house. Nevertheless, her eyes were fixed on the large windows in front of her. With a bit of luck, the reflection would show whether she was right and there was someone staring at her - or would it prove that she really was becoming paranoid?

* * *

Alan Johnson arrived at the hotel shortly after Agnes left. The receptionist told him she had seen her leave a few minutes ago.

"Did she say where she was going," Alan asked.

"No, I'm sorry, she didn't."

Alan was about to ask whether the manager was available, when he suddenly appeared from his office. He looked rather flustered and seemed relieved to see the chief inspector standing in the reception area.

"Chief Inspector Johnson," Mr Jenkins said as he hurried towards him. "There has been another robbery. I was just on my way upstairs, perhaps you could join me."

"What was taken this time? More jewellery?" Alan answered his own question before the manager had time to speak.

"Yes," Jenkins replied, leading the way over to the lift. "This is now much more than a joke. My job and the reputation of this hotel are on the line. Don't you have any idea who might be doing this?"

"I'm afraid not. But we are keen to catch the thief and of course the murderer."

"Please don't mention Mary Swinburne's murder when we are in Mr and Mrs Andersons' room." Mr Jenkins flapped his hands vigorously. "Having a thief in the hotel is bad enough. I don't want them to think we have a murderer staying here, too."

Alan nodded. He could understand the manager's problem. A great deal of money had been spent on making this hotel one of the grandest in the area. Its prime position here on the quayside had, until now, drawn guests from far and wide. However, once word was out that the hotel had a resident thief, not to mention a murderer, visitors to the area would very soon choose somewhere else to stay.

By now, the two men had reached the lift. The attendant stood aside, allowing them to step inside. But Alan's last thought caused him to stop in his tracks. Could that be it? Could that be the purpose of everything, which had happened over the last week? Could there be someone out there, who wanted this hotel threatened with closure?

"Are you coming, chief inspector?"

The sound of the manager's voice hauled Alan back to the present. "Yes," he said, quickly stepping into the lift. "Sorry, I suddenly thought of something that might be relevant."

The lift doors closed and before long Alan and Mr Jenkins had arrived at the appointed floor.

The manager hadn't said anything while they were in the lift, but once they were alone in the corridor, Mr Jenkins wanted to know what the chief inspector thought might be pertinent to the case.

"I can't say anything at the moment," Alan replied. "I need to check a few things out. But I will definitely get back to you."

Alan could see that Jenkins wasn't happy about being left in the dark. But he wasn't sure about anything himself at the moment, so how could he tell him things he didn't know? "I promise I'll get back to you as soon as I have a clearer picture in my mind. Meanwhile, let's go and see the Andersons."

The manager heaved a sigh. The determined look on the inspector's face told him he wasn't going to get anything further and that he should leave it alone. Without another word, he turned and led the way to the room where the Andersons' were waiting.

They were told that the stolen necklace was an heirloom. Mrs Anderson, a woman in her late forties, looked so distraught she could hardly speak. She gestured to her husband to do the talking.

Mr Anderson was about fifty years old. He was going bald. However he had a rather heavy moustache; almost as though it was to make up for the loss of hair. "We haven't had a single problem of theft, robbery, whatever you want to call it, until we came here. That necklace is worth a fortune," he raged. "If we don't get it back we will sue this hotel."

"I'm not sure that's possible," said the manager. "You see we have a safe where all guests are advised to deposit any jewellery, charge cards, anything the guest thinks valuable. If you choose to ignore our advice, then the responsibility is totally left with you."

Alan could tell Mr Anderson was not impressed.

"Don't think for one minute that will let you off the hook." Anderson moved closer to the manager and stared at him in a threatening manner. "I have spoken with my solicitor. He agrees that there is room for doubt about a hotel safe being really safe. Besides, if someone can get into our room without having a key card, how secure is your damn safe?"

Mr Jenkins swallowed hard and pointed towards Alan. "This is Chief Inspector Johnson from CID. He has assured me they will do their utmost to find the culprit and recover your wife's jewellery."

"Is that so?" Mr Anderson turned his attention to Alan. "Well, I do hope so, because when my solicitor has finished with this hotel, he will turn his attention to the Newcastle Police Force. Make no mistake about that!"

Alan was not about to put up with any intimidations from this man. While he understood Mr Anderson being annoyed over the loss of an expensive piece of jewellery, he was not about to be blackmailed. Nor was he going to allow this man to intimidate the manager of the hotel. For goodness sake, guests had to take some responsibility for their possessions; most especially if they were as expensive as they were proclaiming.

"Mr Anderson, you are doing absolutely nothing to help your situation by accusing the hotel manager or the police of responsibility for the stolen jewellery."

"Then who is to blame?" Mr Anderson fumed.

Alan hesitated for a moment before replying. "It could be you; either of you. You both say you brought an heirloom to this hotel; something of immense value. Yet neither of you registered this very expensive piece of jewellery at reception. You didn't even ask to deposit it into the hotel safe, which I know to be very secure." He paused. "How can we be expected to believe such an item exists? And, if it does, how do we know that you even brought it to the hotel? Yet you expect the hotel and the police to jump through hoops to find it, though no one here has actually set eyes on it."

"How dare you speak to us like that?" Mr Anderson spluttered. He glanced at his wife and then back at the chief inspector. "Your superior will hear about this."

"Yes I'm sure he will," Alan replied, calmly. He was beginning to tire of this man's threats. "If not from you; then he will hear it from me." He paused to allow the mood in the room to cool down.

"Now, Mr Anderson, shall we start again?"

Chapter Seventeen

Agnes continued to look at the reflections through the large windows of the museum. At first, she couldn't see anyone standing around across the road. There were quite a few people going about their business and some cars waiting for the lights to change. However, when a car moved away from the traffic lights, she saw someone staring at her. It was David Drummond.

She desperately wanted to turn around and stare back at him; make him aware she knew he was watching her. Perhaps he would slink off somewhere; annoyed with himself at having been caught out. But after taking a moment to sum up her position, she realised that wouldn't be a wise move.

Right now, she knew exactly where he was. Also, he had no idea she was aware he was following her. Therefore it must be in her best interest to carry on as though she hadn't seen him.

She entered the Bessie Surtees Museum and climbed up the wooden stairs. At the top, she headed for the window she had seen being closed a few nights ago. She moved closer and peered down at the pavement where she and Alan had found the body. Then slowly, without moving her head, she raised her eyes towards the spot she had last seen Drummond. He was still there. However, he wasn't looking up at the window. His eyes were fixed on the entrance; he was waiting for her to reappear.

What was he going to do then? Would he continue to follow her for the rest of the day? Every time she turned around, would she see him skulking somewhere a little way behind? She turned away from the window and looked back into the room. At any other time she would have delighted to be drawn back to the days when Bessie Surtees made the decision to elope with the man she loved. But today, Agnes needed to focus on her own future.

* * *

Outside in the street, Drummond's eyes were fixed on the entrance to the museum. He had been on his way to a meeting when he suddenly caught a glimpse of Agnes. She was staring down at the pavement where Mary's body had been found. He was just about to cross the road to speak to her, but he swiftly changed his mind when a woman stopped and began talking to Agnes.

He couldn't hear what they were talking about, but it appeared that Agnes was very interested in what the woman had to say. He glanced at his watch a couple of times; he really didn't have time to stand around here; he was going to be late for his meeting.

At last the woman moved off and he was just about to cross the road when the lights changed and the traffic started to move. "Blast," he murmured to himself, as he saw Agnes disappear into the museum. If only that wretched woman hadn't stopped to talk.

He stood for a few minutes wondering whether to go inside and catch up with her upstairs. But he decided against it. There might be a number of people up there and he really didn't want to be caught talking with her. After a final glance at the door, he set off for his meeting.

* * *

Agnes spent some time wandering around the rooms of the old house; admiring the carvings and architecture. However, as she was about to leave, she began to panic. What if Drummond was still out there? She went back to the window and looked down to where she had last seen him. But he had gone. She wondered whether he might be waiting outside the front door, but, without opening the window and drawing attention to herself, she couldn't see the entrance.

For a moment, she was tempted to ring Alan to tell him she was being watched, but decided against it. If Drummond had gone, there was nothing he could do. Come to think of it, even if Drummond was still outside, neither she nor Alan could prove he had followed her or that he intended to do her any harm.

Her heart was pounding as she set off down the stairs. She took the opportunity of speaking to the man duty to give her the time she needed to peer through the windows and see if Drummond was hovering around. But there was no sign of him. Taking a deep breath, she smiled and nodded at the man, before stepping outside into the sunshine.

Agnes looked up and down the street outside, but Drummond wasn't anywhere in sight. She flagged down a passing taxi cab.

"Where to?" the driver asked, as she clambered inside.

"I have absolutely no idea," said Agnes, settling down into the large comfortable seat. "Just drive. Why not simply give me a tour of the city?"

The driver turned around to look at her in amazement. "You're serious?" Normally the people he picked up were in a hurry to get to somewhere or another – or at least they said they were; probably to cut down on the fare.

"Yes, I'm serious." She shrugged. "Why not? I was born here, but have been away for a long time. Things have changed and I would like to see some of the changes." Agnes thought for a moment. "Can we start by going over the Swing Bridge and then back over the Tyne Bridge?" She giggled. "And then, just for fun, perhaps we could do it all over again before we go on somewhere else."

Just then a car caught her eye. The headlights were flashing as it headed towards the taxi. Was that David Drummond? Had he picked up his car and come back?

"There's another thing you should know. I think I am being followed." She nodded towards the black car, now momentarily stuck in traffic. "Do you want me to get out of your cab and let you go on your way? Or is there a chance you might decide to put your foot down and lose that car?"

The driver smiled before quickly turning back to face the road ahead. He pushed the gear lever into first. "You know something? All the years I've been driving a taxi, no one has ever jumped in and said 'just drive' or 'lose the car behind.' I've seen it in the movies, but I never thought it would happen to me. Lady I've got to say, you have just made my day."

* * *

Back at the hotel, Mr Anderson had calmed down and he began to describe the necklace to the chief inspector.

Alan was rather puzzled when Anderson paused and looked at his wife as though for guidance. Didn't he know what it looked like? However, he didn't get a chance to dwell on it as Anderson suddenly leapt to his feet and began to pull various items from his suitcase.

When at last he found what he was looking for, he shoved a photograph of a necklace into the hands of the chief inspector.

"There!" he said, triumphantly. He flicked his hand across the top of the photograph. "That is the necklace in question. Now perhaps you will believe that this piece of jewellery does exist."

"Yes, I believe there is such a necklace." Alan spoke slowly. The photograph, which had been thrust into his hands, showed the necklace strung around the sort of neckline you see on display in jeweller's window. Alan looked up from the photo. "But I'm not sure how this photo proves it belongs to your wife." He looked at the picture again. "There is absolutely nothing here that indicates it belongs to either of you."

Alan glanced at Mrs Anderson as he spoke. Was he imagining it? Though the tears were still streaming down her face, the distraught look of someone having an heirloom stolen had disappeared. It had been replaced by an expression of fear.

"What the hell are you talking about?" Mr Anderson yelled. He snatched out at the photo Alan was holding.

But the chief inspector was too quick for him. He pulled the photo out of reach.

"I need that for insurance purposes." Anderson made another grab at the photo.

"So do I," Alan replied, taking a step backwards. "I need to confirm that you and your wife are the true owners."

"I'll have your job for this!"

"You wouldn't like it," Alan pulled a face. "The hours are too long and the holidays too short." He knew he was being flippant, but there was something here that wasn't quite right. Naturally, all the people whose jewellery had been taken were upset and angry. Voices had been raised, and there had been the occasional threat, which he knew would never be carried out. But each of those people had been able to prove the jewellery stolen had belonged to them. Most had a photograph of the wife or girlfriend wearing the jewellery, even if the picture was still on the camera phone. This couple had absolutely nothing to show. Therefore, until they were able to produce something to verify the necklace was actually theirs he had no intention of allowing them to leave the hotel.

"That went well," said the hotel manager, once they were outside in the corridor.

"It went rather better than I thought," Alan replied.

"I meant…"

"Yes, I know what you meant. You were being ironic." Alan pushed the button to call the lift.

"So?"

"So, what?" Alan turned to face Jenkins. "If you are asking whether we treat all victims of a crime in that manner, then the answer is no.

However, I am not prepared to discuss this case with you. It is sufficient to say that I feel we are progressing in our investigation and I will keep you informed."

At that point, the lift arrived.

"I'll be in touch," Alan said when the lift stopped at the reception area. Without another word, he strode off towards the entrance.

Outside the hotel, Alan jumped into his car and drove along the quay. He wondered where Agnes might have decided to go today. He knew there were lots of places she wanted to visit. But since this case, she had put all that on hold. He wondered whether she had decided to go back to the Bessie Surtees Museum. Though what she could hope to gain from going there escaped him. The whole area had been checked out by forensics the night he and Agnes found the body. He and other detectives had gone back the following morning to check it out in daylight, yet there had been no evidence of any shots being fired at that spot.

But now, wise to the fact that Agnes was not the kind of person to be put off easily, he realised she could have decided to go back to take another look for herself.

Traffic was busy on the quayside. The Law Courts had been sitting that morning, perhaps there had been more cases than usual. There were certainly a great number people milling around outside the building. Nevertheless it wasn't long before he approached the museum. At first, he couldn't see Agnes, but then quite suddenly she appeared from the museum. Unfortunately, the traffic lights were against him and he had to wait before he could move forward. He was still watching her when he saw her hail a passing taxi. At first, he thought of turning on the flashing blue lights and siren, but decided against it; it wasn't really appropriate.

The lights changed and the traffic began to flow, but by now Agnes was inside the cab, probably giving the driver instructions as to where she wanted to go. He headed towards her flashing his headlights, hoping she would see him and get out of the taxi. However, it didn't work.

The taxi suddenly took off and turned at the corner of the road. It appeared to be heading towards the Swing Bridge.

"Damn!" Alan slammed his hand against the steering wheel. There was nothing he could do. He was facing the wrong way. By the time he found somewhere safe to turn around, the taxi would be long gone.

The sound of car horns blasting all around, told him he needed to move on. 'So much for that,' he thought, as he set off up The Side, towards the city centre. But at least he felt a little relieved at having seen her. She was safe – for the time being, anyway.

Back at the police station, Alan found his sergeant was no further forward. It seemed that no unnamed person had been left at any of the hospitals in the city.

"At the moment, forensics is still trying to match the blood from the scene in Grainger Street to anyone on their database," Andrews said. "But so far they haven't come up with anything." He looked up from his notepad. "Did you learn anything new at the hotel?"

"If you call finding another theft anything new, then yes, I did." Alan slumped into his chair.

"Not another one!"

"Yes, another one," Alan spoke slowly. He was mulling over the conversation he'd had with the Andersons.

"The chief constable is going to go ballistic over this," Andrews replied.

"This one is a little different. I'm not convinced the necklace belonged to Mrs Anderson in the first place."

Andrews looked up sharply. "So you're saying that the necklace stolen from... what's her name?"

"Mrs Anderson." Alan interrupted.

"... Mrs Anderson," the sergeant repeated, "was one you think they might have stolen from someone else."

"That about sums it up," Alan nodded. "And that, Andrews, puts a whole new slant on the case."

"I see." Andrews thought about it for a moment. "No, I'm sorry, I don't see. How does this alter the case of the missing jewellery?"

"Think about it for a minute," said Alan, taking a deep breath. If he couldn't even sell this to his sergeant, what chance did he have with his Superintendent?

"Suppose this particular piece of jewellery is what the thief had been looking for all the time? What if someone was being paid to steal a valuable necklace only to have it stolen from them before they could deliver the goods and collect the money?" He smiled to himself; now he was beginning to sound like Agnes with all these 'what ifs'.

"It's possible," Andrews replied slowly. "But what happened to make you think the Andersons might have stolen this necklace?"

Alan pulled the photograph from his pocket. "When I asked what the necklace looked like, Mr Anderson handed me this – correction, this is what he showed me. He was adamant I should hand it back." Alan passed the picture to Andrews. "But I was just as adamant that I was going to keep it."

Andrews peered closely at the photo, before pulling a magnifying glass from his desk drawer to take a closer look. "Strange. This picture seems to have been taken while the necklace was on display some-where." He pointed to something in the photo and handed to magni-fying glass to Alan. "Look there, beyond the necklace. Could that be another display case in a jeweller's shop?"

"That's exactly what I thought!" Alan replied. "It was the reason I was so determined not to hand back the photo." He paused. "So now I am wondering whether we should be thinking more on the lines of a display of fine jewellery being shown at an exhibition somewhere." He fell silent, giving his sergeant time for the penny to drop.

"There's a rather expensive necklace being included in a show in Central London later this month." Andrews said slowly, He was still staring at the photograph. "My wife is trying to get tickets..." He looked up sharply, suddenly realizing what his boss was getting at. "Good heavens! You don't think the star attraction has been stolen, do you? Surely we would have heard about it. It would have been all over the news if something like that had happened." He looked at the picture again. "Do you really think this is the piece in question? How could anyone have penetrated the high level security?"

"I don't know," Alan shrugged. "However, if someone did manage to steal it before it even went on show, there must be a great number of red faces in London right now. The top brass looking after the jewellery would not want its disappearance broadcast across the world. It would be most embarrassing to explain the theft to the owner. My guess is they are hoping to get it back before the exhibition opens and the owner finds out it is missing." He sniffed. "But it's all speculation. We don't know anything for certain."

"Nevertheless, such a necklace would be worth killing for, if someone got wind it was at the Millennium Hotel here in Newcastle." Andrews said, excitedly. "We could go on the assumption that the murder of Mary Swinburne is linked to the thefts at the hotel. Then there is the blood we found on Grainger Street." He slumped back into his chair at a sudden thought. "Though, we haven't yet found a match for that."

Alan nodded. "Not yet, but…"

* * *

Agnes enjoyed the tour across the Swing Bridge and then the Tyne Bridge. She had told the driver to go as slow as possible, but with traffic piling up behind he was unable to travel too slowly. Hopefully, the next time they drove across both bridges, there wouldn't be quite so many cars.

As they approached the Swing Bridge for the second time, Agnes sat up in her seat and peered from the taxi window. She didn't want to miss a thing. They were almost half way across the bridge when she noticed something in the water. It seemed to be wrapped around one of the bridge supports. She could have sworn it wasn't there the first time they crossed. For a second it seemed to disappear beneath the water, but then resurfaced long enough for her to make out the shape of a body.

Chapter Eighteen

"Stop the cab!" Agnes yelled out to the driver. She wanted to take a better look.

"I can't stop here," said the driver, looking in his reversing mirror. There was a line of traffic behind him.

"You have to stop. Please, just stop!" By now Agnes was kneeling on the back seat frantically searching for where she had last seen the body in the water.

The taxi driver switched on his warning lights and pulled over. Agnes leapt out of the cab and ran back along the bridge, ducking up and down trying to see through the railings.

In the meantime, the taxi continued across the bridge and parked on the other side. The driver then hurried back to find his passenger, he still had no idea what had happened. But from her actions she must have seen something important. By the time he caught up with her she was punching in a number on her mobile phone.

"What happened? Are you okay," he asked.

She nodded, but didn't have time to say any more as she heard Alan's voice on the other end of the phone. "Alan, you have got to get down to the Swing Bridge right now!" She glanced down at the water. "I can see a body in the Tyne," she added, before he could interrupt.

The chief inspector told her he would be there right away.

By now the taxi driver was gazing down at the swirling water. "Where is it? I don't see anything."

"It's there by the joist, support or whatever it is they are called." Agnes pointed to where she had seen the body. "The police are on their way."

For a moment the driver couldn't see anything, but then the body suddenly reappeared. "Yes, yes, I see something now."

* * *

Back at the police station, Alan quickly told his sergeant the reason for Agnes's call. "I'm going down to the Swing Bridge right now. Organize some officers and divers and meet me there as soon as possible. We might just have found our second murder victim."

* * *

The chief inspector opened the door and leapt out of the car before his driver had brought the vehicle to a stop. He saw Agnes and hurried towards her. She was still standing on the bridge, staring down at the water, as though keeping guard over the body.

"It's there." Agnes pointed down toward the massive supports. "It keeps disappearing under the water. Perhaps something is dragging it down."

"Thank you, Agnes." Alan looked at the young, neatly dressed Asian man standing next her. "Who's this?"

"This is my taxi driver. I hired him and his cab to take me around the sights of Newcastle."

"Nice to meet you," the driver smiled and held out his hand. "Call me Ben."

"Hello," Alan smiled as he shook his hand. "I am Chief Inspector Johnson." He turned back to Agnes. "I'll take it from here. Go and see the sights," he urged, though he knew he was on a losing wicket.

"Are you mad?" retorted Agnes. There was no way she was going to leave the scene. "I discovered the body; I am a witness at the scene where a body has been found. Do you honestly believe I am simply going to walk away to look at the sights?"

Alan shook his head before turning his attention to the taxi driver.

"I'm with the lady," said Ben, before Alan could say a word. He grinned. "This is turning out to be quite a day."

By now, Andrews had arrived with other police officers and divers. Alan barked out a few orders. "Keep the traffic moving steadily across the bridge. We don't want traffic backed all the way along the quayside. And keep the people away from the edge of the quay. We can't have anyone falling in the river while trying to take a selfie." He turned to his sergeant and nodded. "See that it's done."

Once everything was under control, Alan led Agnes and Ben to the quay and told the divers to go ahead. Now it was up to them to bring the body aground.

"Where is your taxi?" Alan asked the driver.

Ben pointed across the bridge. "I parked it on the other side, once I let the lady out."

"Please call me Agnes," she said, smiling at Ben. She looked back at Alan and explained how she had ordered him to stop the car when she thought she saw something in the river. "Obviously, he couldn't stay sitting on the bridge as the traffic was beginning to pile up." But then a thought crossed her mind. "Alan, you don't think Ben will get a ticket, do you? Is there a note or something you could give him so he won't be issued with a penalty?"

"See that a police message is placed on the taxi," Alan called out to one of the officers.

Shortly afterwards, the body of a man was lifted onto the quayside. The pathologist, who had now arrived at the scene, was able to tell the chief inspector that the body had been in the water for a few days.

A cord, attached to the waist of the victim, indicated he had been fastened to something; probably a weight to keep the body submerged. However, the cord was frayed. It must have rubbed against something underwater causing it to break.

"Good thing it did," the pathologist concluded. "Otherwise he could have been down there for a very long time."

"That's most likely what the murderer was hoping for," Alan mumbled. "Is there anything else you can tell me before you take the body back to the lab?"

"Only that the poor man was shot." The pathologist pointed to a gunshot wound in the head. "He would have died instantly."

Agnes took a step back. The moment when she and Alan found the body of the woman on the pavement flashed before her. Back then, it had been dark. She hadn't seen the gunshot wound very clearly. Today, despite the clouds overhead, it was still quite bright. Though the wound had been washed by the water in the river, it still looked frightful. But apart from that, the man's eyes were wide open and seemed to be staring up at her. Was this man, even in death, trying to tell her something?

Then something in her mind clicked. She had seen this man before; but where? Agnes closed her eyes. *Think, woman,* she thought. *Think back to where you have been over the last few days*

When Alan saw Agnes standing with her eyes closed, he thought she was suffering from shock at seeing the dead man lying on the pavement. "I think you should go back to the hotel and relax," he said.

"No, Alan. You don't understand. I've seen this man before, but I can't remember where."

Alan glanced at the body. "Is it possible you saw him with Mary Swinburne at the hotel?"

Agnes shook her head. "No. The only time I saw Mary Swinburne was at breakfast one morning, and she was alone."

"What about you?" Alan said, looking at Ben. "Do you recall ever seeing this man in the back of your taxi?"

Ben stared down at the victim. Something was stirring in his memory. "No, not in my taxi, but I do remember seeing him in a restaurant one evening. It was a few days ago." He nodded towards the restaurant across the road. "My wife and I were having a meal to celebrate her birthday," he explained. "I recall this man had an argument with one of the other diners. It got quite vocal and the manager came to ask him to tone it down a little."

Agnes looked across the road towards the restaurant. "That's it," she said. "That's where I saw him." She turned back to Alan. "I was with you, but you had your back to him so you wouldn't have noticed him. He wasn't causing a fuss or anything. He was alone. Though another man came over to his table and had a few words with him." She screwed up her eyes as she recalled the evening. "The victim was wearing a navy blue suit, white shirt and blue tie."

Alan raised his eyebrows.

Agnes shrugged. "So, I like to people-watch."

Alan took a photograph of the victim on his phone. Once the restaurant opened, he would speak to the manager. Maybe he could tell him something about the man. At the moment, no one knew who he was. Any identity he might have been carrying on the night of the murder had been removed from his body before it was dumped into the river.

When the pathologist had done all he could at the scene, the body was lifted into a large van and taken back for a post mortem.

"There's nothing more you can do here, Agnes. Why don't you continue on your trip around the city?"

"But don't you need me back at the station. Surely I need to make a statement or something." Agnes was determined she was not going to be shuttled off. If she hadn't spotted the body, it might have slipped back into the water never to be seen again.

Alan knew that if it had been anyone else, he would have insisted on them making a statement. Nevertheless, he was doing his best to keep Agnes out of the proceedings for her own sake. Though he had to admit, it was becoming increasingly difficult as she seemed to be finding all the evidence.

"Yes, you're right," he conceded. "I'll give you a lift back to the station."

Agnes turned to Ben and opened her bag. "Perhaps I could do the tour thing tomorrow morning." She pointed to the other end of the Quay. "I'm staying at The Millennium, could you pick me up outside the hotel at about ten thirty?" She pulled thirty pounds from her wallet. "Will that cover it for today?"

Ben waved the money aside. "No charge," he said. "It's been quite an experience." He smiled. "I'll see you tomorrow morning."

Agnes insisted he should take the money before watching him disappear back over the bridge. Finally, she turned her attention back to Alan. "Okay, let's go," she said. "Where are you parked?"

* * *

Once the formalities at the police station were over and done with, Alan asked Andrews to check what time the restaurant opened.

"It won't open until five o'clock, but the manager is there now," Andrews said, putting his hand over the mouthpiece. "He is expecting some sort of delivery in the next hour."

"Fine, tell him I am on my way." He looked at Agnes, still sitting in front of his desk. "I can drop you off on the way down there."

Agnes didn't say anything until they were out of the station. "What's all this about dropping me off? I'm coming with you."

Alan opened his mouth to say something, but changed his mind. What was the point? He knew she would go to the restaurant with or without him. At least with him there, he knew she was safe.

"Now let me do the talking," Alan said as he pulled up outside.

"Okay," Agnes said, opening the car door. She walked across to the entrance of the restaurant. "I'll just stand there smiling sweetly."

The manager appeared at the door, making it impossible for Alan to comment further.

"Good afternoon," said the manager holding out his hand. "My name is Gordon Peterson, How can I help youoe?"

"Good afternoon, I am Chief Inspector Johnson." He shook hands with Peterson.

"And this is?" Peterson gestured towards Agnes.

"This is Mrs Lockwood." Alan coughed. "She is assisting us with our enquiries." He paused for a moment. "I don't know whether you have heard, but a body was pulled out of the river earlier today. Over there by the Swing Bridge."

"Yes, I heard something about it on the radio. But what has that to do with me?"

"We hoped you might be able to help us identify the body. It seems the victim used this restaurant a couple of times recently." The chief inspector pulled out his mobile phone and showed the manager the photo he had taken earlier. "Do you recognize him?"

Alan was alarmed when Peterson suddenly turned pale and collapsed into a nearby chair. He hadn't expected such a reaction.

"Yes, I know this man," Peterson said after a long pause. "His name is Dennis Drummond."

There was a gasp from Agnes when she heard the name. She placed her hand on the back of one of the chairs to steady herself. Was it possible Dennis Drummond was related to David Drummond, the man who had been stalking her?

"Would you like to sit down, Agnes?" Alan said, as he pulled out a chair from one of the tables. "Can I get either of you a glass of water?"

"You can get me a brandy." Peterson uttered. He pointed towards the bar as he sat down. "Make it a large one. And have one yourself."

"I'll see to it," Agnes said, as she made her way over to the bar. She certainly needed one.

"I take it from your reaction, Mr Peterson that you knew Dennis Drummond quite well." Alan said.

"He is – was my cousin. We played together when we were kids. He came here for a meal most evenings." He looked up. "Who did this? Why?"

"That's what we want to find out." Alan replied. "Was he married?"

"Would you like a brandy chief inspector?" Agnes held up the bottle. Alan shook his head. "Not on duty."

"Dennis was divorced a little while ago," Peterson replied. He spoke quietly. "I don't think he ever got over it. He still loved Dorothy. I'll need to contact her." He paused, when Agnes handed him the brandy. "Thank you."

"Did he have any siblings?" Alan felt he needed to ask, though he was sure he knew the answer.

"Yes." Peterson took a drink from the glass. "An older brother; his name is David. He lives in London, but he's here in Newcastle at the moment on business. He's staying at The Millennium."

The chief inspector glanced at Agnes By now she was sitting in a chair alongside Peterson. She took a large drink from her glass of brandy.

"Someone told the police that Dennis Drummond was arguing with another diner in this restaurant recently," Alan continued. "They said you stepped in to stop it getting out of control. Do you know who he was arguing with?"

"Yes, it was his brother, David. It wasn't really an argument, just a difference of opinion. They were..." The manager stopped speaking when a sudden thought popped into his head. "You're not suggesting David had anything to do with his brother's murder, are you? Let me tell you, David is not like that. He wouldn't kill his brother. He wouldn't kill anyone."

"Our enquiries are wide open at the moment, Mr Peterson. You must understand we are groping around in the dark here. If you know anything that you think will help us find the killer, then please tell me." Alan paused, allowing his last statement to sink in. "Now, do you know what the difference of opinion was all about?"

The manager took another drink from his glass, before looking away.

"You must try to help the chief inspector," Agnes intervened. She had noticed Alan was beginning to look a little frustrated at Mr Peterson's reluctance to answer his question. "It was I who spotted your cousin's body in the river this morning and called the police. I am doing everything I possibly can to help the police to find out who did this dreadful thing, even though it is none of my business. But you are related to Dennis Drummond. He is your cousin; someone you know and love. You should do everything you can to help."

The manager took another drink from the glass. "Yes, you are right. I'm sorry, but I just don't believe David could do something like this. He and Dennis always got on so well."

"Okay. I understand that," said Alan. He had remained standing so far, but now he sat down. Perhaps it would look less formal. "So tell me what happened that night, here in the restaurant."

"The difference of opinion was about their sister," Peterson replied.

"There was a sister?" Alan wanted to say more, but Agnes flashed him a glance that said 'shut up, you're ruining everything'. He apologized for the interruption and gestured for Peterson to carry on.

"Yes. Dennis and David had a sister." The manager continued. "She was called, Mary. Mary Swinburne." He paused for a few seconds, reflecting on his cousin. "She is such a lovely lady. She married when she was quite young and I gather they were very happy together, until her husband died suddenly. They didn't have any children. She is going to take this news very hard when she..." He broke off when he noticed the chief inspector and Agnes staring at each other. "What am I missing?"

"Don't you know?" Alan said, slowly.

"Know what?" Peterson replied. But he quickly guessed it wasn't going to be good news when Agnes reached out and clasped her hands around his.

Alan took a deep breath. There was no easy way to say this. "I'm sorry to be the one to tell you, but Mary Swinburne was found murdered a few nights ago. She had been shot; the same as Dennis."

"No! Not Mary, too!" Peterson wailed. "I don't believe this is happening." He gulped down the remaining brandy in his glass.

Alan allowed the news to sink in before speaking again. "I'm sorry for your loss. But, I have to ask how you hadn't heard about her death."

Peterson took a deep breath and handed his glass to Agnes. "Another – and, please, just help yourself." He looked back at Alan. "I've been away for a few days. I was at some damn new-fangled conference for restaurant managers and owners. There was to be no contact with the outside world. The idea was that we concentrate solely on the course." He shrugged. "Learn how to lure customers into our restaurants and keep them coming back. That sort of thing; it was all supposed to help with the business." He paused. "I shouldn't have gone. I should have been here."

"A few days?" Alan prompted.

"It was rubbish. Utter rubbish," Peterson ranted. "I don't know why I signed up. I learned nothing new. For a start, they told me that, as the owner of the restaurant, I should not take any nonsense from my staff. I already knew that." He closed his eyes. "I'm sorry, I'm just so shocked. It was a three day course held in London. I got back from the last workshop at about lunch time today only to be informed by my head chef I needed to be here to take in a delivery this afternoon." He shook his head. "I know. I'm stupid. Isn't that what the course was all about? Perhaps it wasn't rubbish after all. Maybe I am too soft. What the hell do I have staff for? They should have been here today for the delivery. I really need to sort them out!"

"Yes, you do." Alan agreed. "But that's not what this is about. We are talking about your two cousins, both of whom have been found murdered. Both were shot. At this moment, our pathologist is looking at the possibility that they were shot with the same gun. Now, think about this before you speak; is there anyone out there who can verify you were where you said you were over the last few days?"

Agnes took a sip from her glass of brandy. Okay, she was feeling a little squiffy; she had topped up her glass when she did a refill for Mr Peterson. Yet she wasn't so far gone that she couldn't see the interview with the restaurant manager wasn't going well. She set her glass down on the table nearest to her and suggested she and Alan have a word in private.

"Nothing important," she said, as she stood up and moved out of earshot.

"What the hell are you doing?" Alan said when he caught up with Agnes. "This guy is a prime suspect."

"No, he isn't!" Agnes retorted. "You saw how shocked he was when you told him the news about his cousins. But then I noticed a look of fear sweep across his face."

"That could all have been an act. I still need to verify his alibi." Alan sighed.

"Alan, you still don't see what I'm getting at. Mr Peterson's two cousins have been murdered. He might be thinking that he could be next."

"But why would he be next? What were his cousins mixed up in?"

"That is what we have to find out."

"We?" Alan quizzed. But before he could add anything further, Agnes had already turned away and was walking back towards Mr Peterson.

"Can you tell us what Mary had done to cause her brothers to argue?" Agnes asked, as she sat down beside the restaurant manager. But then another thought crossed her mind. "The police were informed that the man, who was arguing with Dennis, had been sitting at another table. Didn't you think it strange that they weren't dining at the same table?" She glanced at Alan. "I mean, being brothers and all, anyone would have thought..."

"I know what you mean," Mr Peterson interrupted. He gulped down the remaining brandy and slowly lowered the empty glass onto the table. "Dennis and David were great brothers," he continued. "Always fooling around and having fun together. I used to join them, but somehow, I got on better with Dennis. We seemed to be on the same wavelength." Gordon Peterson fell silent for a moment, as he reflected on the past. "David was always the leader. Dennis and I," he paused, "well I suppose we sort of fell in with whatever he suggested." He looked up quickly. "Don't get me wrong. David was great; we both admired him and were quite happy to follow his lead. There was never any animosity between us. But then Mary came on the scene."

Tears welled in Gordon's eyes and he pulled a handkerchief from his pocket. "I'm sorry, this is all getting too much for me," he said, as he wiped the tears from his eyes. "Mary was the only girl to be born into the family," he continued. "She was lovely and everyone made a big fuss over her. I suppose she was spoiled really. In other words, she got everything she wanted. Nevertheless, I have to admit that her brothers and I thought the world of her."

"But then we grew up. Dennis had always wanted to join the Air Force, but he was turned down due to health reasons." Peterson shook his head. "It turned out that he had a heart problem no one knew about. It wasn't something really life-threatening. But he was told he would never be allowed to fly. Dennis didn't want a desk job – not in the Air force, anyway." Gordon broke off and wiped his eyes again. "I still can't believe they are gone," he said. "Anyway Dennis gave up his dream and went into the insurance business. A bit of a come-down, but I think he did well over the years.

"Mary was personal assistant to the chairman of a large company in Newcastle until she was married. She and her husband moved to Yorkshire. She continued to live there after Peter died. However, she often returned to Newcastle to catch up with her old friends. I know she liked to stay at the Millennium Hotel.

"What about David?" Alan asked. He was keen to learn something about him. "Is he in the insurance business, too?"

Peterson burst out laughing. "David, in business of any kind, is a no-no." He looked around making sure no one had entered the restaurant while they had been talking. "This must go no further. If anything happens to David because of what I tell you, I will hold you both responsible. Is that clear?"

He looked at both Agnes and Alan in turn. When they both assured him that they would not repeat a word, he continued.

"As a kid, David always admired the character James Bond. He read the books and saw all the films several times. Suddenly, one day he told his parents he wanted to be a spy. Naturally we all laughed at him. His parents thought it was a phase he was going through and would grow out of it. They wanted him to get a normal job, find a lovely wife, settle down and have children. You know, the usual things people do.

"But David stuck to his guns, so to speak. One day, on impulse he went to see his MP and, after a few meetings with various people, somehow or another David got his way." He paused. "I don't know where it came from; no one in any of our family was into codes, electronics or anything like that. Yet David was really good at that sort of thing. He could pick locks, hack into computers; all sorts of things. Perhaps that's why they decided to give him a chance."

"So, David Drummond is a member of Her Majesty's Secret Service?" Alan looked at Agnes in amazement. Had they really got this man so wrong?

"Yes, didn't I just say that?" Peterson frowned. "Though I doubt he is working on a case at the moment. I understand he was here to catch up with Dennis, Mary and me. Mary had written to tell him she would be in Newcastle this week."

"Mr Peterson," Agnes held up her glass. "Your news has come as a great surprise to me. Would you mind if I have another glass of your excellent brandy – a small one?"

"Help yourself." Peterson gestured towards the bar. "What about you, chief inspector?"

Though Alan would have loved a drink at that very moment, he declined. He really needed to keep his wits about him. There were so many things to think about. Could David be here on a case despite him telling his relatives it was a holiday? If so, could the case David was working on be linked to the stolen jewellery at the hotel?

Come to think of it, did he check in before or after the first theft? But surely the secret service wouldn't send one of their men to the hotel because the Chief Constable was concerned about Mrs Hargreaves's missing necklace. No, the presence of an MI5 agent at the hotel would have to be for something much bigger than that. Was it possible he was here because of the latest theft?

If he was right, and the necklace the Andersons claimed to have been stolen from them was actually the one stolen in London, then there was no doubt that the government would do everything possible to get it back. That would even include using members of the Secret Service.

Alan glanced back at the restaurant manager. Did he really believe David was here on holiday in Newcastle? Or could he be just saying that? Though, if David Drummond was a good agent, he would be able to fool them all.

By now, Agnes had poured herself another drink and was back sitting in her chair. Alan was surprised she hadn't said anything. Despite what he said, she always chipped in when she felt there was something missing. Or something she disagreed with. Like earlier, when they were almost playing, good cop, bad cop.

"I need to get back to the station," Alan suddenly announced. He felt he needed to talk this whole thing over with his sergeant. "Can I drop you off somewhere, Agnes?"

"Yes, please." Agnes said. "Would you be so kind as to drop me off at my hotel?" She swiftly finished her brandy and turned to Peterson. "I really am sorry for your loss. It's unbelievable that you should lose two close relatives in such a short time. No doubt David will be in touch once he knows you are back in the city."

A sudden thought crossed her mind and she shot a glance at Alan, but decided to wait until they were alone before saying anything.

They were both seated in the car before either of them said a word. It was Alan who spoke first. "I have got to have a word with David Drummond. "Yes, I agree you need to find out what is going on with Drummond," Agnes replied.

"You do?" Alan was rather surprised. So far, she had rarely agreed with him on any matter pertaining to the case.

"Yes. But I don't think you should speak to David. I think it should be me." She saw he was about to interrupt, so she quickly continued. "Think about it, Alan. If he is up here on a case, then he is working undercover. Your face is well known at the hotel now. If anyone saw you talking to him, his cover could be blown."

"Your face is known at the hotel, too."

"Yes, but I am a guest, not a member of the police force. Anyone who sees Drummond with me, they might think I am flirting with the guy."

Alan realised what she was saying made sense. But he was concerned about her getting even more involved. "Surely a plain-clothed woman police officer could do the same thing."

"No it wouldn't be the same thing at all. As you said, I am known at the hotel. People recognize me now. The lift attendant, room service and reception all know me. Is your officer going to walk into the hotel alone one evening and have a meal on the off chance David is there? What if he isn't? Will she keep trying until the hotel staff becomes suspicious at seeing a woman calling in for dinner every night?" Agnes giggled. They might think she is a lady of the night? Come on, Alan you know I'm right."

Alan did know she was right. But he was still not happy with what she was suggesting. He sighed heavily. "Okay," he said, somewhat reluctantly.

"Great. Now I have something else to run past you."

Alan pulled the car over to the side of the road and switched off the engine. "What do you want to do now?"

"Nothing, I promise." Agnes grinned. "I simply had a thought when I was talking to Mr Peterson. "What if... ""

Alan groaned. "Not again."

"What if," Agnes repeated, ignoring Alan's remark, "Dennis and Mary were shot at the same time? Their bodies could have been stuffed into a car or van to be taken down to the quayside and dumped in the river. But... ""

"For some reason, the van doors swung open and Mary's body fell out onto the pavement," Alan finished her sentence. "You could be right. The pathologist at the crime scene stated that the body, who we now know to be Dennis Drummond, had been in the river for a few days. It could have been the same night we found Mary's body outside Bessie Surtees House."

"The killers might even have stopped the van around the corner and returned to pick up the body." Agnes picked up the story. "But they were too late. They found us standing over the victim, so crept back to the van and continued on their way, hoping the police would never find Dennis and link the two together."

"Agnes, I could kiss you," Alan blurted out the words before he could stop himself. He stared through the windscreen of the car, desperately trying to think of something else to say to fill the silence that followed.

"Now, don't you think I ought to get back to the hotel and try to figure out a way of bumping into David Drummond?" Agnes changed the subject. That was the second time Alan had said that he could kiss her. Did he really mean it? Or was it more a figure of speech? Something he had heard on TV?

"Yes, you're right." Relieved Agnes hadn't questioned him about his remark Alan restarted the car and set off towards The Millennium Hotel.

Chapter Nineteen

During the short drive back to the hotel, Agnes outlined her plan to meet up with David Drummond that evening. She explained that she would dine alone in the hotel restaurant; it was the most likely place to 'accidentally bump' into him. Failing that, she might find him in the Drawing Room or even the bar.

"Rest assured, Alan. If he is spending some time in the hotel this evening, I will catch up with him," she said as she stepped out of the car.

There was no doubt in Alan's mind that she would. The only good thing about this arrangement was that she was meeting him in a hotel full of people. Nevertheless, he still couldn't help feeling uneasy about the whole thing.

"Remember, don't hesitate to call me if you feel upset about anything," he replied.

She nodded before she turned and hurried into the hotel.

Upstairs in her room, Agnes pulled several fashionable dresses out of the wardrobe and threw them onto the bed. She loved them all. But this evening was different. Though she hated to admit it, she was a lady looking to get together with a man younger than herself – much younger than herself. Not that she was looking for anything other than to talk. Nevertheless, she would still need to wear something stunning to attract David's attention.

She sat on the bed, slowly sorting through the clothes. But then she stood up quickly. What the hell was wrong with her? David had been trying to 'bump' into her for the last few days. She didn't need to do or wear anything special to catch his attention. She could be wearing moth-eaten old rags, yet the moment he saw her sitting alone, the chances were he would grab the opportunity to join her.

Nevertheless, she still chose to wear a rather revealing, low-cut lace dress. The shade of blue rather suited her. Besides, if the grey hair was starting to take a hold, the dress wouldn't really be suitable. Or was she being too pessimistic?

Alan wouldn't approve, but, what the hell. Jim always recited an old saying, 'If you want to win a fight, you have got to give them something first.' She closed her eyes for a moment as she thought about Jim. If he had been looking down on her this afternoon, what would he have thought if Alan had actually leant across the car and kissed her? Or more to the point, what would he have thought if she had simply told Alan to go ahead and do it?

* * *

Back at the police station, Alan found his sergeant on the phone.

"I was just about to ring you, sir. Forensics has been on the phone. They have found a match between the blood taken from the pavement in Grainger Street and that of the victim we pulled from the river earlier today. They're going to send the paperwork, but they know how urgent this case is, therefore they rang to bring us up to speed."

Alan slowly lowered himself into his chair. He needed time to think. If Dennis and Mary were together the night they were killed, as Agnes had surmised, why wasn't Mary's blood found on the pavement, too? Was it possible that they had been out together for the evening before the murderer caught up with them? Perhaps the plan was to get them both into the van, drive off and kill them somewhere else; somewhere more secluded. But maybe the brother and sister had started to call out for help, leading the killer to panic and shoot Dennis on the spot and bundle his body into the van. Mary could have been in a state of shock at seeing her brother shot dead in front of her, making it easy to haul her in after him.

"Sir," Sergeant Andrews interrupted his thoughts. "Did you hear what I said? The blood was a..."

Alan looked up. "Yes, I heard you. Sorry, I was just thinking through something Mrs Lockwood said today."

"Is it something you would like to share with me?" Andrews' tone indicated he was being left out of the investigation.

Alan coughed. "Yes, of course, Michael." It wasn't very often that he called his sergeant by his Christian name. But it seemed appropriate right now. "I was simply trying to get it sorted out in my head first." He went on to tell Andrews what he had learned from the restaurant manager about the two brothers and their sister. Finally he came to the part where Agnes had come up with the suggestion that Dennis and Mary might have been killed at the same time.

"Like Mrs Lockwood said, the murderer could have been on his way to dispose of the bodies in the river. But for some reason, the van door burst open and Mary's body fell out. After all, the pathologist at the scene did say he thought the body we fished out of the river had been there for a few days."

Andrews pondered on what he had been told. He would have loved to have been in the position to tell the chief inspector that the whole idea was rubbish. But he didn't have anything better to offer. Besides, it all sounded feasible. The van door might not have been closed properly and the driver, in his haste to get the bodies out of the van, could have taken the corner too fast.

After a long pause, Andrews cleared his throat. "Yes, I agree. Mrs Lockwood could be right. But, I think there had to be at least two people involved. One person could not have lifted the dead body into the van by himself. There had to be another person there, especially as there would have been two bodies to throw into the river."

"Okay, we are clear on that," said Alan, thankful there wasn't going to be a skirmish with his sergeant. "But is the murder of these two people linked to the thefts at the hotel and," he paused, "where the hell does an MI5 agent come into all this?"

"Do you want me to go to the hotel and speak to David Drummond?" By now Andrews was already on his feet.

The chief inspector closed his eyes. How on earth was he going to explain to his sergeant that Agnes was already on the case?

Chapter Twenty

Agnes went downstairs intending to do everything possible to accidentally bump into David Drummond. Quite a change from her normal pattern; until now she had tried to avoid him.

She hoped he was having dinner in the hotel this evening. It would make it much easier to meet up with him and have a chat. Nevertheless, even if he were merely to pass through the reception on his way out of the building, he would suddenly find her somewhere in his path. There was no way he was going miss her.

Stepping out of the lift, she made her way over to the bar. For a moment, it had unnerved her to find, Larry, the usual lift attendant wasn't on duty. Since the episode with Drummond a few nights ago, they had become quite friendly.

He had told her his name the following day when they were in the lift together and now she looked forward to his pleasant chatter. However, she learned he would be back on duty at seven. It was good to know he would be around if her meeting with David didn't go well.

She was surprised to find the bar almost empty. Where was everyone? Most people stopped off for a drink in here before dinner. Most especially if they were staying in the hotel for a meal. It meant they didn't have to worry about driving under the influence of alcohol.

Agnes ordered a drink at the bar and sat down at one of the many empty tables and waited for it to be brought across to her. She had only asked for a Tonic Water with ice and lemon as she wanted to keep a clear head if David was to show up.

Alan had given her clear instructions when he dropped her off. Do not leave the hotel with this man. On no account go to his room; be sure to stay in public rooms where you are in sight of other guests at all times. We need to be sure he is who he says he is. If you are in any doubt at all, call me immediately. He had even insisted that she add his number to the speed dial on her phone. "You can't be too careful," he had said.

The waiter brought her drink and set it down on the table. He smiled as he handed her the bill to sign. Back at the bar it would be added to her hotel account.

"You don't seem to be very busy this evening," she said, once she had signed the paperwork. He looked fairly young and had a pleasant smile. He was dressed in the bar staff uniform, made up of a white shirt and black trousers. He was definitely foreign; Egyptian, she thought, very likely making his way around the world, learning various jobs in the catering trade.

"No." He glanced back towards the bar to make sure no one was watching him. "Quite a number of people have checked out and a few reservations were cancelled, after the word got around about the thefts."

"Really?" Agnes was genuinely surprised. She hadn't realised that the word had got out yet. She had seen no mention of it on television. But, on reflection, when had she been in her room long enough to watch the television news? She had been out most days – and evenings, come to that. In between, she had been in the process of getting ready to go out somewhere or other.

He glanced towards the bar again.

She followed his gaze, half expecting to see some ogre of a Bar Manager glaring at him for wasting time. But no one seemed to be taking any notice. Why would they? They weren't exactly rushed off their feet. So why was he so concerned?

"There are lots of people working here who are very anxious about their jobs."

He looked around the room again and when he saw no one was looking, he sat down. "Do you have any idea who the thief might be?"

"Me?" Agnes was most surprised. "You are asking me who the thief is. How would I know?"

The waiter shrugged. "You seem to be very friendly with the policeman. I thought he might have told you something." He leaned forward in his chair. "I would like to know what the police are doing about the thefts."

Agnes was beginning to feel a little uncomfortable about this man's attitude. He was getting way beyond his station. But then she tried to relax. Like he said, he was probably worried about his job.

"Well, I am sorry to disappoint you, but I am afraid the police haven't told me anything I don't know already." That much was true. Come to think about it, most of what they knew was because she had told them – not the other way around.

"And what is it you know?" the waiter asked. A grim expression crossed his face.

"The same as you, I imagine." Agnes replied. *This man needed to work on his communication skills,* she thought. *Waiters were not supposed to interrogate guests in this manner.* Was he fishing around for something? Or was he genuinely concerned about what the robberies were doing to the hotel's reputation? She heaved a sigh of relief when she saw two other guests walk into the bar and sit down at the other side of the room.

"I think you have another customer, Achmed," she said, making a note of the name pinned to his shirt

He glanced at the people and frowned. Agnes thought he looked angry that he had to move on.

"Maybe we can speak later, just you and me."

Not if I can help it, Agnes thought, as she watched him walk across the bar. What was that all about? Was he genuinely trying to find out information from her because he was worried about his job? Or was there another reason? Something more sinister? It was hard to tell. Foreigners, still learning a new language, sometimes sounded aggressive when they were trying to translate sentences in their head.

She recalled the very same thing had happened to her when she and Jim were abroad. One occasion in particular sprang to mind. She had thought she was asking politely for something in one of the gift shops, while really she was almost demanding that the shopkeeper gave it to her free of charge. It had taken another customer, who spoke both languages fluently, to calm the man down and stop him from raising the alarm. If it hadn't been for that lady, she and Jim might have missed their flight home, while she was languishing in a foreign jail awaiting trial. Since then, she had always tried to give everyone learning a new language the benefit of the doubt.

Agnes was still mulling these thoughts around in her head when she saw David Drummond emerge from the lift. She had purposely placed herself in a position in the bar where she could see, not only people stepping out of the lift, but also those who were entering the hotel. The latter was due to one of the mirrors adorning the walls of the hotel. The location of this one gave an excellent view of the double doors at the entrance. She recalled how when she had first seen them, she had felt uncomfortable, but now she loved them. By placing herself in the right position, she could see the Bar and the Reception from various angles.

Not wanting Mr Drummond to see she was looking at him, she turned away and began to fumble with her handbag, making sure that a few things fell to the floor. She then went on to make a drama of picking everything up, hoping to attract his attention. She may not want him to see her peering at him, but she certainly wanted him to notice her.

It worked. The next thing she heard was his voice asking if he could be of assistance.

"Thank you," Agnes replied. She gave him one of her most winning smiles. "I was simply looking for a handkerchief, when everything seemed to fall out onto the floor."

"I think that's it," Drummond said, placing everything onto the table. "I can't see anything else. I always thought that women's handbags were a bottomless pit. Rather like the one Mary Poppins had."

Agnes noticed that his eyes lingered on her mobile phone for longer than necessary. She laughed as she placed her belongings back into her bag. "Yes, they are. The problem is, when we go out for the evening, we tend to change to a much smaller handbag, yet want to carry the same number of things – whether we will need them or not."

Drummond looked around and seeing there were so few in the bar, he asked if he might join her.

"Yes, please do." Agnes gestured towards the seat opposite her. However, he chose to sit in the chair nearest to her.

For a moment she was caught unawares. Facing him across the table was one thing, but having him sit right next to her was something else. What if he was a double agent? What if he had been waiting for this very moment over the last few days and suddenly pulled a gun with an enormous silencer and shot her dead? It was possible. These things happened all the time in *James Bond* films.

Agnes swallowed hard. She needed to get a grip. It was she who had volunteered to do this. Alan had wanted to send in an undercover policewoman to speak to Drummond. But she had talked him out of it. Now she needed to pull herself together and get on with finding out why he was here and, more importantly, why he was fixating on her.

By the time Agnes agreed to him taking the seat next to her, he was already seated. He gestured towards the waiter and ordered himself a drink. "And you," he said, pointing at her glass. "Would you like a refill?"

"Yes please," she said, glancing at Drummond. But when she was sure he was looking the other way, she held her finger and thumb close together, indicating to Achmed that she wanted a small one.

"Are you enjoying your stay in Newcastle?" Drummond said, once the waiter had returned to the bar. "By the way, my name is Drummond, David Drummond." He held out his hand.

"Hello, David." She replied, trying desperately not to laugh at how he had introduced himself. Did this guy really see himself as James Bond? "I hope you don't mind me calling you…" She coughed … "David." She hoped he hadn't noticed her slight hesitation. She had been on the brink of calling him James. "I am Agnes Lockwood. But please, call me Agnes. Yes, I am enjoying my visit." She explained how she had been born here in the north east, but had left the area many years ago. "Now I am simply trying to catch up with my past."

She smiled at the waiter, who had suddenly returned with their drinks. "Thank you," she said, graciously, as he placed a glass in front of her. His interruption had broken David's train of thought, allowing Agnes the chance to turn the subject around.

"Cheers," she said, raising her glass. "And you, David?" Agnes questioned. "Are you here on holiday?" She took a drink from her glass of gin and tonic and almost choked. Hadn't she made it clear she wanted a small measure?

"Cheers," David answered, picking up his double whisky. "I came to visit my family." He took a large swig from the glass and then swallowed another before he continued.

"Like you, I came here to catch up with the past." He held up his hand to attract the waiter's attention." He pointed at his glass. "Another. What about you?" he added, nodding towards Agnes's glass.

"I'm fine," she replied, placing the palm of her hand over her glass. "And have you?" Agnes prompted. "Caught up with your past?"

David eyed Agnes thoughtfully. He had spent the last few days trying to catch up with this woman. She had an image of him on her phone and he needed to remove it. Now he had finally caught up with her, all they were talking about was catching up with their past.

He picked up the remainder of his whisky and swirled it around in the glass. "I think in my case, my past caught up with me," he said.

Before he could say anything further, Achmed placed a glass in front of him. David signed the bill with a flourish and then turned back to Agnes. "Haven't we met before?"

Agnes took a sip of her gin and tonic to give her time to think about how to answer. If she was correct in that he had mistaken her for the woman who had taken his photo a few nights ago, then that needed to come from him.

"I believe we bumped into each other in the lift the other night," she said at last. "But I don't think we spoke. I recall the lift attendant did all of the talking."

"Yes, he did rather, didn't he?" David shifted uncomfortably in his chair. This wasn't going well. Either she had no idea what she was talking about or she was a damn good actress.

"But I wasn't referring to when we were in the lift together," David continued. "I recall seeing you a few evenings earlier. It was near Grainger Street and it was rather late."

"No. I don't think so," Agnes replied, slowly. She shook her head. "You see, I haven't been in the city centre late at night. I have had a few evenings out with an old friend from my past, but we ate in restaurants here on the quayside."

Although she could see David was puzzled, she wasn't about to help him out. She was here to learn a few things from him. This whole meeting was meant to be an exchange of information – though he didn't know it – yet.

"You must be mistaken," she said.

"But I could have sworn I saw you," he blustered. "You even took a photograph of me on your mobile phone." The last sentence was out before he could stop himself.

"Now I know you have made a mistake." Agnes picked up her hand-bag and removed her mobile phone. "I don't have any photographs of you. Take a look for yourself." She handed him her phone.

Agnes watched David as he looked through the photos and videos. Thankfully, she had erased the video she had taken of him the day he followed her across the Millennium Bridge. Once it had been trans-ferred to Alan's phone, she had deleted it in case there was ever a moment, such as this.

"I don't know what to say." David handed the phone back to her. "I can only apologize. I felt sure it was you I saw."

"Why is it so important, anyway?" Agnes shrugged, trying to be flippant. "I mean, what if I had taken a photo of you? Would it really have been such a big issue?"

"No, I suppose not." David laughed.

But Agnes could tell his laughter was forced.

"I thought we had met before," he continued. "Obviously I was wrong. It must have been someone else I saw that evening."

Agnes watched him as she dropped the phone into her handbag. He seemed satisfied that she hadn't seen him hurrying up the road that night. But she could tell he was now concerned that there was some other person out there who had evidence which could place him near the scene of the crime. But this was not the time to dwell on that. She needed to gain his confidence if there was to be any chance of her learning something that might be useful to the police.

She was wondering what to say next, when he interrupted her thoughts.

"There have been a few thefts at the hotel," he said. "Has any of your jewellery been taken?"

"No, thank goodness," she replied. "Ever since Mrs Hargreaves reported her necklace stolen, I have carried my jewellery around with me. Not that I have anything really valuable in a monetary sense," she added hastily. "But what I have is precious to me as they were gifts from my late husband."

"I'm sorry for your loss." David muttered the usual MI5 comment for such news.

"It was over a year ago now," Agnes said, quietly. "But I am still trying to get used to him not being with me. We did everything together."

Agnes cringed when David looked at his watch. Had she blown it? Was he looking for some means of escape?

"Are you dining here in the hotel this evening," David asked. "If so, I thought we might have dinner together."

"Yes, thank you. That's a wonderful idea." Agnes was relieved. Dinner together was what she had been hoping for. People with secrets tended to loosen up over dinner. Fine wine and good food was well known for making people relax – especially, fine wine. Things were often said over dinner that might otherwise have been left unsaid.

"I thought I was going to have to dine alone this evening," she said, as she gathered her things together.

Chapter Twenty-One

In the dining room, Agnes was careful not to carry on the conversation where they had left off. Though she would have been happy to talk about Jim, she was aware that she needed to keep David chatting, not send him to sleep.

Instead, she talked about how she was enjoying her stay in Newcastle, telling him about her visits to both the art gallery and the Sage. "Both were most interesting. I'm sure you would enjoy seeing them."

Agnes noticed him flinch slightly when she mentioned her trip across the Millennium Bridge. That was the day he had followed her. Nevertheless, she carried on as though nothing had happened.

"What about you? Are you here on business or pleasure," she asked.

"Both," he replied. "I live in London, so I jumped at the chance of doing some business here in the north, as it gave me the opportunity to meet up with my brother and sister."

"That's nice. I don't suppose you will get to see them very often." Her heart quickened a pace. They were now moving towards the reason why she had met him that evening. How would he react? Would he simply agree with her and swing the conversation over to another subject?

"No, we didn't meet up enough," he said, thoughtfully. "And now I won't see them ever again." The words were out before he'd had time to think about what he was saying.

"Why is that? Are they moving abroad?" Agnes asked the question even though she already knew the answers. By now her heart was pounding. Would he tell her the truth? Or would he make up some story about them moving half way across the world to Australia or New Zealand.

* * *

David studied Agnes from across the table; he wondered how to answer her question. The Home Office, already aware of his brother and sister's death had warned him to stay silent on the issue. Therefore, he knew he should change the subject; move the conversation on to something else.

Normally he wouldn't find it a problem. Part of his training had been to learn how to turn a subject around without anyone noticing and, over the years, he had done exactly that without a problem. Yet, he had the feeling this time, his audience wouldn't be hanging onto his every word.

Agnes Lockwood had been going out with the chief inspector. He had seen them together. No doubt the detective had discussed some aspects of the case with her – if not all; even if a man in his position wasn't supposed to. Agnes was probably a very persuasive woman.

He took a deep breath. He knew that whatever he said next had to sound very convincing.

* * *

Agnes sat quietly, slowly sipping her wine. She wondered what was going on in David's head, when suddenly he slammed his hand down on the table, making her jump. The glasses and cutlery rattled so loudly, a few of the other diners looked around to see who was causing the disturbance.

"Sorry," he mumbled to Agnes. "Sorry," David nodded towards the people at the tables closest to him.

Agnes didn't say anything. Truthfully, she didn't know what to say. Not expecting such an outburst, she hadn't prepared herself for the sudden explosion from across the table. Maybe this hadn't been a good idea after all. A policewoman would have known what to do in such a situation.

She raised her glass to her lips again and took a couple of sips of wine. The brief interval would give her the chance to think through what to say next. However there was no need, as David took up the conversation.

"Both my brother and sister were murdered last week." He looked away, as though trying to hide the tears in his eyes. "And it was my fault."

Though David merely mumbled those last few words, Agnes picked them up. She wanted to ask why he had come to that conclusion, but decided to wait until later. Instead, she reached across the table and took his hand in sympathy.

"Oh my goodness, David, I am so very sorry. You must be devastated." Even though she knew in advance of David's loss, she had not been prepared for his display of grief. He looked absolutely devastated.

Agnes swallowed hard.

"If it would help you to talk about it, then I am here." Agnes suddenly felt guilty at her attempt to be a shoulder to cry on. What would David Drummond think of her when he found out she had known the two murdered people were his siblings all the time. And she was here tonight on an errand to prise information from him to pass on to the police. It was almost certain he would find out – it was only a matter of time.

She was already surprised his cousin hadn't been in touch to tell him about her visit, together with the chief inspector, to his restaurant that very afternoon. Alan had introduced her as Mrs Lockwood, so the restaurant manager had her name.

But even if Mr Peterson had forgotten her name due to their stressful conversation, surely David would have guessed it was her. He wasn't an idiot – he was an undercover spy for the Secret Service, for goodness sake.

She covered her mouth to hide a smile when a thought suddenly ran through her mind. This could almost be the day that *James Bond* took *Miss Marple* to dinner. Yet, even with that comical thought in mind, something troubled her. If David really was here in Newcastle in an official capacity for MI5, why would he be using his real name?

* * *

When they had finished dinner, Agnes and David went back into the bar. Agnes was a little disappointed that he hadn't opened up further. The evening was drawing to a close and she still hadn't found out what he was working on and why he felt the murder of his brother and sister was his fault.

David had taken the opportunity to change the subject entirely when the waiter brought their meal to the table and had kept away from the issue of his family ever since. Instead, he had been more interested in hearing about her stay in Newcastle. She was going to have to try again over drinks in the bar otherwise all this had been a complete waste of time.

"I have just had a thought." She waited for a few seconds, hoping he would think she was still running the idea through her mind. "Is it possible that the murder of your brother and sister had anything to do with the thefts here at the hotel?"

Agnes sat waiting patiently for him to reply. She didn't take her eyes off him for one second, fearing it might give him the chance he was waiting for: to call the waiter or to wave to some non-existent person passing the bar doorway. Anything at all that might give him even half a chance to distract her from the question she had asked.

From his glazed expression, she could tell he was thinking it all through. Yet the very fact he was taking so long to reply, told her the murders did have something to do with the thefts – regardless of which way he might respond at the end of his lengthy deliberation. Therefore, there would be a problem with whatever he said.

If he were to say there was absolutely no connection at all then she would have to go down the road of enquiring why he was so certain one had nothing to do with the other. Hoping it would lead him into giving her some sort of explanation he'd had to make up on the spur of the moment, which would ultimately lead him into saying more than he wanted to say.

Her eyes never left him as she reached for her glass and took a sip of her gin and tonic. It tasted good; so cold and refreshing. She had found it rather warm in the Dining Room and it wasn't much cooler in here. She took another drink, a larger one this time, before setting her glass back on the table.

David had still not uttered a word. Why didn't he say something? This was getting more complicated by the minute. Now, even she was beginning to lose the plot. Her head was starting to spin. Why was that? Had she had too much to drink? No! She had kept her hand over the glass when David had reached over to top up her wine glass. Could he have spiked her drink when she wasn't looking? No. Again that wasn't possible. All through dinner, she had never taken her eyes off him.

Yet, if this guy was as cunning as MI5 agents were supposed to be, then he could have waited for the right moment to add a few drops of something into her glass without her even knowing about it. Fearing such a thing might have happened, her mind raced through some of the James Bond movies she had seen. She needed to think; keep her mind occupied. The character in the films had used fountain pens, and many other such gadgets devised by Q to drop something into the victim's drink to put them into some sort of a coma.

However, in all cases James Bond always had to lean close to his victim. Agnes tried to focus her mind on whether David had leaned over her glass during the evening? But she couldn't remember. She didn't think he had, but how near would anyone have to be to drop something into her drink?

Her head was spinning faster now and the voices of the other people in the bar sounded distorted. In that instant, she knew she was in trouble and needed to call Alan. But if David had spiked her drink, he wouldn't allow her to leave the table, even if she told him she was going to Ladies Room. So instead she raised her arm and called for a passing waiter. It was Achmed, the waiter she had spoken to earlier that evening. "Please, I feel poorly," she gasped. "I need someone to help me up to my room."

A few minutes later, Agnes found herself stretched out on her bed in her hotel room. Two ladies from the reception area were kneeling beside her, while the hotel manager hovered in the background.

"Where is my phone?" she called out.

"I don't think having your phone is a good idea," the manager replied. "You need to stay calm. We'll call an ambulance."

"I don't want an ambulance. Just give me my damn phone," Agnes screamed. "I need to have a friend here beside me."

"Okay! Okay!" The manager nodded to one of his staff and she handed Agnes her handbag.

Agnes didn't notice the manager and his staff leaving the room as she fumbled around and found her phone. She pressed the button on her speed dial which would immediately connect her to Alan and yelled down the phone the moment he answered. This was not the time for pleasantries. "Alan, I am feeling so unwell. Help me. I think I have..." But that was all she was allowed to say, before someone yanked the phone from her hand.

Chapter Twenty-Two

Alan had felt uneasy all evening. Truthfully, he had been uncomfortable from the very moment he had agreed to Agnes meeting up with David Drummond. Even more so since his sergeant had suggested they were playing a dangerous game. But as the evening had worn on, his discomfort had grown worse.

He knew Andrews was unhappy at being left out when the decision had been made. His sergeant had made that very clear; even though he had agreed that the reasoning behind the decision was good. "But it should have been one of the team," he'd insisted. "Not a member of the public."

Andrews had gone on to suggest that Agnes could be out of her depth. "Drummond could be a rogue agent; a double agent, working for and against the United Kingdom.

Though Alan had played down such thoughts at the time, they were still mulling around in his head when he arrived home. What on earth had he been thinking to allow Agnes to meet up with this man? But since first seeing her, he seemed to have forgotten that he was a chief inspector in charge of a murder investigation. He should be the one taking control. Yet he was allowing her to run rings around him.

Of course Andrews was right to be annoyed. He was a good sergeant and would be promoted to inspector when an opportunity arose. He had already passed the necessary exams. Alan knew that he would have been quite hurt if his previous chief inspector had cut him out of any investigation. He was going to have to make it up to Andrews. But right now, his attention needed to be focused on Agnes and her meeting with Drummond.

It was at that very moment his phone began to ring. Flipping it open, he immediately saw that the caller was Agnes. He didn't have time for any pleasantries as her voice came down the line the moment they were connected. He was stunned; she was crying out for him to come to the hotel right away as she needed help.

"I think I have..." she screamed. Then there was silence.

"Agnes! Agnes," he yelled into the phone. There was no reply.

He quickly phoned her back and tapped his fingers on the table impatiently while he waited for her to answer. But when it stopped ringing it went to voicemail.

Alan grabbed his car keys and headed out of the door and hurried towards his car, still parked in the drive. As he started the engine, he called Andrews. "Get to The Millennium Hotel right away. Agnes is in trouble. Meet you there." Without another word, he threw the phone onto the passenger seat, lobbed the gear of the car into reverse and backed out of the drive.

Both Alan and Andrews arrived at the hotel at the same time. As they ran through the doors, Alan told his sergeant about Agnes's phone call. "I don't know any more. She was cut off in mid-sentence. The phone could have been snatched from her hand."

Andrews nodded. He noted the look of anguish on the chief inspector's face. This was not the time to say, 'I told you so.' Instead he said, "I called for backup once I was on my way."

"Good. We may need it."

The two police officers entered the building and took the lift up to the fourth floor. The lift attendant was no-where to be seen, so there was no need for small talk. As they moved nearer to Agnes's room, Alan pulled a gun from his pocket. It had still been locked in the glove compartment. He had forgotten to remove it when he had arrived home earlier that evening. But on the way to the hotel, he remembered it was there and thought it might be a handy thing to have around – just in case.

Andrews raised his eyebrows when he saw it in Alan's hand.

"Don't ask," Alan said, as he moved slowly towards Agnes's room. He shouldn't have a gun with him; though he did have a license to carry one.

"I won't," Andrews said, following his boss down the hall. Over the last few hours, he had seen a whole new side of Chief Inspector Johnson.

"Okay, stand to one side of the door, Alan whispered, raising his gun. "When I nod, knock and call out room service."

Andrews stared at Alan with a blank expression on his face. Was this for real?

"Just do it." Alan hissed.

"Room service," Andrews called out as he knocked on the door.

There was no reply.

Alan lowered his gun and knocked on the door again. But there was still no reply. He tried the handle yet the door remained closed. They needed a damn keycard.

Alan remained where he was, while Andrews went downstairs to the reception.

A few minutes later Andrews arrived back holding a keycard. He pushed it into the lock and removed it. A brief nod from Alan told him to turn the handle and open the door. Alan hurled himself through the door only to find the room was empty.

Chapter Twenty-Three

Agnes awoke with a splitting headache. It took her a few seconds to realise she wasn't in her hotel room. She sat up slowly and tried to look around. But she couldn't see much as it was so dark; there was only one small window high above her and there was very little light coming from there. Where the hell was she?

The last thing she remembered was being in the bar talking to David Drummond. What had happened in between then and now? But her head was still hurting so much, she was forced to lie back down and close her eyes.

Slowly, she began to recall the events of the evening. She'd had dinner with David Drummond and then she had agreed to go back to the bar for a drink to round off the evening. There were still many things she needed to learn from him and that final drink in the bar might have helped.

Her eyes snapped open. It was all coming back to her. It was while she and David had been in the bar that she began to feel unwell. Had he dropped something into her drink? But now, on reflection, why would he do that? According to Gordon Peterson, he was a government agent. Unless, of course, David wasn't really the man his cousin thought him to be.

She groaned and closed her eyes, when a searing pain ran through her head. However, as the pain subsided, she continued running things through her mind.

Two ladies from reception had escorted her upstairs to her room; even the manager had appeared when he heard the news. It was clear they all thought she'd had too much to drink. Though she knew that wasn't the case. She had been very careful. She'd been determined to stay alert during her conversation with David Drummond.

Her mobile phone had been placed in her hands when she demanded it and all three had left the room while she was making the call to Alan. The next thing she remembered was someone snatching the phone from her before she fell unconscious.

So where was she now? Surely she still had to be in the hotel somewhere. No one could have dragged her from her room, into the lift and out through reception without being seen. Next question: who had done this to her and why? Could it be David Drummond? Had she been right when she suspected it was he who had spiked her drink? Yet there was still something nagging at her. Something was telling her she was on the wrong track with Drummond. If only her head would stop pounding, she might remember more.

* * *

The two detectives hurried back downstairs. Alan was keen to speak to the staff on the reception desk. The two ladies were just about to go off duty but were happy to help with the police enquiries. They explained how they had helped Agnes upstairs to her room.

"Didn't you think to call an ambulance?" Alan asked

"No. We simply thought she'd had too much to drink," one of them told him. "Though, in light of what you say, we regret not doing that now. If we had, Mrs Lockwood might have been taken to hospital and not have gone missing."

"You think?" Alan muttered. "Have either of you seen her since you came back downstairs." Alan's tone was brusque.

The two receptionists looked at each other. They were really worried now. Had they missed something? Yet they had been here all evening. One of them would have seen her.

"No, she certainly hasn't come through the reception since we left her." It was the other lady speaking now.

"Unless she sneaked by and went back into the bar. I believe the young man she was with is still in there." The first receptionist added, trying to be helpful.

"What about your lift attendant?" Alan suddenly remembered he hadn't been on duty when they arrived. "He might have seen something."

"Larry was called away while we were upstairs," said one of the receptionists. "I gather his mother had an accident."

Alan looked at his sergeant. That sounded rather suspicious. However, he didn't get a chance to say anything further, as the backup team arrived. Sergeant Andrews went over to speak to them.

"Did the young man in the bar escort you up to the room when you helped Mrs Lockwood upstairs?" Alan turned his attention back to the receptionists.

"No." The first lady looked at her colleague for confirmation. "No," she repeated, when her colleague shook her head. "We are certain about that. However, Mr Jenkins must have heard about what had happened from the bar staff because he arrived a few minutes after we got to her room. We all left when she used her phone to call someone."

Alan asked them if they had seen anyone in the corridor when they were leaving. But they shook their heads and told him the corridor was empty. After thanking them both, Alan moved across to where Andrews was talking with the backup crew.

"Okay, I want to you to spread out and check all the public rooms and store cupboards and talk to the staff, but do it discreetly. We won't get anywhere by jumping in and stamping our feet. But bear in mind, there have been several thefts at this hotel, one of the guests has been murdered and now another has gone missing. Be discreet – but thorough."

Once the team had set off on their mission, Alan and Andrews went across to the bar. They needed to speak to David Drummond.

They found him still sitting where Agnes had left him.

* * *

David Drummond hadn't moved from the Bar since Agnes left. Earlier, one of the ladies from reception had called in to tell him that she and her colleague had taken Mrs Lockwood up to her room. Asking if Agnes would be alright, the receptionist had told him she was on the phone when they left. She also told him that Mr Jenkins knew of the situation and he was sure that Mrs Lockwood had simply had a little too much to drink.

Since then David had sat patiently in the bar sipping his drink. He had been expecting the police to arrive ever since he had heard that Agnes had started to make a phone call.

He wasn't an idiot. He had known all the time that she was fishing around. Looking for something to give her a clue as to what was going on. After he had seen her phone, he knew she wasn't the woman who had taken his photo a few evenings before. Yet he was certain she was aware of the person who had. His training with MI5 had taught him how to pick out the truth from everything he was told.

Yes, she could have deleted the photo. But something told him she hadn't been the woman he'd seen that night when he was fleeing from the murder scene.

He had been told to pack and head back to London when his boss had learned of the murder. But so far he had managed to hang on by ignoring their calls. Too much was at stake for him to leave now and even if he did leave the area, he wouldn't be going to London. He had somewhere else in mind.

He knew it wouldn't be long before MI5 picked up on this and sent two men to escort him back to London. Therefore he needed to finish this as soon as possible and get out.

David Drummond recognised Detective Chief Inspector Johnson when he slid into the seat opposite him. He had seen him several times while investigating the thefts at the hotel.

* * *

"Can I help you guys?" David asked.

"I hope so," said Alan. "I understand that you were having dinner with Mrs Lockwood earlier this evening."

"Yes," David replied. "She suddenly felt unwell so two members of staff helped her upstairs." He paused for a moment and allowed a puzzled expression to cross his face. "She's okay, isn't she? I mean she looked a little pale when she left, but I didn't think it was anything serious. She had been fine all during dinner."

Alan looked up at his sergeant. Though it might look like he was seeking advice from Andrews as to how far he should trust this man, the movement was to give him a moment or two to think.

Drummond had sounded genuinely surprised at them asking about Agnes. Yet, he now knew this man was a trained agent. He had probably been taught how to conduct himself whatever occasion arose. He needed to find Agnes before she came to any harm. Therefore, though he was reluctant to do so, he was going to have to trust this man.

"Mrs Lockwood has gone missing," Alan said at last. "She called my mobile saying she needed help, but then the call was disconnected. We got here as quickly as we could, but Mrs Lockwood's room is empty. The staff on reception told us they haven't seen her since they helped her upstairs." He paused for one brief moment. "Is there anything you can tell us that would help find her before anything terrible happens."

Drummond opened his mouth to say something, but held back when he noticed a new waiter wiping a table nearby.

Alan guessed Drummond was waiting for the waiter to finish before saying anything. In his job, he would need to be vigilant. However, the waiter lingered on; continuing to spray the table with some sort of antiseptic liquid and wipe away non-existent germs. Either that table was totally septic or the guy was trying to make a good impression with the bar manager.

"I'm afraid I can't help you," Drummond said after a long pause. He spoke a little louder than he had done before, as though he wanted to make sure everyone in the bar heard every word. "Once Agnes was hurried away to her room, I waited here hoping it was a simple problem and she would be back soon."

At that point, the waiter took a step backwards and looked down at the gleaming table. Satisfied with his work, he moved across to where a couple of new customers had just sat down.

Now that the overelaborate waiter had moved on, David rose to his feet. "I'm sorry; I need to go now. I'm waiting for a phone call, which I need to take in my room." He was still speaking loudly. He smiled and shook hands with Alan. "I hope you find Agnes very soon."

Then, as he turned to shake hands with Sergeant Andrews, he lowered his voice. "Meet me in my room in ten minutes." He gave his room number before leaving the bar.

The chief inspector and his sergeant sat down and looked at each other for a few seconds.

Alan was the first to speak. "I'm not sure which way to take that man. At first I thought he was a little edgy because the waiter was too close. But then I wondered whether he was interested in how well the man was cleaning the table. Or could it be that he was buying time."

Andrews nodded. "Could be all three! Now he is buying even more time by leaving us here sitting here while he goes up to his room and makes sure there isn't anything incriminating lying around."

"Or maybe Drummond noticed something going on with the waiter earlier in the evening, and was being cautious." Alan added slowly.

"I don't buy it," said Andrews. "The waiter was simply doing his job. I was watching him the whole time Drummond was holding back. That waiter didn't even look in our direction. His attention was focused on cleaning the table." He paused. "Agent or not, I still don't trust David Drummond."

* * *

The sergeant looked away. It was true. He didn't trust the man; though he had no real reason not to. Yet there was something that didn't sound right and now the wretched man was moving in and taking over their case. So far, Agnes Lockwood had managed to worm her way into every aspect of the investigation. Now they had David Drummond butting his way in and it seemed that his boss was simply accepting it without question.

"I'm sorry, sir," Andrews said. "I just feel we are being taken for a ride by this so called agent."

* * *

"No need to be sorry, Michael, I understand how you feel." Alan smiled. "However, as detectives, we have to go with what information is thrown towards us." He paused. "We weed through any information thrown in our direction. Obviously, we find some of it to be stuff we already know to be totally useless. There are some things we will find will help, but only for a short time. Then there are the odd scraps of info that will move us a step closer to the truth. Even one shred of information could lead us to someone who knows more than we do." Alan shrugged. "In our present case, that someone could be Drummond. He might have noticed something happening earlier this evening, something which could help with our investigation." By now Alan was staring at Andrews. "So, tell me, do you really want to dismiss anything he has to offer, because he is a so called, secret agent?"

Andrews swallowed hard. He hadn't realised his envy of Drummond had been so obvious.

"Okay, Sergeant. I think we have given Drummond enough time. We'd better head upstairs." He paused. "However, let me tell you something. I, too, am not convinced about this man. I suggest we listen to what he has to say and then make our own judgement."

Out in the reception area the detectives found the backup team hovering around. Their report wasn't good. No one had seen Mrs Lockwood. Alan was told that a forensics guy was still in her hotel room looking for fingerprints.

The chief inspector nodded, but he felt sure the man wouldn't find anything. He suspected that whoever had abducted Agnes, would have taken great care not to leave a trace of his identity.

After sending the men back to the police station, the chief inspector looked back into the bar. He wanted to make sure no one was watching them as he and Andrews went upstairs to talk to Drummond. He saw the two waiters standing at the bar with their backs towards the door. No doubt they were waiting for their orders to be fulfilled. As for the customers, they were so involved with the conversation going on around them, they wouldn't have noticed if a famous film star had walked into the room.

Alan nodded to Andrews and they both quickly made their way across to the stairs.

Chapter Twenty-Four

Agnes looked up at the small window. It was still dark outside. How long had she been here? Was this the same night she had met David Drummond. Or, could she have been up here for a full twenty-four hours?

Her head was still hurting. Though it wasn't quite as bad as it had been earlier, it was still very painful. Nevertheless she needed to find out where she was. But it was still so black in here. Perhaps there was a light switch somewhere. Very carefully, she swung her legs over the sofa or whatever it was she was lying on, and rose to her feet. She would have to step very carefully. If this was some kind of a storeroom, there could be things lying around the floor. First of all, she would have to find a wall. From there, maybe she could feel her way around the room until she found a light switch or even a door. Though she guessed it would be locked.

Very slowly, she placed one foot in front of the other and began to move away from the sofa. This could take a long time depending on how big the room was. But she knew she couldn't hurry. If she fell over something, she might hurt herself. Her head was painful enough without having something else to worry about. She took a few more tiny steps without any problems; so far, so good. She raised her arms out in front of her and groped around in the darkness, feeling out for something solid. She knew she could do this. But she had to stay calm.

Even imprisoned in this dark room, she managed a slight smile as she thought back to the small plaque hanging on her kitchen wall. Keep Calm and Carry On, it read. Those words had been written for an instance such as this.

* * *

David Drummond opened his door the moment Andrews knocked. He quickly ushered the two detectives into the room. He had been hovering around waiting for them to appear, the fewer people who saw them together the better. Guests arrived back at the hotel from various clubs or parties at all hours. Most of them were too inebriated to notice anything or probably wouldn't care if they did. But his job had taught him to be wary of everyone. His goal was so close; he had no intention of losing out now.

"Okay, what can you tell us about what has happened to Mrs Lockwood?" It was Andrews who asked the question. He got straight to the point once the door was closed. "And what has the waiter got to do with anything?"

"Please sit down." Drummond gestured towards a large sofa.

The two detectives sat down.

"I can't say anything for certain, but I believe one of the waiters knows something," David said as he lowered his large frame into an armchair. "During our conversation over dinner, Agnes commented that the waiter, Achmed, in the bar had been a little presumptuous before I arrived. She didn't say much more, but I got the impression she had been rather perturbed, when he took it upon himself to sit down beside her and begin asking questions."

"What sort of questions?" It was Alan who spoke now.

David shrugged. "She told me he had been asking her what she and the police had found out regarding the thefts. I understand, she stated she had no idea what the police had discovered or how far they were with their investigation." He paused. "She laughed it off, saying that he was probably having trouble with the language, but I was not so sure.

I would like to have asked a couple of questions about his manner, but she refused to talk about it any longer. Saying it was probably a misunderstanding."

"But you don't think so?" Alan asked. "You think there is more to it than a mere mistake."

Drummond nodded. "There is something about the waiter that I am not comfortable with. When Agnes called him over saying she was feeling unwell, he didn't look surprised. I watched him while she was being escorted upstairs.

I wanted to see whether he left the bar area."

"And did he?" Andrews asked.

"Yes, he went out into room behind the bar, but was only gone for a couple of minutes. When he came back he was carrying a crate of beer for the waitress at the bar. If he had been gone any longer, I would have gone out there to see what he was up to. I know for a fact that there is a staircase out there which leads upstairs."

"So, if Mrs Lockwood didn't think the waiter was a problem, and you didn't lose sight of him for more than a couple of minutes, why do you still think he might have been involved with her disappearance. I mean, that's why you asked us to come up here, right?" Andrews was itching to get one over on the MI5 guy. "Or have I completely lost the plot somewhere down the line."

"Is your sergeant always this abrasive," said David, looking at the chief inspector.

"No, not always," Alan replied, "just when he doesn't see where the conversation is going." He paused. "I have to admit, I, myself, am beginning to wonder why we are here – and, if it was Achmed Mrs Lockwood told you about, why did the new waiter interest you so much?"

"I invited you here to tell you I was already watching Achmed long before Agnes told me about his behaviour this evening." Drummond shrugged. "The other waiter simply amused me." He turned his attention to the sergeant. "However, when you started asking the questions, I thought I would play along until you caught up." He paused. "Would either of you like to join me in a drink?"

Alan looked at his wristwatch. It was well past midnight now. How much longer would this take? "Do you think this is a joke, Drummond? A woman has been kidnapped here in the hotel under your nose and you are asking us to join you in a drink! For goodness sake, man, tell us everything you know."

* * *

Agnes was still groping around in the dark room. She had almost fallen over a couple of things. Thankfully she had been taking it very slowly, so no harm was done. The room must be extremely large. Either that or she was going around in circles. In which case, she wasn't going to get anywhere fast. Perhaps she should wait for the sun to rise.

But she knew she simply couldn't sit here waiting for something to happen. Someone could be back at any time and she didn't want to take the risk of being murdered without having made some attempt to save herself.

At last she came to what felt like a wall. It was certainly very solid. Now, if she slowly followed it around the room, while feeling up and down for a light switch, she might actually get somewhere.

After what seemed like an eternity, Agnes' fingers touched a switch. Until that moment, she had begun to think she was wandering around the room covering the same ground over and over again. She flicked the switch and a bulb above head her sprang to life.

At first she couldn't see anything; the sudden glare of light blinded her. But then slowly, as her eyes grew accustomed to the brightness she was able to take in her surroundings. It was quite a large room and the floor was covered with boxes. How she hadn't tripped and fallen at every step was a miracle. Looking up, she could see that the light was fastened to one of the many large beams which held up the pitched roof. The window she had seen earlier was set at the top of the wall just below where the roof began to slide upwards. The window was tiny in comparison to the size of the room. It was little wonder that she couldn't see the glow from any streetlights.

Her head was still hurting, but she fought off the pain. She needed to get a grip; she needed to think. Her very life might depend on what she could remember. She thought back over the days when she had walked along the quayside looking towards the hotel. There had been the odd times when she'd seen someone leaning out of a window. On those occasions, had she allowed her eyes to stray above the windows to the roof?

Yes! She suddenly remembered seeing a union flag on a long pole flying above the hotel. The pole had been perched on what looked something like a church steeple, though much shorter. She looked up at the ceiling again; peering through the darkness beyond where the beams from the light reached. After a few moments, she was able to make out that the wooden supports rose gently to a point in the centre of the room. So, she was still in the hotel. She hadn't been carted off to some old storehouse that no one used any more. Now, somehow or another, she needed to get out of here before her captor came back.

She swept her eyes around the room. At one side were some chairs; the same as those currently used in the Dining Room. Obviously they were spares in case something happened to the ones downstairs. There were a couple of leather sofas and lots of cushions. And then there were the boxes; countless boxes. They probably held crockery and kitchen ware.

There were two doors in the room. The first one she tried was locked. It held firmly as she tugged at the handle. She held her breath as she crossed the room towards the other door. If this didn't work, she was going to have to look for some other means of escape. When she reached the door, she stretched out and turned the handle. Damn! It was locked, too. What else could she have expected? No one takes a prisoner and then leaves the door unlocked.

She was about to move away, when she noticed that this door was taller than the other one and it had a bolt at the top and bottom. However, it didn't have a keyhole, which meant if she could draw back the bolts, she could possibly see what was on the other side; unless it had bolts on the other side as well.

The bottom bolt was no problem, it slid back quite easily. However, she would need to stand on something to reach the top one.

Glancing around the room, her eyes fell on the chairs. She already knew they were heavy. She had tried to move one on her first evening at the hotel and found it extremely difficult. It was little wonder the waiters in the Dining Room pulled back the chairs for the lady diners to be seated. Nevertheless, if she was to get out of here she needed to stand on something to reach the damn bolt.

She began to pull the chair across the room towards the door, but stopped when she realised it was making too much noise. She had no idea of the whereabouts of her kidnapper. He could be outside the locked door or in a room somewhere beneath her. She would need to carry it. Grasping the chair with both hands she lifted it from the floor and began to stagger across the large room. Why did they have to make these chairs so heavy?

Her mind flittered back to the call she had made to Alan. If only she knew whether he had heard her plea for help before the phone was snatched from her hands and she received a blow to her head. However, she had to go on the assumption he hadn't. Therefore, she must believe she was on her own and do everything she could to help herself.

At last she reached the door. Now she had to move quickly. Even if the person who had drugged and brought her up here wasn't somewhere nearby, he could come back at any time.

She heaved herself onto the chair and slid back the bolt. Jumping back down, she heaved the chair to one side and turned the handle. The door opened and she found herself at the bottom of some steps. A quick glance told her there was nowhere else to go but up. Even though she still had a headache, made worse by heaving the chair across the room, she ran up the steps.

At the top, there was another door, which, thankfully wasn't locked. Pulling it open, she found herself on the roof of the hotel. Agnes crept gingerly across to the edge. If it had been raining, the surface could be slippery. Once she reached the edge of the roof, she rested her hands on the parapet and leaned over.

The quayside lay out before her. She was looking towards all four bridges and they looked even more magnificent from up here. But this wasn't the time to admire the view. She needed to attract the attention of someone below – anyone. But who would be down there at this time of night? There was no sign of life. Even the bars and clubs would be closed by now. The only person she could rely on was the person on night duty in the hotel reception or, maybe, the Millennium Bridge. She couldn't remember whether anyone was on duty overnight on the bridge. Nevertheless, she still had to workout a way of making someone look up here.

For a moment Agnes began to panic. All that trouble had been for nothing. She was still trapped. She took a deep breath. She needed to keep her wits about her. It wouldn't help if she were to lose her nerve now.

Looking back down at the bridges and the streetlights, she guessed that the front entrance into the hotel must be somewhere below where she was standing. So, how could she attract the attention of whoever was on night duty at the reception desk? If she called out, it was possible that the man who had locked her up here might hear her and hurry upstairs to find out what she was doing. She looked down at the quayside, stretched out below. But there was still no sign of any movement. No late night stragglers struggling to stay on their feet after a night on the town.

She needed to think. Thankfully, her head wasn't hurting so much now. The cool night air must be helping to alleviate the pain. *Come on, Agnes. You have got this far, you can't give up now.* A few moments later, she turned and hurried back into the storeroom. She'd had an idea.

* * *

The hotel reception area was quiet. As usual, by this time of night, most of the guests who had gone out for the evening had returned and were either tucked up in bed or were enjoying a nightcap in their room. Any last minute stragglers would need to ring the bell to be admitted.

John Harrison, the night security officer, had just returned to the reception desk after making a tour of the ground floor public rooms. He seldom changed his routine. Being an ex-military man, he felt it was his duty to make regular checks ensuring there were no intruders – even though other members of staff often told him he was too vigilant.

"Once you have locked the front door, no one can get in," his opposite number had told him. "You should relax a little." However, John Harrison had never relaxed while on duty, and he wasn't about to start now.

Still following his normal routine, he took a bunch of keys from the desk drawer and made his way across to the hotel entrance. He unlocked the front door and peered around outside on the off chance that a guest might have pressed the bell during the few minutes he was out of earshot. Satisfied no one was waiting to come in, he began to push the door shut. But a thump from somewhere outside caused him to hesitate.

He cocked his head on one side and listened. But there was silence. He shrugged and began to close the door again when he heard another thud; only this time it was louder.

"What the hell…?" Harrison murmured to himself. Pulling the door open, he stepped outside onto the pavement and looked around. Just out of sight of the hotel door he saw three or four boxes lying on the ground. Cautiously, he took a step towards them and only just missed being hit by another box as it fell to the ground. Harrison stepped onto the road and looked up to the roof of the hotel. At first he didn't see anything, but then he caught a glimpse of someone waving their arms at him.

"What the hell are you playing at," he called out. "Get yourself down here right now."

"I can't," Agnes shouted back down at him. "Someone has locked me in the room up here. Please help me."

"I'll be up in a few minutes," he yelled.

He hurried back into the hotel, making sure the door was firmly locked behind him. If this was a ploy for someone to creep in when he wasn't looking, then it was about to backfire.

He pulled another bunch of keys from the desk before making his way across to the lift. One of the keys should fit into the security lock in the lift. Once the lock was turned, the lift would take him to the floors beyond the limit of the guests. He could only hope that whoever had locked the door of the storeroom had left the key in the lock. He had no idea whether any of the keys he had with him would actually open the door.

At the top of the building, he pressed a button that would hold the lift in place with the door open. Until he found the light switch on the landing, he would have to make do with the light escaping from the lift. Tomorrow morning, he would inform the manager that the night staff should be issued with torches.

"Where are you?" he called out, as he fumbled around looking for the light switch.

"I'm in here," Agnes replied. By now she had returned to the storeroom and was waiting by the door. She rattled the door handle. Harrison made his way across to the door straight opposite the lift. Thankfully, he saw that the key was still in the lock and no sooner had he turned it, than the door burst open and Agnes ran out.

"What on earth were you doing in there in the first place?" he scolded. "Guests are not allowed into this part of the hotel."

"I didn't come up here of my own free will. Someone drugged me and when I awoke I found myself locked in the room." Agnes didn't know whether to laugh or cry. She wanted to laugh at how she had managed to escape by having the idea of throwing some of the smaller boxes off the roof. But at the same time, she wanted to sit down and cry at how close she had come to being murdered.

At first Harrison found it hard to believe that anyone would lock one of the guests up here. This was a very high-class hotel. People, who came to hotels such as this, didn't do that sort of thing. But then he thought about the thefts, which had taken place over the last week. Perhaps the woman was telling the truth after all.

"I must get to a phone. I need to call my friend; he's a police detective. The man who locked me in there took my phone from me."

Harrison nodded. He didn't waste any more time. He ushered her into the lift and pressed the button for the ground floor. "You can use the phone on the desk," he told her, as the lift began to descend. "And while you are contacting the police, I will get you a brandy from the bar. I think you could use one." He paused. Just as a matter of interest, do you have any idea who locked you up there?"

"Yes," she answered slowly. "I think I do. I have had plenty of time to think about it." She paused. "I'll pass on the brandy; I still have a headache. Some mineral water would be good."

Harrison nodded. He didn't press her any further. It was plain she wasn't going to divulge any further information to him.

In the reception area, the night security officer pointed towards the desk and told her to make the call. He made his way over to the front door and brought in the four parcels still lying on the pavement. Two of them had burst open and several pieces of crockery were scattered around. He would need to sweep them up.

Once he was satisfied everything was in order he went into the bar and got a bottle of water for Agnes. The events of the evening were still running through his mind.

He was tempted to pour himself a small brandy, but changed his mind. He had never had a drink while on duty and he wasn't going to start now.

Chapter Twenty-Five

Upstairs Drummond explained why he had been sent to Newcastle.

"How the hell did you know that?"

Drummond almost leapt out of his chair, when Alan told him they'd had their suspicions regarding the necklace stolen in London.

"No one is supposed to know," he continued. "The whole thing has been kept very quiet. Not one single word has been uttered outside the locked rooms where meetings were held to discuss how this could have happened and, more importantly, how they were going to get it back."

Drummond sat back in his chair and shook his head. "If the media get hold of this, then it will be splashed all over every newspaper in the world. How many other people know?"

"Apart from whoever stole it, I think we are the only two people who have guessed." It was Andrews who answered. He took pleasure in being able to tell the secret agent, that he and his boss were ahead of him on that one.

"Okay," Drummond said, "tell me how you knew about it."

"That's not why we are here." The chief inspector was beginning to get annoyed. A woman's life was at stake here. He couldn't give a damn about a bloody necklace no matter how much it was worth. "You were going to help us find Mrs Lockwood, not talk about some damn necklace."

"Some damn necklace, you say!" Drummond roared. "That damn necklace is worth around five million pound. The loss of that necklace could cause diplomatic relations between the Arab countries and the United Kingdom to fall apart."

"In that case the powers that be should have thought twice before asking for it to be included in the exhibition." Alan spoke calmly, though he was seething inside. "They should have at least decided how best to keep the necklace safe once it arrived in the country. Instead, it seems everyone assumed that no one would even think about stealing it and left it unguarded – well," he shrugged, "perhaps they didn't leave it unguarded, but obviously it hadn't been safely enshrined in a vault. Nevertheless, they were wrong in their assumption. Someone did steal it and now people are being murdered because of it."

Alan thumped his fist on the arm of his chair making both Drummond and Andrews jump. "Perhaps now you will get to the point of this meeting and tell us something that will help us to find Mrs Lockwood before she ends up murdered like your brother and sister." He paused. "What happened over dinner this evening? Are you behind her sudden disappearance? So help me, Drummond, if you don't tell us what we need to know right now, I will arrest you for withholding information in a possible murder enquiry."

"Dinner with Mrs Lockwood went well," he said, looking at the chief inspector. "We chatted for a while; I drank too much, but that was all. Agnes didn't really drink very much at all, so I didn't really believe it when someone told me she'd had too much to drink and needed to be left alone to sleep it off."

"Yet, knowing she wasn't drunk, you simply accepted what they told you," the sergeant broke in. "You didn't even think to go to upstairs and check up on her?"

"I was keeping an eye on the waiter."

"So now we are back to the waiter." Alan burst in. "Okay, so what has the waiter got to do with all this?"

Drummond sighed.

"The waiter in the bar here in The Millennium Hotel has been under surveillance for some time," Drummond said at last. "Achmed is a thief. But he is a very clever thief. No one has ever been able to prove anything against him. He arrived in the United Kingdom shortly after the agreement for the safety of the necklace was signed. He was using false papers and passport. Agents abroad had warned us that he was on his way. They believed he was coming either to steal the necklace or meet up with the person who did." He held up his hand when Andrews was about to interrupted. "Don't ask me how they knew this was about to happen. That information is top secret. Even a hint at who they are, could blow their cover. They have worked too hard to be accepted as part of the regime only for them to be found out now. They would be stuck out there at the mercy of the people they had deceived."

Alan nodded. He wasn't convinced this man was telling the absolute truth. Something about his manner didn't ring true. However, being an ex-soldier, he understood how these things worked. For the moment he would give Drummond the benefit of the doubt.

"Leave it, Andrews. He's right."

"Yes, sir," Andrews coughed and gestured towards Drummond to carry on.

"It was thought this man would hang around in London waiting for the opportunity to steal this valuable piece of jewellery," Drummond continued. "But he didn't. He made his way up here to Newcastle and applied for a job at this hotel – and before you ask, we believe the hotel manager has no idea that this man isn't who he says he is. He interviewed him along with three others and found him to be more than capable of doing the job, albeit he is still learning the English language."

"I take it you were then sent up here to keep an eye on him," said Alan.

Drummond nodded. "Yes, except I volunteered to come here. I was anxious to catch up with my brother and sister. It had been quite some while since we'd had a get-together."

"Which is why you are using your own name?" Andrews couldn't resist butting in.

Again Drummond nodded. "But now I wish I'd let someone else do the job. My being here probably caused their deaths."

"So where does the waiter fit into all this?" Alan was tired of all this beating around the bush. Agnes could be lying dead somewhere and he was sitting here talking about a damn waiter. "Do you think he murdered your family?"

"No. We don't think so. We believe the sole purpose of him being here in Newcastle was to pick up the necklace from whoever stole it. Until that happens, we think he was meant to keep out of trouble simply by doing his job as a waiter." Drummond paused. "My guess is, since the robberies in the hotel, he's seen Agnes talking to you and got hold of the wrong end of the stick. I believe he thought she was onto him and he panicked. Hence the questions he asked her earlier this evening. I firmly believe he had something to do with her disappearance. Perhaps he wasn't convinced by her answers to his questions. Or, maybe he saw her talking to me and came to the conclusion he was right to be concerned about her. For all he knew, she could be an undercover detective or even a member of my team. That being the case, he might have acted on the spur of the moment and decided to do something drastic."

"But you said he didn't leave the bar when Mrs Lockwood was escorted up to her room," said Alan. "Yet you still think he had something to do with what happened to her."

"I certainly believe he put something into her drink."

"Can I ask why you started a conversation with Mrs Lockwood this evening?" The chief inspector asked. "I am assuming it was you who first approached her and not the other way around."

"It was because of a photograph." Drummond decided to take the honest route on this one. "I thought I saw her take a photo of me the night my brother and sister were murdered. But she assured me she hadn't. She even showed me her phone to prove it."

Alan took out his mobile phone. "Do you mean this one?" He showed David the picture he had copied from Alice Thurgood's phone, the woman who had inadvertently taken it as Drummond ran past her that fateful night.

"So Agnes did take the photo after all." Drummond's smile was cynical as he handed the phone back to Alan. "She's a good liar."

"No, it wasn't Agnes." Alan replied. He snapped his phone shut and placed it in his pocket. "A person showed me the photo the day we found the blood on the pavement in Grainger Street. That person, who shall remain nameless, hadn't thought much about it until she saw us at the scene. However, she deleted it from her phone the moment I copied it; I saw her do it, so you have no need to worry. It's not still floating around out there."

"You say the waiter might have thought Mrs Lockwood was an undercover cop or part of your team?" Andrews had waited patiently until the chief inspector had finished speaking. "Or part of your team," he repeated, slowly. "That seems to indicate he knew who you were and why you were here. For a waiter, who, by your own admission, hardly leaves the bar area and whose English is not good, he seems to have picked up a great deal of information about you – especially as you are supposed to be – undercover."

Andrews had said that last word slowly and distinctly.

Drummond could have kicked himself. How could he have made such a stupid error? It wasn't like him at all. But what really surprised him was that it had been an ordinary sergeant in the Newcastle Police force who had picked it up. His mere slip of the tongue could bring his dream to an end. What he said next could heal the wound or open it up completely.

"That's true." Alan peered at Drummond. He had to admit his sergeant had really done well to pick up on that.

"A bad choice of words," Drummond laughed heartedly. "For goodness sake, Andrews, all I am trying to say is that Achmed is clever. I have watched him closely as instructed. Maybe he saw me watching him; I didn't think he had, but who knows." He shrugged.

"Quite honestly, Drummond, you have told us absolutely nothing we don't know already." Alan rose to his feet. "You know the waiter is involved in something to do with the necklace and you believe he spiked Mrs Lockwood's drink, though you didn't see him do it. But apart from that you haven't a clue how she went missing. This has been a whole waste of time and..."

Alan broke off when his phone began to ring. He opened it quickly, hoping to see Agnes' number showing, but it was one he didn't recognize.

"Alan, it's me, Agnes. I need your help. Can you come quickly?"

"Where are you?" Alan bellowed down the phone.

"I'm in the hotel reception."

She hardly had the words out of her mouth, when Alan interrupted. "I'll be right there."

"It's Agnes. She's in the reception." Alan called out as he hurried towards the door. "Andrews, get some men back here – and the paramedics!"

In his haste to get downstairs, Alan did not see the swift expression of anger which crossed Drummond's face. It was only there for one split second, before he changed it to a look of concern, but it hadn't gone unnoticed by Sergeant Andrews.

Alan arrived at the reception area first. Fearing the lift would be too slow, he had raced downstairs two at a time. His sergeant and Drummond followed close behind.

Agnes rushed across the reception towards Alan. "I was drugged and locked in the attic," she cried, wrapping her arms around him. "If it hadn't been for the guy on night duty, I might be still up there.

Suddenly she saw Drummond arrive on the scene. "I was with you. Why the hell didn't you do something? You knew I hadn't had much alcohol, yet they were saying I was drunk. You could have told them."

"I thought you would be safe upstairs in your room..."

"Safe! Safe?" Agnes retorted. "I was taken from my room and dumped somewhere in the attic. I could have been murdered up there."

She paused. "I might still have been if the night security man hadn't been so alert."

"I have just heard the news." Mr Jenkins called out, as he hurried across to Agnes. He gestured towards Harrison. "Our security officer has just told me what happened. I really don't know what to say, Mrs Lockwood. We simply thought you'd had a little too much to drink and needed to sleep it off. If..."

"Will everyone stop saying I was drunk!" Agnes yelled. "I was not drunk. Your damn waiter put something in my drink and then came up to my room, pulled the phone away when I was talking to the chief inspector and then hit me over the head."

"I agree the waiter might have added something to your drink. But he can't have been in your room." It was Drummond speaking now. "The waiter never left the bar. I saw him the whole time you were upstairs. I thought you would be fine in your room."

"There, you see, Mrs Lockwood, it can't have been the waiter. You must have been mistaken." Mr Jenkins sounded relieved to learn that a member of his staff was not to blame.

"I didn't say that!" Drummond pounced. "I said your waiter never left the bar area. But he may have added something to Mrs Lockwood's drink."

Mr Jenkins was relieved when he heard the police and the ambulance pull up outside. For the moment he was off the hook.

"Who needs an ambulance?" Agnes glanced around the reception area expecting to see someone lying on one of the sofas. "Has someone been hurt?"

"The ambulance is for you," Alan replied, calmly. "I didn't know what state you were in, so I asked Sergeant Andrews to arrange for paramedics to check you out."

"I'm fine," she retorted.

Alan raised his eyebrows.

"Yes, I was a little panicky when I spoke to you on the phone a few minutes ago," she admitted. "But that was because I wanted you to get here before the waiter went upstairs and found I had escaped. Though if he is up there now, he will be wondering how I did it. I turned the key in the lock after I had been rescued."

Alan nodded towards the police officers as they entered the building. "Go up to the storeroom in the attic and take a look around. If you find anyone up there, bring them back down here for questioning. I think we are pretty safe in assuming that at this hour, any honest person will be tucked up in bed." There wasn't time to brief the men any further. He wanted to catch whoever was responsible.

Harrison led some of the police officers across to the lift and handed them the key, which would allow them to reach the storeroom.

Alan turned back to Agnes as the ambulance crew entered the hotel. They had taken a few extra seconds to gather what equipment they might need once they found their patient.

"I really think you should let the Paramedics take a look at you, just to be sure." He knew it was useless insisting she should go to hospital. But at the very least he wanted to be sure that the drug had worn off and she wasn't still in shock.

Though she thought it was a waste of time, she agreed to be escorted to her room and checked over. "But I am coming straight back down here. We are not finished yet," she added, pointing a finger at Drummond.

"Do you have your room key?" One of the paramedics interrupted her train of thought.

With everything churning through her mind, she hadn't realised they had reached her room. It took her a few seconds to remember she didn't have her bag. "I'm sorry, but whoever hauled me off to the attic either has my bag with my key inside or both are still inside my room."

"Go back downstairs and get a spare or even a master keycard," he said, to his colleague. "We'll wait here."

"Sorry," Agnes said to the paramedic as his partner walked back along the corridor towards the lift. "I should have thought about that before we set off up here."

The man smiled. "No worries. After what you've been through, stuck up there in the attic, not knowing what was going on, I would be a little forgetful, too."

Agnes didn't reply. Something else was worrying her now. If Achmed had her key, he could get into her room at any time. He could be there waiting for her one evening when she arrived back after dinner. He could even creep in one night while she was asleep. The thoughts running through her head terrified her. Perhaps it was time to change her hotel.

A short while later all three were inside Agnes's hotel room. She spotted her bag lying on the bed and found that nothing had been taken. Even her keycard was still inside.

After a few checks, the paramedics told Agnes that she was okay. "Though, we think should let us take you to the hospital for an x-ray." one of then told her.

"Are you kidding me?" Agnes laughed. "I feel fine now, so I'm going back downstairs to join the others." She picked up her bag and followed the ambulance crew through the door and out into the hall.

Downstairs, she found the detectives, Drummond and Mr Jenkins had all moved into the Drawing Room. A few of the police officers, who had been called to the scene, were milling around in the reception. She guessed the others were still up in the attic, looking for clues and taking fingerprints.

"I'm back. They told me I was okay." Agnes announced, as she stepped through the door.

"Are you sure?" Alan looked towards the paramedics. They were standing a few feet behind Agnes.

"Yes, we are satisfied that Mrs Lockwood isn't suffering from shock or concussion," the senior paramedic replied. "We suggested she should have an x-ray, but she declined. She wanted to get back downstairs and be involved."

"Sounds familiar," Alan muttered. He was looking at Agnes now and, from her grin, he knew she had heard his remark. "Thank you for your assistance," he added, his attention now focused back on the ambulance crew.

"So, what have I missed?" Agnes glided across the room and sat down on one of the large sofas. "Bring me up to date on what you have established since I left."

"Mrs Lockwood, I really don't think that you should be involved in this police investigation..."

"I'm sorry," Agnes interrupted. "Remind me. You are?"

Alan groaned inwardly. His sergeant had much to learn about being tactful. He was a good detective sergeant and would make a great inspector, but he still had much to learn about how to handle the public, especially people like Agnes Lockwood.

"I'm Detective Sergeant Andrews. I am working on this case with Chief Inspector Johnson." He paused. He had fallen into her trap. By making him state who he was, he had made himself the outsider – not her. "But you know that already. This isn't some sort of a game!"

"You are right, sergeant." Agnes clutched her handbag.

For a moment, Andrews thought she was giving in and was about to leave. But he was wrong.

"It isn't a game." Agnes continued. "Two people have been murdered already and I could have very easily followed the same fate this evening. I think that is a good reason for me to be here."

Agnes turned her attention back to Alan, not giving Andrews a chance to reply. "While I was stuck up there in the attic my head was hurting so much I had to just lie there hoping it would go away. But it gave me time to think about what had happened to me. I know that my drink must have been spiked. I certainly didn't have much to drink, so I knew I wasn't drunk. At first I thought David might have done it, even though I had watched him carefully all during the evening. But up there, once I was able to gather my wits together, I realised it must have been the waiter."

Drummond nodded. "That's who I believe was behind it. He had access to both our drinks, but I seem to be okay, so it must have been you he was targeting."

"But why? What has he got against me?"

"I think he thought you were working with me and the chief inspector," Drummond said.

"Then if he knows you are an agent, why didn't he go after us both?" Agnes replied.

There were a few sounds coming from reception.

"The cleaning staff will be starting to come on duty," the manager explained. "I need to go out there and inform them we don't want to be disturbed in here. They can clean this room later." He stopped when he reached the door. "What about the police? There are some officers still hanging around out here."

Alan instructed Andrews to tell them to wait in their cars. He had already told two men to wait up in the attic in case the offender returned to check on his victim.

"Do you remember anything else, Agnes?" Alan asked once Jenkins was back.

"I vaguely recall seeing someone when he snatched the phone away from me. I'm certain it was Achmed." She glanced at the manager expecting him to insist it was not one of his staff. But it was Drummond who interrupted intervened.

"That's impossible," David replied. "I was watching him. He never left the bar. Your experience upstairs has got you all mixed up."

"I can only tell you what I saw."

"Even if we believe you saw the waiter, how did he get into your room?" the manager asked Agnes. "He doesn't have access to the hotel rooms and you were alone when the two receptionists and I left you. You were on the phone at the time."

"I don't know how he got into my room," said Agnes. "Perhaps you left the door to swing shut on its own and he was able to reach it before it actually closed. They do close very slowly."

"I'm sure we closed the door properly when we left. I instruct all my domestic staff to make sure the bedroom doors are firmly closed when they have finished cleaning the rooms." The manager ran a finger around his collar.

Alan watched Jenkins as he continued to fumble with his collar and then straighten his tie. Despite what this man was saying it was obvious to him that the manager was having doubts as to whether he had actually pulled the door shut behind him or had hurried off leaving it to close in its own time.

The chief inspector was angry that such a stupid mistake could very nearly have cost Agnes her life. Thankfully she had managed to get out unharmed. But what would happen when whoever had hauled her up to the attic found she wasn't a captive any longer and was now talking to the police. Would she be safe staying here in the hotel? Should he insist that she return back to Essex?

But then, thinking it through, would she be safe in Essex? The hotel usually kept a record of who had made bookings. Was it possible that whoever was behind this whole affair, could gain access to the records and find her address? This was going from bad to worse. He shouldn't have made contact with her the night he first recognised her. Or, having made contact, he shouldn't have allowed her to become embroiled in either the jewellery thefts or the murder inquiries.

Andrews was right. This was a police investigation and she shouldn't be involved in any way. But it was too late now. She was in the thick of it and whether his sergeant liked it or not, she had been a big help with their investigations.

"I am absolutely certain it was the waiter I saw before I blacked out," Agnes said firmly. She stared at David. "You must have seen another waiter in the bar and mistaken him for the one we saw earlier."

"The other waiter on duty last night was Terry." The manager said, looking at his note book. "But he only started here a couple of days ago. It's unlikely he is familiar to any of the guests yet." He looked up. "Does that help?"

Drummond opened his mouth to speak, but Agnes beat him to it.

"I still say, it was Achmed who came into my room last night," she said firmly.

"I think we should leave it there for the moment." Not for one minute was Alan going to leave the investigation at this point. But he knew

Agnes must be tired. She might not realise it now, but she would as the day wore on. This was a conversation he and Andrews could carry on back at the station. He rose to his feet. "Agnes, allow me to escort you to your room."

Agnes would have liked to have argued with him, but tiredness had crept up on her and she was beginning to feel weary. "Thank you," she said. She stood up slowly. "Thank you everyone and goodnight." She giggled as she caught a glimpse of the sun rising. "Or should that be good morning?"

Upstairs in her room, Alan checked the bathroom, and all cupboards large enough to hide a person. However, no one was lurking around. "Agnes, it might be a good idea if you went back to Essex after all." he said. He tried to make it sound casual, as though he had just thought up the idea. "If someone is watching you, then it might be the safer option."

Agnes had just been about to sit down, but changed her mind. "No, Alan. I want to see this through. Yes, I was scared when I found myself locked in that dark room. But I still have no intention of running away." She pointed towards the door. Whenever I am in here, I'll make sure the safety chain is in place. At least if anyone tries to get in I'll hear them."

"Okay." Alan shrugged. In one way he was delighted that she wasn't leaving, but at the same time he was worried about her. "But promise me; at the first sound of trouble you will give me a call."

"I promise," She replied and she meant it. She would scream the place down if anyone got anywhere near her.

* * *

All the way back to the police station, Alan and his sergeant mulled over the events of last evening. Alan had left his car outside the hotel and joined Andrews for the short journey back so they could confer notes. He would pick it up sometime tomorrow.

"The Millennium Hotel certainly hasn't had much luck since it opened," Andrews said. "First jewellery thefts, then the murder of one of the guests and now the abduction of another guest, it certainly won't look good on TripAdvisor. It rather looks as though someone has got it in for the place."

"That's exactly what I thought when the robberies began. I wondered whether it was possible someone was trying to ruin its reputation. But since the theft of the necklace in London, I'm not so sure." Alan sighed. "If they had to steal the damn thing, why the hell did they have to bring it to Newcastle?"

Chapter Twenty-Six

Despite feeling so tired, Agnes couldn't sleep. The best she could do was to snuggle down in bed and try to relax. Everything that had happened since she arrived at the hotel kept churning through her mind in a continuous loop.

The first couple of days had been peaceful enough, but since the theft of Mrs Hargreaves's necklace, she felt as though she had been caught up in an ever circling whirlwind. After an hour, she decided it was useless to lie any longer. What was the point? She was more restless now than she was before she climbed between the sheets.

In the shower, the warm water rained down on her and she began to unwind. She should have had a shower earlier instead of going straight to bed. By tonight, she would probably fall asleep while sitting in the front row during a performance of the massed bands, but at the moment she was ready to face the world.

Once she was dressed, she stepped out into the corridor where she noticed a 'Do Not Disturb' notice hanging outside her door. She smiled to herself. Alan must have done that thinking she would sleep soundly until midafternoon. She unhooked the sign and placed it inside her room.

Making sure that the door to her room was firmly closed, she set off down the corridor. There were a couple of trollies standing outside rooms further down. Obviously the domestic staff hadn't finished their duties yet. The first room she passed, she saw a lady stripping the bed. Obviously the guest had checked out and the sheets needed to be changed. The lady saw her and smiled. Agnes smiled back at her before carrying on down the hall.

The next trolley she came to was slightly larger and jutted so far out into the corridor she had to maneuver her way past. When architects started drawing up the plans for new buildings, why on earth didn't they make the corridors wider? How could someone in a wheelchair get down the corridor with one of these damn trolleys stuck in front of them?

Squeezing past the trolley, Agnes couldn't help seeing inside the room. She expected to see one of the domestic staff making the bed or dusting the dressing table, but no one was there. Then Agnes heard the shrill voice of a woman singing to herself. The sound appeared to come from somewhere within the room. From the vibrations she must be in the bathroom.

Agnes grinned as she moved on down the corridor. At least someone was happy in their work.

Downstairs, she made her way to the dining room. She wasn't sure whether they would still be serving breakfast, but perhaps they might be talked into making her some coffee and toast. She kept a sharp lookout for the waiter, Achmed. She would rather not bump into him at all. But if it were to happen, she wanted to see him before he saw her. She didn't want any surprises. Despite what David had said last night, she was convinced it was Achmed who had stolen his way into her room.

The Dining Room was empty when she arrived, but one of the wait-resses clearing the tables told her she would be happy to bring her fresh coffee and toast. Agnes had only taken a sip of her coffee when she saw Alan peering through the doorway.

"I wasn't sure you would be up yet," he said, as he joined her at the table. "You remember Sergeant Andrews," he winked and gestured to the detective hovering behind him.

"Yes, of course I do," Agnes replied. She was tempted to add a little quip about how he had introduced himself the previous evening, but decided to let it rest. "Please sit down, both of you."

"We can't stay long," Alan said, pulling out a chair. "I just wanted to make sure you weren't having any after effects this morning."

"No, I'm fine. Though I'm not sure what I'll be like by this evening. However, I don't plan to do anything strenuous today, so hopefully I will last out." She hesitated. "Have you come to any conclusions about the case? By that, I mean any part of the investigation. The thefts, the murders or even what happened to me? I still can't see why I was targeted. Even if I was part of David Drummond's team, why would they attack me and not him? Whoever is doing this seems to be trying to get rid of the people close to Drummond. Yet it seems to be important to them that he stays alive."

Andrews glanced at his chief inspector. They'd had the very same conversation at the police station in the early hours of this morning. Perhaps Mrs Lockwood was on the ball and wasn't the interfering woman he'd first made her out to be.

Alan coughed. "That's what we are working on at the moment. Meanwhile, is there anything you can tell us about Drummond that we don't know already? For instance, when you were having dinner, did he say anything about the murder of his brother and sister? Always assuming, of course, you were able to get him to say anything at all."

"Yes," she replied, thinking back to last night. So much had happened since she had spoken with him at dinner, it was difficult to remember. "He said the two people who had been found murdered were his brother and sister. I let him believe I had no idea they were his relatives, hoping to pick up more information. I recall him saying that their deaths were his fault. Though I don't think I was meant to hear that remark. At the time, I thought David was referring to the fact he was a member of the British Secret Service and whoever pulled the trigger was under the impression they might know something about whatever their brother was working on. Maybe they tortured Dennis before they killed him hoping he would tell them something. They might have planned to torture Mary in front of Dennis, but their plan went wrong." She shook her head. "Does any of that make sense to you?"

"So what do you think now?" Sergeant Andrews asked.

"I'm sorry?" Agnes quizzed.

Andrews looked at his pad; he had been making notes. "You mentioned how you thought David was referring to the fact he was a member of the British Secret Service and that whoever killed his siblings assumed they might know what their brother was working on." He paused. Out of the corner of his eye, he could see his boss watching him. But this was a fair question. If it had been anyone else had been sitting in that chair, the chief inspector would have asked the question himself. "I simply wondered whether you have a different theory now and, if so, what is it?"

"It is difficult to explain," Agnes replied. She thought back to when David mentioned the two people murdered were members of his family. "Don't get me wrong, David looked genuinely devastated by the deaths of his brother and sister. The man was almost in tears when he spoke of their murder." She swallowed hard.

Alan took her slight hesitation to mean she was too stressed to carry on. Who could blame her? She could even be dead if she hadn't had her wits about her and managed to attract the attention of Harrison. Thank goodness the man was so vigilant about his duties otherwise the police might have found her washed up somewhere along the quayside.

"I think that will be all for the moment. We can continue this..." Alan began.

"No, Alan." Agnes interrupted. "Sergeant Andrews is right. I need to do this before I forget it altogether."

She looked back at the sergeant. "The problem is I have nothing to substantiate the doubts I have about what David said. I simply have a nagging feeling there is more to it than he told me." She sighed. "I would hate you to go off with the idea that I think he murdered his own family. How could anyone do that? I just feel he knows he could have done something to stop it from happening."

"Maybe he knew he should have asked London for help earlier on, but had held back because he didn't want to admit he was out of his depth." Alan said, thoughtfully.

"Yes, that's possible," Agnes replied.

"We don't seem to be getting anywhere with this case," the sergeant grumbled. "First, there were the jewellery thefts and we still don't know how the culprit got into the rooms, let alone who he is. Then there were two murders and now a priceless necklace, due to go on display in London has been stolen. The Newcastle Police force is going to look like a bunch of idiots."

Alan couldn't argue with his sergeant. They weren't any further forward today than they were a week ago. "If we could figure out how the thief got into the rooms, we might be able to work out something from there. The manager is adamant that the master keycards can be accounted for at all times. He insists that the guests are accountable for their cards during their stay at the hotel and no one has reported their card missing or stolen. The credentials of all domestic staff are thoroughly checked before they are given a job. Other staff does not have access to the master keycards. Therefore, how the hell can anyone get access to a room and steal the jewellery?"

Agnes kept silent during Alan's summing up of the situation at the hotel. She was thinking back to something she had witnessed that morning. It was a long shot, but it was possible.

"You're very quiet." Alan grinned. "It's not like you at all. Are you sure you are okay?"

"Yes, it's just that I have suddenly come up with an idea as to how he or she is getting into the rooms without needing a keycard," she said. "It is something I noticed this morning, though I didn't think anything of it at the time." Agnes went on to explain how she had passed two rooms being cleaned as she was walking down the corridor and how both the doors were wide open. "I saw one lady in full view of the door. She was changing the bed. But the other lady was cleaning the bathroom; I couldn't see her, but I could hear her singing."

"And that tells us...?" Andrews broke in. His impatience was beginning to show on his face. "Are you saying the domestics are the thieves? As the chief inspector has just said, Mr Jenkins is certain they are not involved."

"No, I'm not saying that at all." Agnes retorted. "What I am trying to say, if you will let me finish, is that while the lady was cleaning the bathroom, she wouldn't know if someone had crept into the room with the intention to steal something. They could even hide in the large wardrobe until she had finished and left the room. They would then have ample time to search the room for whatever it was they were looking for."

The look of scorn on Andrews face was replaced with an expression of admiration. "I think you might have something there, Mrs Lockwood," he said.

Alan agreed. "It's cunning and yet so damn easy. Now we need to catch the person in the act and then we have both who and the how," he said. "We need to think about how best to do this, Sergeant." He rose to his feet. "We had better get on. I wanted to call here first to make sure you were alright."

"Can I assume that there has been another theft in the hotel since the Andersons reported their missing jewellery?" Agnes asked.

The two detectives looked at each other before Alan replied. "Yes, it was reported yesterday morning. How did you know?"

"I didn't." Agnes grinned. "You just told me."

* * *

"How did she figure that out?" Andrews said as he climbed into his car.

"Don't ask," Alan replied. "I have learned two things about Agnes Lockwood over the last week: never argue with her and never try to figure out the workings of her mind."

Andrews grinned. "From what I have seen of her so far, I have to say, I agree."

Chapter Twenty-Seven

Once Alan and his sergeant had left, Agnes moved through to the Drawing Room. It was a lovely day outside. It would be nice to take a stroll along the quayside and finish off by sitting with a nice glass of wine outside the café close to the hotel. Yet, at the same time, she wanted to stay where she was and think everything through.

She had been involved in this case since the beginning. She knew everything the police did. Therefore there was no reason why she couldn't piece the bits together herself. But where should she start?

She knew nothing about what might have happened at the hotel before she arrived. But, obviously it hadn't involved calling in the police. Alan would have told her. Therefore she could only assume the whole chain of events, ending with finding herself locked in the attic, had begun with Mrs Hargreaves's missing necklace.

Had Mrs Hargreaves's room been particularly chosen that day? Or had the thief simply been lucky?

Moving on to the theft of the necklace stolen in London, MI5 seemed to believe it had been brought to this hotel. Why this hotel? Was it because of its closeness to the open sea? But then many other hotels were situated close to rivers leading down to the sea and some were far nearer to London than Newcastle.

However, she decided not to go down the road of trying to decide why they had chosen The Millennium Hotel as their dumping base.

The fact was they had. For the moment, she decided to focus on what she did know – and that led her straight back to the thefts at the hotel.

Now she was going around in circles. Yet she was determined not to give up.

She beckoned a passing waiter and ordered a large, strong black coffee. That was exactly what she needed right now. It would keep her alert. While placing her order, she casually mentioned Achmed's name.

"I'm sorry, Madam, but Achmed won't be on duty until five o'clock this evening."

"No problem at all, Paul," she said, peering at the name pinned on his shirt. "I agree; everyone needs time off to unwind." At least she wouldn't have to watch what she ate or drank before he came on duty. After that, she would eat out. There was no way she wanted to meet him again.

She thought back to the matter in hand. Could it be possible that the thief stealing the necklaces from the rooms of this hotel was part of the gang that stole the valuable necklace in London? She wasn't sure where that little spark of inspiration came from. Her strong coffee hadn't even arrived yet. Nevertheless it was worth more thought.

Was it conceivable that whoever was stealing the necklaces from guests staying at the hotel was simply doing so to distract attention from the theft of a really valuable piece being removed at a later date?

The waiter set her coffee down on the table in front of her. She signed the bill and, reaching into her handbag, she gave him a large tip. "Thank you," she said, smiling up at him.

"No, Madam. Thank you," he replied.

Agnes took a sip of her coffee as thoughts continued to flutter though her mind. Alan had told her how Mr Anderson had almost blown his stack when he reported the robbery of his wife's necklace. But then who wouldn't, if something expensive had been stolen from a hotel room. But the chief inspector had had grave doubts about whether the Andersons were telling the truth.

She recalled the picture of the necklace, which Alan had shown her. "Look at how it is being presented, Agnes," he had said stabbing his finger on the picture. "It is standing alone. Other jewellery on display is set well back from this one piece."

He was right. Most jewellery shop windows didn't have space for such an arrangement. Even displays inside the shops weren't so elaborate. Therefore the piece Mr Anderson was claiming to have belonged to his wife could be the valuable necklace stolen in London. It must have been on show somewhere in the world for him to have a photograph of it. If so, the police needed to find out where. Then they could trace Andersons' movements and find out whether he took the photo himself or if it had been given to him by whoever he might be working for.

But why would the Andersons draw attention to the necklace if it didn't belong to them in the first place? What did they expect to gain? Did they think the police would believe they had been robbed, which would allow them to claim for insurance? Yet surely the insurance company would have seen Mrs Andersons' piece of jewellery before agreeing to insure it. Consequently, they would know whether or not the piece in the photo was the same as the one on their files.

She sighed. She was getting nowhere and to make things worse, she was beginning to get a headache. Perhaps it would help clear her head if she were to take a walk in the sunshine.

Chapter Twenty-Eight

Chief Inspector Johnson had instructed plain clothed officers to watch Achmed, the waiter. Men were stationed a short distance from his flat and were to follow him wherever he went. Alan had made it clear he didn't want him picked up until they had absolute evidence that he was responsible for kidnapping Agnes. He certainly didn't want the man to get off on some technicality.

After the meeting had broken up in the early hours of the morning, he and Sergeant Andrews had agreed that Achmed should not be arrested or questioned about Agnes. Before they had left the hotel, Drummond had made it clear that if the waiter was involved with the theft of the necklace in London, it was important to let him believe he had got away with it. "It would be foolhardy to arrest him now. Besides, he didn't have anything to do with Mrs Lockwood's kidnapping." he had said.

Nevertheless, when Alan said he understood the reasoning behind the suggestion, it was clear in his own mind that if Achmed became the slightest threat to Agnes, he would arrest the wretched man himself.

Alan was also aware that the officers, who had hung around in the storeroom in the hope of catching the kidnapper, had arrived back at the station empty handed. The first person to enter the storeroom was the storekeeper's young assistant and he had nearly jumped out of his skin when the officers pounced on him.

It was evident that either the culprit already knew Agnes had escaped and the police were on the scene or he hadn't planned to go back at all; leaving it for the day staff to find her. Maybe he was teaching her a lesson for getting involved in the first place.

"Where do we go from here?" Sergeant Andrews scattered his paperwork across his desk. "This case is getting more ridiculous by the hour." He shook his head. "How are we supposed to write up the case when all we have are questions and no answers?" He shook his head. "Let's face it; we haven't a clue about what is really going on."

Alan empathized with his sergeant. Most cases they had worked on, there had been at least one clue they could ponder over. From there, they had gone on to solve the case together. There was no doubt they were missing something. He leaned back in his chair and clasped his hands behind his head. What the hell were they missing?

* * *

David Drummond watched the two men as they stepped into the hotel. His eyes followed them as they strode across to the reception desk to check in. These were the two agents sent to escort him back to London. Once they caught up with him, all he had worked for would be lost. His replacement was probably already on their way to Newcastle with full instructions to find the missing necklace at all costs. He had to keep out of their way until he finished what he had set out to do.

The annoying thing was, everything had been going so well, until someone had taken that damn photo. From then on, he had messed up big time.

He watched the men sign for the keycards, before making their way across to the lift. They already had his room number, so he guessed once they dropped off their cases they would head for his room.

But he wouldn't be there. He had also switched off his mobile phone, so they couldn't contact him that way. He still had a little time left to play the winning hand; so long as nothing else got in the way. He hadn't checked out of the hotel. That would have been too obvious.

But he had filled his briefcase with essential items of clothing in the hope he might find somewhere nearby to stay for the night. One more day and he would be home and free.

It was then that he saw Agnes walking across the reception towards the hotel entrance. It was obvious she hadn't seen him and he wanted to keep it that way until the two agents were in the lift. Once the lift doors had closed and it had started to move, he picked up his briefcase and hurried out onto the quayside. Agnes wasn't too far ahead and he quickly caught up with her.

"Weren't you meeting up with your replacements today?" She was rather surprised to see him suddenly appear at his side.

"I decided to keep out of their way for a while. I'm not keen on letting go of this case yet." David looked over his shoulder towards the hotel as though expecting to see one of agents watching them. "Can we have a drink or something, somewhere? I don't want them to see me."

Agnes pointed towards the café she had often used over the last week. "We could go there. I usually sit outside and people watch, but I'm sure we could find a secluded table somewhere inside. It gets rather busy so I don't think anyone will take any notice of us."

A few minutes later they were seated in the café. David had already been to the bar and ordered a bottle of wine and two glasses. "It's a bit early, but at least the sun is over the yardarm," he joked.

"So, what do you want to talk to me about?" Agnes asked. "I thought we had discussed everything earlier this morning while we were with the two detectives."

"Yes, I appreciate that. But..." He paused as the waiter brought the wine to the table and opened the bottle.

"But?" Agnes queried, once the waiter was out of earshot. There was no way she was going to allow him to wriggle out of what he had been about to say due to the brief interruption. More might have been said the previous evening if it hadn't been for her being drugged and kidnapped. Even now she was free she shivered at the thought of how it could have ended.

"But, I'm afraid I haven't been quite so honest with you – or the police."

Agnes took a sip of her wine before saying anything. She wanted to give him time to follow up on his statement. But he didn't add anything further.

"So, what aren't you telling us?" Agnes ventured. She spoke quietly, not wanting to sound threatening. Yet she wanted to know what was going on. It was obvious David had wanted to talk to her about something; it was he who had caught up with her and suggested this rendezvous. Therefore, why was he still being so cagey? Or was it an act? She wasn't sure where that last thought had come from.

Drummond took a large gulp of wine before he spoke. "I don't believe the thefts at the hotel have anything to do with the necklace stolen in London." He glanced towards the door for a second before continuing.

"From what I can gather, since the police picked up the scent of the theft in London, they seem to think there might be a connection between the two. But I maintain they are totally unconnected."

"What makes you think that?" Agnes asked. Her mind was racing back over the last few days. It was when the Andersons reported the theft of their necklace and Alan had seen the photograph in their possession that he had suspected there might be a connection. He had wondered whether the hotel thefts had been set up to draw attention away from the big haul in London – especially since learning that the priceless necklace had found its way to Newcastle.

"I was watching George Hargreaves when his wife's necklace was stolen." David interrupted her thoughts. "He didn't seem remotely concerned about the theft. He even tried to stop his wife from contacting the police. But she did call them and he kept well away from the investigation. Why?"

"So what are you saying?"

"I don't know – yet. But there has to be a reason why he was so against calling the police."

Agnes took a sip of her wine to give her a moment to collect her thoughts. Yes, she agreed George Hargreaves had tried to calm his wife down by telling her she had simply mislaid the necklace and was making a fuss about nothing. She had heard them both arguing outside her room on the evening in question.

"Don't you think he was acting rather strange for a man whose wife's necklace had been stolen?" David continued. "Think about it, Agnes. Would your husband have acted so casual if a necklace he had given you for a present had been stolen from a hotel room while on holiday?"

For a moment, Agnes wanted to reach across the table and punch David on his nose. How dare he bring Jim into this conversation! But then she realised what he said was true. There was no way her husband would have dismissed her claim so casually. Even if he hadn't bought the piece of jewellery in question, he would have stuck by her side during the whole investigation. He would never have slunk off to the bar to get drunk and left her to deal with the police alone.

David had a point. Agnes's eyes flashed from side to side as she thought about it. Why would Hargreaves want his wife to believe her necklace hadn't been stolen? Why didn't he want her to call the police? Surely any husband would want the theft of his wife's jewellery to be investigated, especially if it was as expensive as Mrs Hargreaves claimed. She clicked her fingers as the penny dropped.

"He took it himself," she said, triumphantly. "He took it and tried to have her believe she had mislaid it. But his wife wasn't having any of that and demanded the police should be called in."

"Why would he do that?" David asked. "Yes, I can see where you are coming from, but why?"

"Perhaps he needed the money," she replied. "Maybe he sold it to pay off some gambling debts. Or it could be that his business, if he has one, isn't doing too well at the moment." She hesitated as another thought ran through her mind. "However, once the police were involved, George might have panicked fearing he could be found out.

Therefore, that's when he decided to make it more convincing by stealing jewellery from other guests."

"You know I think you might be onto something there." Drummond stroked his chin as he stared at Agnes.

"But that's not all." Her eyes were gleaming with excitement as she continued. "I still don't know for certain whether the Andersons' are involved with the necklace stolen in London. However, assuming they are involved and they had it hidden in their room waiting for someone to collect it, then it could have been George who took it. He probably had no idea how much it was worth when he stole it."

"Well George is in for a nasty surprise when he tries to sell it." David replied. "I'll have to try to catch up with him and have a quiet word. If he is the thief at the hotel and he took the necklace from the Andersons' room, I can only hope he still has it."

"And I'll have to have a word with the chief inspector. But before we part company, can I ask how your family fits into all this?" Agnes paused. "Okay, George may have stolen the jewellery, but I really can't see him as a murderer. Nor do I believe he had anything to do with me being kidnapped. So why were they targeted and by whom?"

"I disagree with you on that. People do many things to cover up a crime – some even commit murder." He shrugged. "Who would have thought of George as a thief? But now you think he stole his wife's necklace and then a few others to put the police off the scent. Anyway, I don't want you to get involved."

"But I am already involved," Agnes insisted. "I was at the scene when both bodies were found. I was drugged and stuck upstairs in the storeroom at the hotel and previous to that, you were following me around as you suspected I had taken a photo of you leaving the scene of where one of your siblings was killed; surely I couldn't be any more involved." She looked around hoping no one had heard her last statement. But everyone seemed to be too preoccupied with their own conversations.

"Please, just leave it. Let me sort it out. I haven't got much time. I can't evade my replacements for much longer." He sighed. "I really need to find somewhere else to stay for tonight. I can't stay in my own room as they will know my room number. It needs to be close by…"

"You can stay in my room, if you can get up there without being seen," Agnes interrupted. "You'll have to sleep on the sofa, which I know isn't too comfortable, but at least you will still be in the same hotel."

"I don't like to impose. What about your reputation?"

"If no one is to know you are there, then my reputation will be intact."

"Then I would be grateful to take you up on your offer. I can't see me getting away with it for more that twenty-four hours, so the closer I am to the scene of the events, the better."

"Good! Now that's sorted, you will be able to fill me in on all the details tonight." She had a sudden thought. "You don't snore, do you?"

Chapter Twenty-Nine

Once David had left the café, Agnes pulled out her mobile phone to call Alan. David had urged her to wait until he'd had a chance to speak to George Hargreaves first. But she had disagreed telling him that the police had a right to know her thoughts on the matter.

Once Alan answered her call, she told him about her meeting with David and then went on to say who she thought might be the thief and the reasoning behind her idea.

"David has gone off to try to find George right now. He's keen to know whether George has the necklace stolen from the Andersons' room. I gather that the two agents replacing him have arrived at the hotel. So far, he has managed to avoid them. He is determined to solve the case he was sent here to investigate before they take over." Did that make sense? Agnes knew she was gabbling, but she wanted to get her message over as quickly as possible.

"Yes, I understand what you are saying." Alan was furious with himself. Why hadn't he thought that George Hargreaves might have had an ulterior motive for his reluctance to get involved in the theft? He threw a paperclip at Andrews to get his attention and then nodded towards the extension phone on his sergeant's desk; suggesting he should listen in.

"So you think George Hargreaves stole his wife's necklace because he was in debt," said Alan, hoping his sergeant would be able to pick up on the conversation.

"Yes, didn't I just say that?" Agnes removed the phone from her ear and stared at it for a moment.

"Sorry, Agnes, I just wanted my sergeant to catch up with the conversation.

"Fine," said Agnes. "Anyway, Drummond agrees with me and like I said, he has gone off to find George."

"So what is Drummond doing about his replacements? No doubt they have his room number and will be waiting for him.

"Yes, that's what David is afraid of. That's why I said he could spend the night on the sofa in my room."

Once the conversation had ended, Agnes sat back in her seat to finish her wine. Alan hadn't sounded too pleased about David spending the night in her room. But he hadn't made a big fuss about it. How could he? It wasn't really any of his business. However, what he had said had made a great deal of sense and had left her wondering whether she had done the right thing.

Alan was concerned that as David's siblings had both been murdered, it was possible the killer might now be watching David. He could well be the next target.

Agnes swallowed hard. Alan could be right. If that was the case, she would be putting herself in the line of fire. She looked at the bottle on the table. There was still a little wine left in there. With a sigh, she swiftly refilled her glass and took a large gulp.

She had been too hasty with the invitation. She knew that now. Yet she had simply wanted to help David out of a jam. But since her conversation with the chief inspector, something else was starting to niggle away at the back of her mind.

David hadn't answered her question about how his family became so involved with the case that they were murdered. He had skipped over that one pretty quickly, suggesting he didn't want her any further involved. But if that was the case, why had he agreed to spend the night in her room? Surely that was involving her more than ever.

Agnes took a sip of her wine. She was beginning to feel very uneasy about the night ahead. She decided to put it out of her mind by focusing on how to spend the rest of the day. However, for the first time since arriving in Newcastle, she felt at a loss as to what to do.

Until now, her days had been filled with various aspects of the case – usually with Alan at her side – and she had felt quite excited about it all. But today, it seemed she was being left out. Once she had spoken to Alan, he and his sergeant had rushed off to seek out George Hargreaves. No doubt they wanted to find him before Drummond caught up with him.

They were probably all at the hotel now having a heated argument as to who should be the first to interrogate Hargreaves. She would have liked to have seen the fiasco, but after speaking to Alan, she wasn't keen to meet up with Drummond at the moment. Alan had suggested dinner that evening before hanging up and she agreed. Therefore she was going to wait until she had spoken to him before bumping into Drummond.

Agnes finished her drink and left the café. She was just about to turn back towards the hotel, when she saw George Hargreaves. Obviously neither Drummond nor the police had caught up with him as he seemed quite at ease talking to a man near the Millennium Bridge.

As she watched the two men in conversation, Agnes had a strange feeling that she had seen the man before. But as she couldn't place where that might have been, she dismissed the idea. She pulled out her phone to call Alan and let him know where George was, but on a sudden impulse, she decided to take a photograph of the two men talking together. It might be very useful at some point.

* * *

There was no reply when Sergeant Andrews knocked on the door of George Hargreaves's room. He tried again; thumping the door hard with his fist and calling out "Police, open the door." But there was still no response.

"I wonder whether Drummond has already caught up with him." Alan was thinking aloud.

"We could try Drummond's room," said Andrews. "He might have taken Hargreaves there to interrogate him."

Alan shook his head. "Drummond won't be there. He's lying low at the moment, trying to avoid the two agents sent to replace him."

He quickly explained how the agent wanted a little more time in Newcastle to solve the case. "Once he talks to his replacements, his orders are to return to London immediately."

"So has he moved out of the hotel? If so, does anyone know where he's gone?" Andrews asked.

Alan sighed. "Mrs Lockwood told him he could spend the night on the sofa in her room."

"What!" Andrews yelled. "And you're okay with that!"

"No, I'm not okay with it! It's a bad idea!" Alan retorted.

He didn't usually raise his voice to anyone. In the army, he had been renowned for keeping a cool head under all circumstances. So why was he so on edge now? Was he so frustrated with this damn case he couldn't help himself? Or was there more to it than that? Had his feelings for Agnes totally mixed him up? No woman had had that effect on him before.

He shook his head. "But I can't tell her what to do. What the hell can I do about it?"

"I have picked up on how you feel about Mrs Lockwood," Andrews said slowly. "But I'm not talking about that. I'm talking about whether you, me, The Newcastle Police can really trust this man, Drummond." He took a deep breath and looked around. They were still standing in the corridor outside Hargreaves's room. Was this the best place to have this conversation? "Can we go somewhere less conspicuous?"

Alan nodded. A few minutes later they were downstairs in the manager's office.

Mr Jenkins had ushered them in, saying he was more than happy to allow the detectives the privacy of his room to discuss the case of the missing jewellery.

"Right! What do you want to tell me?" Alan's tone was brusque. He hated being dictated to, especially by a subordinate. He could take it from his superiors; well he had to. That was part of the job. But spoken down to by his sergeant; that was something else.

He watched Andrews look away for a moment, as though he was unsure of where to start.

"I know you had started to trust David Drummond," Andrews began. He held up his hand when Alan was about to interrupt. "And, yes, after he explained himself, so did I – to a certain extent. But I have spent a great deal of time thinking about this case and I am beginning to wonder whether he is quite as legitimate as he makes out to be."

"Are you suggesting he is not with MI5?" Alan asked. "Because I can assure you he is. I checked it out a few days ago." It had taken him some time to get through the security protocol, but he had stuck with it and found David Drummond was indeed an agent with MI5.

"That did cross my mind at one point. But, no, I am wondering whether Drummond is an honest agent working for the good of the country or rather someone out there in the field looking out for himself." Andrews paused. "I'm not saying his intentions weren't good in the beginning. He was probably a good agent – a good man, but people change and not always for the better. I think Drummond changed for the worst over the years." The sergeant sighed. "Look, I know you thought I was jealous, envious or whatever of his position as an agent, and yes, I admit, I was – slightly. But this is not about that, sir. This is about me coming up with the idea that this guy might be playing us from both sides. Once I had that notion fixed in my mind, I began to wonder whether he might have persuaded his superiors he was the best person to check out the missing necklace because of his connections in the north. He could have swayed them by saying how easy it would be for him to pose as someone visiting his family. Yet, all the time, he had been involved with the theft in London and wanted to be here to make sure he collected his share of the money."

"Sounds plausible," said Alan, thinking it through. "But..."

"There's more." Andrews held up his hand. "Don't you think it strange that the very evening Mrs Lockwood had dinner with him, she ended up drugged and locked in the storeroom?"

Again Alan was about to interrupt, but Andrews got in first.

"I know. Mrs Lockwood swears it was Achmed she saw in her room just before she was struck on the head. But Drummond repudiates that. He insists Achmed never left the bar area long enough for him to go up to her room and take her to the storeroom. Who do we believe? If I am right about Drummond, he and Achmed could be working together and if that is the case, then surely Drummond would vouch for him. He couldn't allow Achmed to be arrested. He would realise that should the waiter confess everything for a deal with the Law Court, it would put him at the centre of the theft in London."

"But it was Drummond who told us the waiter was an MI5 suspect in the first place," said Alan.

"Yes, that's true." Andrews agreed. "But, looking it from another angle, might he simply have been trying to gain our confidence by giving us a name to be going on with?? Isn't that what double agents do? Therefore, with that in mind, if we think back to the moment Achmed came under suspicion for kidnapping Mrs Lockwood, who leapt to his defence? None other than Drummond." Andrews answered his own question. "He was adamant Achmed couldn't have done it because he had sight of him all the time. I accepted that – we all accepted that; except Mrs Lockwood. She never wavered. Even now, she is still convinced it was Achmed who had entered her room that night."

Andrews paused to allow his boss to say something. But Alan gestured he should carry on.

"Okay." Andrews continued. "If what I have said so far is correct, then it's entirely possible that London have already come to the same conclusions. They could have been watching him for some time and now realise he is not all he makes out to be. This leads me to believe that the two, so called, replacements are not here simply to take over the case, as he has us believe, but are really here to escort him back to London. It's also likely MI5 have already sent an undercover agent to carry on with the case. I would assume that the identity of this new agent will have been kept from Drummond and anyone else working on the case. The man or woman could already be at the hotel, as we speak; they might even have been there for several days watching Drummond and trying to pick up the threads of what happened to the necklace after it arrived in Newcastle."

Alan had listened intently and was impressed with his sergeant's conclusions. But at the same time he was annoyed he hadn't picked all this up himself. He was a darn good police officer. How could he have missed so much of what was staring him in the face all the time? Had he been so wrapped up with his childhood crush on Agnes he had let so many things slide past him? He had to admit; even she was coming up with answers to the case before he did.

"But there's something else," Andrews broke into Alan's thoughts. "And this takes us back to the beginning of this conversation."

"What else could there be?" Alan sighed, heavily. As far as he could see, his sergeant had already summed it up.

"Assuming I'm right about Drummond," Andrews continued. "Then, shouldn't we be more than a little concerned that he has managed to worm his way into spending the night in Mrs Lockwood's room."

Alan shot a glance at Andrews before reaching into his pocket for his phone. "You're right! We have got to warn her – and we have got to find Drummond."

Chapter Thirty

Agnes had just taken the photograph of George Hargreaves and the man he was talking to, when her phone rang.

"Hello Alan. I was just about to call you..."

"Agnes, stop talking and listen to me. I will bring you up to speed when I see you. But in the meantime, whatever you do, don't allow Drummond into your room today, tonight or any time. Stay away from him. My sergeant has a theory about him and he could be right. Meanwhile, we are in the hotel and Hargreaves isn't here. We are going off to try to find both him and Drummond."

"That's what I was about to tell you. George Hargreaves is outside the hotel as I speak. I can see him. He's right by the Millennium Bridge and he's talking to another man. Hurry before they move off!"

"Okay we're on our way." Alan didn't hesitate. He flipped his phone shut and swiftly made his way out of the office. "Hargreaves is outside," he called out to his sergeant, as he crossed the reception area and hurried towards the hotel entrance.

A few minutes later Alan and Andrews emerged from the hotel and saw Agnes standing across the street. When she spotted them, she pointed to where George and the other man were still deep in conversation.

The chief inspector motioned Andrews to approach the two men from behind.

"Good afternoon, Mr Hargreaves," Alan said, once Andrews was in place.

"Err, Chief Inspector," George mumbled. For a moment he looked a little taken aback. But he recovered quickly and glanced at the man standing beside him. "Chief Inspector Johnson is working on the case of my wife's missing jewellery." He explained. "I suppose he wants to bring me up to date." He looked back at Alan. "How is it going? Have you anything to report?"

"That's what we would like to talk to you about," Alan replied.

He turned towards the man George had been talking to.

The man was clean-shaven and wearing a smart, navy blue suit. He wasn't tall, which meant he had to look up slightly to meet the inspector's gaze. However, he was heavily built and looked as though he spent several hours each week at the gym.

"And you are?" Alan asked.

"I'm just an old friend of George," he replied, hastily. "We play golf and often go to the races together. We just happened to bump into each other. If that's all, Chief Inspector, I'll leave you two to talk."

The man nodded at George and would have moved away if Sergeant Andrews hadn't been blocking his path.

"I think we should have a little chat at the police station." Alan took George by the arm. This man had run circles around him already, there was no way he was going to give him the slightest chance to run off and be lost in the crowds.

"You can't do this. My wife is expecting me to join her for lunch shortly," George blustered. He looked at his friend. "James, you will have to meet her and explain what has happened."

Alan glanced at his sergeant and shook his head.

"I'm afraid your friend can't do that. He is coming with us," said Andrews taking the hint. He stepped alongside James and took his arm.

"Don't worry, Mr Hargreaves. Tell us where your wife is and we'll organize a policewoman to meet her and explain what has happened."

* * *

Agnes watched the proceeding from the other side of the road. She hoped she was right about George Hargreaves. It would be awful if he was being arrested for something he didn't do. Yet the more she thought about it, the more convinced she was that it was he who had taken his wife's necklace.

She traced her thoughts back to when she had seen him in the city centre. At the time, she had put his look of sheer frustration down to the way his wife had spoken to him before she stormed off into the jewellery shop. But today, when she was rethinking things through in the café with David Drummond, she had hit on the idea that he might have been angry because his wife was going to spend more money and put him into further trouble.

It was at that moment she caught sight of Drummond. He was partly secluded because he was hovering in a shop doorway a few yards from where she was standing. Nevertheless, she could see he was looking very angry about something – most likely because the police had caught up with Hargreaves before he'd had a chance to talk to him.

Not wanting him to see her, Agnes swiftly took a couple of steps backwards and ducked behind a parked lorry. When she saw him striding off down the road, she emerged from her hiding place and started to walk back to the hotel. But, on a sudden impulse, she turned around and began to follow Drummond.

Chapter Thirty-One

"What is this all about? Why am I here?" George Hargreaves demanded, once they were at the police station. Have I been arrested? If so, then I want to see a solicitor. I know my rights!"

"I think you know what this is about, Mr Hargreaves," Alan replied, calmly. He had decided to question Hargreaves, while his sergeant had a word with James.

"I don't know what you are talking about!"

"I'm talking about your wife's missing necklace." The chief inspector leaned across the table. "Where is it?"

"How do I know?" Hargreaves replied. "You know it was stolen. It's probably been passed on to some fence or whatever it is you call them. It could be anywhere by now."

Alan watched as Hargreaves took out a handkerchief and mopped his brow.

"I think you know, because I believe you stole it in the first place."

"No! That wasn't me…"

"I believe it was you. Then you tried to throw the scent off yourself by stealing a few more items from the other guests at the hotel." Alan sat back in his chair and watched Hargreaves fiddle with his handkerchief.

For a moment Alan felt sorry for him. It was obvious George had never been in trouble with the law before. This was definitely a first for him. Nevertheless, he was a thief and he would have to pay the price.

"Then we come to the two murders," Alan said, slowly. "Now I'm beginning to wonder whether you might be our killer. For instance, the victims could have found out you were the thief and were going to inform the police. But you killed them both before they had the chance."

Alan didn't really believe Hargreaves was the murderer. He was simply using the notion to lever him into confessing to the thefts.

"After all, the murdered woman was a guest at the hotel," he continued, "and, as it turns out, the murdered man was her brother. If she had seen you, she might have passed the information to her brother and then you would have had to kill them both."

"No! I didn't murder anyone." Hargreaves wailed.

"It sounds very plausible to me," Alan shrugged. "And it means that we have solved both cases with one shot."

"No! No!" You have got it wrong," George exclaimed.

"Which part?" Alan asked.

* * *

Hargreaves looked away for a moment. He had never meant it to come to this. All he wanted was a little money to pay off a gambling debt. Then he'd had the idea of stealing his wife's necklace and selling it. The money from the sale, together with the insurance for the stolen necklace meant he would have been home and dry. But when his wife created such a fuss and called the police he had panicked; terrified he would be the suspect. He had then decided to steal one more necklace in an effort to make the police look elsewhere. It had been so easy. Why not do it one more time?

He knew now he should have quit while he was ahead. It was during the last theft that a man caught him leaving the room. He still didn't know how the man knew it wasn't his own room he was leaving. He had approached him and said he knew someone who would pay well for the jewellery and was willing to pass on the information – but there was a price.

"Okay, I'll confess I took the jewellery," Hargreaves said at last. He swallowed hard. "But I swear on my children's life, I didn't kill anyone. No one saw me leaving the rooms. No one threatened to expose me. I am not your killer."

By now he was sobbing. His mention of his children had made him realise he had let them down. What had he been thinking? Why had he allowed himself to be drawn into the gambling ring in the first place?

But he knew why. He had thought he could win. And, yes, he had won a few times and the feeling had been good. Yet he had never won as much money as he had lost. Now he had lost everything. What would his family think of him?

"I never ever thought it would come to this," Hargreaves uttered. "I simply wanted to pay off my debt and get the man off my back. He was going to ask my wife for the money. I couldn't let him do that. I didn't want her to know. I swore that once the money was paid I would never gamble again. You have to believe me."

"What about the necklace you stole from Mr and Mrs Andersons' room?" Alan asked.

Hargreaves sighed. "I sold it to the same man who bought the others."

"Would that be James, the man you were talking to earlier?" Alan asked.

"No." Hargreaves shook his head. "I was paying him. He works for the man I owe the money to." He looked away for a moment, before turning back to face the chief inspector. "It would have all been over today. Once I paid him what I owed, there would have been a little left over. I could have gone home with my wife at the weekend a happy man. But now…"

"If you hadn't stolen from the other guests, I'm sure your wife would have dropped all charges and you would have been free to go," said Alan. "But as it is, I am going to have to arrest you for multiple thefts at the hotel. I doubt the other people you stole from will be willing to drop the charges." He paused. "I will leave the murder charge – for the time being. But right now you can help yourself by telling me how we might contact the man you sold the jewellery to."

* * *

In another room at the police station, Sergeant Andrews had just finished questioning James. It turned out his name was James Hitchens. He admitted that he wasn't really a friend of Hargreaves. In fact he had never met the man until that day. He had simply been sent to Newcastle to catch up with Hargreaves, collect the money owing to his boss and return to London.

"Why send you all the way up here?" Andrews had asked. "Surely Hargreaves would have returned to London once their stay was over."

However Hitchens had merely shrugged, saying his boss must have had a reason and he hadn't asked. "I don't ask questions. I simply do as my boss instructs. Then I get paid."

When the sergeant had asked him to hand over the money he had obtained from Hargreaves, he had been reluctant to part with it, saying, the money belonged to his boss now. But Sergeant Andrews had argued that the money had been illegally gained and not wanting to be held at the police station any longer than necessary he had complied. No doubt his boss wouldn't want to become embroiled with the Newcastle Police.

However, Hitchens refused to give the name of his boss when Andrews asked. "There is absolutely no need to bring my boss into this. He is not involved with whatever Hargreaves did here in Newcastle – and neither am I. Therefore if you are quite finished, I would like to leave."

Andrews knew he didn't have any reason to keep Hitchens at the station. Yet he was loath to let him go without learning what Hargreaves had told the chief inspector. "I'm sure you would, but I need you to wait here until I find out what Hargreaves has had to say."

Without another word, he opened the door and instructed the uniformed officer waiting outside to go in and stand guard until he returned.

* * *

Down the corridor, Andrews entered a side room and peered through the one way glass window. The chief inspector was still talking to Hargreaves. He switched on the speaker and heard Alan asking the name of the man who had bought the stolen jewellery.

Obviously Hargreaves had confessed to being the thief.

Without any hesitation, Hargreaves gave a name and phone number.

"How did you come to hear about this Mr O'Donnell?" Alan asked. "Did you know of him before you arrived at the hotel or," he paused for effect, "did someone suggest to you that this man might be interested in buying the jewellery you had stolen? If that is the case, then I need to know the name of this other person and how he became aware you had stolen jewellery to sell. A few minutes ago, you told me that no one had seen you leaving the rooms with the missing necklaces."

Andrews watched Hargreaves as he held up his hands in terror. "Okay, okay. One person saw me leaving a room. It was the day I stole the first piece after my wife discovered her necklace had gone missing. Like I said, I wanted to throw the police away from me. I saw an open door and found it easy to creep inside while the lady cleaned the bathroom. I hid until she left and then had ample time to look around the room. At the time I had no idea how I was going to sell my wife's necklace, let alone the second one. In the beginning I had hoped that my creditor would take my wife's necklace as payment of my debt. But then this man appeared as I was making my escape. He didn't threaten to go to the police. Instead he said he knew someone who would be happy to pay me for the jewellery I had taken." Hargreaves paused and loosened his tie.

The chief inspector motioned for the uniformed officer at the door to ask for a glass of water for the suspect.

"Go on," said Alan after Hargreaves had drunk some of the water.

"I asked what I had to do to get the name of this person," George continued. "I thought he was going to want half of whatever I got, but he didn't ask for that. The price was that I would need to rob a few more rooms, whichever I liked. I could keep whatever money I received from this man. But the last theft had to be the room number he would give me in due course. I would receive a payment as usual and then walk away."

"And if you didn't agree to his proposal," Alan prompted. "Did he threaten you in any way?"

"He said he would meet up with my wife in a dark corner and..." Hargreaves broke off. "I couldn't let that happen."

"What was the name of this person?" Alan was trying to keep his patience.

"I don't know," Hargreaves uttered. "He wouldn't tell me." He placed his head in his hands. "Believe me I didn't want all this. I love Angela, I love my family. I never wanted them to be involved in my stupidity." He looked up suddenly. "I don't know his name, but I've seen him around the hotel a few times since he approached me. He doesn't acknowledge me, or I him. He's always alone, so I was surprised to see him with another guest the other evening – a woman. I only hope he hasn't got his claws into her."

"This woman," said Alan. "Do you know her name?"

"No," Hargreaves replied, thoughtfully. "But you must know her. I've seen you talking to her a couple of times."

Alan leapt to his feet. "Do you mean Mrs Lockwood?"

"Yes, that's her name." said Hargreaves. "I remember now. Lockwood, there was a film star by that name many years ago."

Andrews was still listening in the next room. He gasped when he heard Hargreaves's last remark. Could the man who made Hargreaves steal the necklace from the Andersons' be David Drummond? He saw the chief inspector make a dive for the door and hurried out into the corridor meet up with him.

"I heard the tail end of that," said Andrews. "Drummond really is behind all this."

The chief inspector was only half listening. He had already pulled out his phone and was entering Agnes's number. "I'm calling Agnes. She mustn't go anywhere near that man." He held the phone to his ear and waited for her to answer.

A few moments later he snapped his phone shut. "There's no reply. I'm going to the hotel"

"It could be that her phone is on charge," said Andrews. "Why not trying ringing her room at the hotel?"

Alan nodded. Picking up the nearest phone he asked to be put through to The Millennium Hotel. The moment he was connected he asked for Agnes's room. But again there was no reply.

"She could still be somewhere in the hotel," said Sergeant Andrews.

"Yes, but I need to be sure. I've got a bad feeling about all this." Alan called out for one of the officers to stay with Hargreaves. "Take his details and then lock him up. If he asks for a solicitor, get him one."

"What should I do about James Hitchens," Andrews asked. "He's handed over the money he received from Hargreaves. But he won't give the name of the man who sent him here."

"Tell the officer with him to get all his details, where he's staying etc., and then let him go. But he's not to leave the area. Then come with me to the hotel."

Chapter Thirty-Two

Agnes kept a good distance between herself and David Drummond as she followed him along the quayside. If he paused for any reason, she stopped and looked in a shop window until he moved off again. One time, while waiting for him to move on, she had asked herself why she was doing this.

He could simply be taking a stroll to work off the frustration of seeing the chief inspector catch up with Hargreaves before he did. Maybe he was simply going to call in to see his cousin in the restaurant. There were probably lots of reasons why he was ambling along the road. After all, where else did he have to go? If he went back to the hotel, he would very likely run into his two replacements. Therefore, given all that, why was she still following him? Nevertheless, here she was, trailing him along the road towards the Tyne Bridge.

Once he reached the foot of one of the towers supporting the Tyne Bridge he suddenly disappeared out of sight.

Blast, she thought, as she moved towards where she had last seen him. Where had he gone? She started to walk slowly around the tower when someone grabbed her arm. She tried to call out for help, but before she could utter a sound, she was dragged into the base of the tower and the door was slammed shut.

It was cold chill inside the tower and there was a musty smell of dampness. The lift that had once carried people from the quayside up to the bridge had gone, leaving only the empty shaft.

"What are you doing?" Agnes cried out as she swung around and came face to face with David Drummond.

"I could ask you the same question," he replied, smugly. "After all, you are the one following me."

Agnes was about to deny it, but then she realised he must have seen her at some point. "Okay," she rubbed her arm where he had grabbed her. It was quite painful. "Sorry about that. It's just that I had nothing going on this afternoon and when I saw you…Look," she spread out her hands and changed her approach. All she wanted was to get out of here. This hadn't been a wise move. "I've said I'm sorry, can I go now?"

"I don't think so." Drummond held out his hand in front of him and inspected his finger nails. "Once you get out of here you'll look for the kindly chief inspector. The man who has been drooling over you since you met up in the hotel the night George took his dear wife's necklace to pay off his mounting debts."

Agnes's eyes widened. "You already knew George had taken his wife's necklace? She narrowed her eyes. "Then why did you come to me earlier today seeking help?"

"Don't flatter yourself, Agnes," He snarled. "I didn't come to you looking for help. For goodness sake, I do this for a living. I simply came to find out what you already knew. Or, with some prompting from me, what you might surmise if given a little information to work on."

Agnes swallowed hard. She knew now that Alan had been right all the time. She should have stayed well away from his case and she should certainly have heeded his warning about Drummond. Yet she had enjoyed being involved with the investigation. And, as for his warning – well, it was definitely too late to back out now. However, if she was to get out of this alive, she needed to play for time.

Her mind was racing. Alan was going to meet her at the hotel for dinner, though that wouldn't be for another few hours. But then another thought crossed her mind. The door to the tower had been locked the last time she had tried opening it. At the time, she had been curious as to whether there was still a lift from the quayside to the road above.

However after a couple of enquiries at the hotel, she had learned the door to the tower was permanently locked now.

The hotel staff had gone on to tell her that the doors were only opened three or four times a year when the building was being checked over. But once the man was inside, he was supposed to lock it after him as it was likely he would be using the door on the bridge to walk along to the next tower. It had sounded complicated, but she had got their drift, well, sort of.

So, somewhere in all that speculation, did it mean that if Drummond had been able to gain access today, was there someone checking the tower and had they forgotten to lock the door? Was that person still somewhere above at this moment? But, more importantly, would they hear what was being said, get suspicious, and ring the police?

"Hang on a minute," she said, raising her voice in the hope someone was up there. At that moment she felt her phone vibrate in her pocket. She had turned it off while she was in the café and had forgotten to switch it back on. She hoped Drummond hadn't heard it. If he had, he would take it from her and destroy it. While she still had a phone in her pocket, she felt there was hope. "Earlier you said the chief inspector was drooling over me," she continued. "Is that really true? Have I missed something? Alan really likes me?" She giggled, trying to make it sound as though she didn't know about Alan's feeling towards her, though she had picked up on a few signs during the evenings they had spent together. "That is so interesting. I should have paid more attention. I just thought he was being polite."

"You know he likes you. Stop fooling me around. I could kill you with one shot." He pulled a gun from his pocket

"Then why haven't you?" Agnes drew herself up to her full height, hoping to look more confident than she felt. "Why did you drag me in here, if not to kill me? You could have killed me the moment you pulled me into this tower and walked out without anyone seeing you." She looked around the small space. "The walls are so thick no one would hear a gunshot, except, maybe, the birds." It was true; the towers were filled with kittiwakes. They had made the place their home over the years. "Yet you haven't pulled the trigger, why?"

Drummond held the gun to her forehead. "Before I kill you, I need you understand why I went off the rails, as they like to call it these days. I want you to know what my life has been like since I left Newcastle to train to be an agent. Yes, I got my dream job; a job I had always wanted. I worked damned hard to get out there in the field. But I found it wasn't anything like I imagined."

"By that, do you mean it was nothing like the *James Bond* films you used to admire?" Agnes said. "Did you think you would be sent overseas on a mission to save the world?"

"I see my cousin has been talking too much." His grin was sinister. "But, in answer to your question, if you had a dream, wouldn't you have been disappointed if it hadn't worked out? I wanted people to know who I was and why I was there. I wanted to be appreciated – admired. But…" Drummond paused momentarily. He lowered the gun as he reflected on the past.

Agnes took those few seconds to glance around the floor, hoping to see something she could grab to defend herself. She was disappointed; there wasn't anything except the piles of dust, which had been blown under the door due to high winds and the mass of bird droppings, all waiting to be cleared away by whoever did the job. "But," she prompted. She had to keep him talking.

"But nobody gave a damn," he yelled. "Nobody knew who the hell I was – and why would they? I was undercover all the time. To them I was simply another Brit in a suit. I was there to look out for them, but they didn't know it or if they did, they didn't give a damn. At first, I thought the pay would compensate for my disappointment, but it didn't. So I decided to turn things around. I devised a plan to use everything I had learned at MI5 to benefit me."

"So what did you do?"

"I think you have already guessed what I did!" Drummond pointed the gun at her again.

Agnes had begun to put the pieces together, but if she was to get through this she was going to have to keep him talking – even if it meant she had to listen to him crowing about how he pulled off the greatest robbery since… the movie, *The Italian Job.* "If I am about to die, then surely I am entitled to know how you stole the necklace from the museum. I'm sure it must have been very well guarded, you must have had an ingenious plan." She hated buttering up to this monster, but if it gave her a few more minutes, then she would keep up the small talk.

"I watched, listened and learned," he replied. "By doing that I found a loophole in their security. They all sat back and drank a champagne toast once they thought everything was in place. They said no one could possibly infiltrate the sanctuary they had created." He smiled. "Yet I did. I did it!"

"So where does Achmed fit into all this?" Agnes asked. She pointed towards the steps leading to the top of the tower. One of them wasn't quite as filthy as the others. "Do you mind if I sit down?"

Drummond waved the gun towards the steps. "Yes, sit down." He laughed. "At least you won't have so far to fall when I pull the trigger."

Agnes wanted to scream out at him. Tell him he was insane. But that would only make him angry and more likely to pull the trigger there and then. Instead, she moved across to the steps and sat down.

"Now where were we?" Drummond flapped the gun around as though it was a toy. "Ah, yes, Achmed. He helped me put my plan into action. He helped me get the necklace out of the building in London. Now he's here in Newcastle to make sure nothing goes wrong. I paid him to come here and get a job at the hotel so he would be nearby should I need him. Once I get the money for the necklace, I'll give him what we agreed and we will part company forever. But I will never forget him. He did well."

"What about the Andersons'?" Agnes asked. "Where do they fit into all this?"

Drummond sighed. "The Andersons' were simply the carriers. They brought the necklace to Newcastle. No one would suspect them of having anything to do with the theft. They are just a married couple on a short trip to see the sights of this northern city." He paused. "Anderson was meant to raise the alarm about the necklace being taken from his room. But he was not supposed to go overboard. It was just supposed to be another theft, plain and simple. Instead he went into hysterics."

"When questioned by the police Mr Anderson produced a photograph to prove it was his," said Agnes.

"He wasn't meant to show the damn picture to anyone." Drummond hissed. "I told him to take a photo of his wife wearing the necklace as proof it belonged to her. But he didn't. He damn well didn't!" He almost spat out the words. "If he had, the police would have accepted it and got on with the enquiry. Instead, the fool showed Chief Inspector Johnson the photo of the necklace in the massive display cabinet at the museum. Anyone with half a brain would have picked up on the true value of the necklace and worked out where the photo was taken."

"Why did you give him the photo in the first place? I mean, like you said, he could have taken one himself." Agnes spoke quietly and calmly. She had to keep him talking, but she couldn't afford to antagonize him any further. He was acting in a very volatile manner already. He didn't need any extra help from her.

"It was because he wanted something for a souvenir to remind him he had been at the heart of one of the biggest heists this country has ever seen. He said a photo on his camera wouldn't have convinced his friends he had been part of the theft. I insisted he must not bring the picture with him in case it was found. Once I was out of the country in some safe haven and Achmed was back to his homeland, Anderson could do what the hell he liked with it. He would be the one to take the consequences. Yet he brought it with him and then he showed it to a police detective." He shook his head. "I couldn't believe it."

For a moment he was silent. Then he glared at Agnes. "And as if that wasn't bad enough, you decided to poke your nose in. Why did you choose this week to come to Newcastle?"

There was a sound from somewhere above and Agnes turned to look up the staircase.

Drummond laughed. "Don't get your hopes up. It's only the birds. This place has been empty for years. I doubt your Prince Charming detective is going to float down and whisk you off to safety. At the moment he is probably interrogating George Hargreaves and whoever it was George was talking to."

Agnes knew that to be true. Her only hope was whoever might be working further up in the tower might hear them. "I'm sorry if my being here in Newcastle spoilt your plans," she said.

"It wasn't your being here that spoilt everything. It was your inquisitive mind. You could have stayed in the background like any normal person on holiday. But instead, you insisted on accompanying the detective wherever he went, especially after the pair of you found my bloody sister's body," he snarled. "Then you set about figuring how the thief got into the rooms and again, today at the café, working out who the thief was."

"I just happened to be with Alan when the body was found," said Agnes, hotly. "I certainly didn't go out that night with the intention of finding someone lying on dead on the pavement." She paused. "I'm sorry. It's your sister you're talking about, we should show some respect. I do hope they find the murderer."

Drummond shrugged his shoulders.

Agnes was appalled at his attitude. "Don't you care? Your sister and brother have both been murdered and all you can do is shrug. Why aren't you out there looking for the killer? The same person probably killed them both."

"Probably." He pulled a face and shrugged again.

"Go on. Think about it," he encouraged her. "I'm sure you will get there in the end."

Agnes leapt to her feet as the penny dropped. "It was you!" she yelled. "You killed both your brother and your sister. How could you do such a terrible thing?"

Drummond laughed. "It was easy. Look, I'll show you."

Agnes closed her eyes as he lifted the gun to her forehead.

"Open your eyes. Don't you want to see how it's done?"

Chapter Thirty-Three

Chief Inspector Johnson and his sergeant pulled up outside the hotel and hurried inside. In his mind, he knew he wasn't going to find Agnes there, but they had to start somewhere.

"No, she isn't in her room," said the receptionist, replacing the phone on its cradle. "Could she be in one of the public rooms?"

"She isn't in any of the rooms." Sergeant Andrews shook his head as he rejoined his boss. He had gone off to peer into the rooms on the ground floor while Alan made enquiries at the desk. "Perhaps she's just gone for a walk," he suggested.

"Then why didn't she answer her phone?"

"The battery might have run out."

"It can't have. She told me she charges her phone every night."

"Maybe she forgot last night." Andrews ventured.

"No. Her phone rang, but she didn't answer and it went to voicemail. If it was dead it would have gone straight to voicemail – okay?" Alan looked around the reception area as he had a thought. "Where's Drummond?" He turned back to the lady on the desk. "Would you please try David Drummond's room?" It was a long shot, knowing the agent was trying to keep away from the hotel. But he had to try all options.

"No reply," she said a few minutes later. "He must have gone out."

"I didn't see him in any of the rooms," said Andrews.

Alan turned away from the desk. "He's most likely looking for Hargreaves." He thought for a moment. "Unless he already knows we've got him."

"So you think he might have seen us escorting him and the man he was talking to back to the car?"

Alan nodded. "And if he saw that happen, then he knew Agnes had spoken to us; telling us about what she suspected." This was getting ridiculous. Having a sudden thought, he suddenly swung around and spoke to the receptionist. "Where is Achmed?"

"Achmed?" she asked "You mean the waiter who works in the bar?"

"Yes. Where is he?"

"I'll check," she said, picking up the phone.

Alan turned back to his sergeant. "If you're right and he is mixed up in this, then he has got to know something about Drummond that we don't."

"He'll be on duty in about five minutes," the receptionist said, glancing at the clock on the wall above her head. "He wasn't due to be here until five this afternoon, but someone has called in sick, so..."

"Right, we'll wait for him in the bar," Alan interrupted. "But if you see him before we do, don't make him aware we are waiting for him. This is police business."

The receptionist nodded.

In the bar, the two detectives chose a table at the back where they hoped they wouldn't be seen by anyone walking in the door.

"These damn mirrors might look very nice, but they aren't helping us at the moment." The chief inspector gestured towards the large ornate mirrors. "Hopefully they won't give us away until it is too late."

They didn't have to wait long before Achmed strode through the door. He was whistling to himself as though he hadn't a care in the world.

Alan waited until the waiter was well into the room before glancing at Andrews and nodding towards the door. He didn't want to give Achmed a chance to make a run for it once he knew they were waiting for him.

"Good afternoon," said Alan. "I'd like to have a word

Achmed jumped at the sudden sound of the detective's voice. He swung around and would have made a run for the door if Andrews wasn't barring his path.

"How can I help you, Chief Inspector?" Achmed asked.

"You can start by telling me where David Drummond is."

"Who?" Achmed asked.

"You know who I mean. David Drummond, your partner in crime." Alan paused. He didn't have time for all this playing around. "Before you carry on denying you know the man, let me tell you that he has already told us about you. He told us it was part of his job to follow you here because you were suspected in the theft of a valuable necklace." He looked at his sergeant. "However Sergeant Andrews has a theory and I think he is onto something." He nodded towards Andrews. "He believes you weren't working alone. He thinks Drummond was fully involved in the theft. That he probably masterminded the whole thing. But we also believe he will do anything to throw us off his scent even if it means betraying you."

"I don't know what you are talking about." Achmed was growing agitated. He waved his arms around. "I came to England to make a new life for myself. When I saw they were advertising for a bar waiter here at this hotel, I applied for the job and I got it. I have worked hard. Ask anyone – ask the manager, he will tell you."

"Achmed, you're not listening. Drummond has already given you up. He's looking out for himself. He is playing it from both sides. How else would we have known about you? Why are you still defending him?" Alan gestured towards a chair. "Sit down and think it through."

Achmed sunk into the chair and fell silent.

Alan could tell he was weighing up his situation. Achmed was probably trying to figure out how much Drummond had told them.

"I don't know where he is," Achmed said at last. He wasn't going to take the fall for this man. "That's the truth." He hesitated. "However, whatever David might have told you, I want you to be clear about one thing; I did not kill those people."

"You mean Drummond's brother and sister? Alan asked. He glanced at his sergeant. He hadn't expected Achmed to come out with something like that.

"They were his brother and sister?" Achmed leapt to his feet. "Are you telling me that the two people he shot dead were members of his own family?"

"Let's be clear on this, are you telling us Drummond was the killer?" Sergeant Andrews jumped in before Alan could open his mouth. "It was David's cousin, Gordon Peterson, who told the chief inspector the two murdered people were Drummond's family. But you are saying it was Drummond who pulled the trigger?"

Achmed flopped back into the chair. "He killed them," he sobbed. "I was with him when he did it. I told him at the very beginning, I would help him steal the necklace from the museum. I would help him to get away. But I was adamant I would not kill anyone. I am not a murderer. He brushed my concerns aside, saying murder would never be on the cards if we stuck to his plan. It was foolproof." He paused and cast his eyes down towards the floor. "Yet two people picked up on what he was doing or should I say, on what he had done." He covered his face with his hands.

Alan looked across at his sergeant. This was all very helpful, but if Drummond was capable of killing his own family, then he was more than capable of killing Agnes. She had been a thorn in Drummond's side from the very beginning. He had to find her. But where did he start?

"Okay, I accept you don't know where Drummond is," Alan said. "But is there anything you can tell me that will help me to find him before he kills someone else?"

"You think he is going to kill again?" Achmed looked up sharply.

"I think he might, if someone gets in his way."

"You mean the woman." Achmed sighed.

"You tell me," Alan shrugged, though he was seething inside. He had to get the truth from this man, even if it meant him sounding nonchalant.

"There was a woman staying at the hotel who was," he paused, thinking of the right words, "getting under his skin. He thought she had something on him, but he didn't tell me more. He asked me to drop something in her drink to make her a little unstable." He swayed his hand back and forth as he spoke. "He even gave me the little white pill. It was very small." Now he held his finger and thumb together to indicate the size of the pill. "He told me to go into her room once the staff had left and take her up to the storeroom at the top of the hotel. I said it wouldn't be easy to get into her room, but he assured me I would figure it out. That was all I had to do. He would do the rest."

"So, what do you suppose the rest was?" Andrews asked.

Achmed shrugged. "I don't know. But it could have meant he was going to kill her."

"And you didn't have a problem with that?" Alan snapped.

"Why should I? He had already killed two other people." Achmed paused. "But I didn't know they were his family."

"So it's alright to kill people as long as they aren't members of your family?" Alan would have loved to punch this man in the face. But he held back. If Achmed was to say he had been mistreated in any way all his evidence would be dismissed as harassment by the police.

"No. That's not what I meant at all. I just told you; I said at the outset I wouldn't kill anyone."

"Yet you didn't object to being there at the murders or helping Drummond dispose of the bodies." Andrews said. "As a matter of interest, what was the plan to dispose of Mrs Lockwood's body once Drummond had killed her?

"He wasn't going to kill her, as you would say; he was going to throw her off the roof. It would have looked like an accident. She was a nosey lady. She could have gone upstairs to see what was there and then accidentally fallen off the roof."

"So in your book, throwing someone off a roof with the intent to see them dead, isn't murder? Tell me, what would the people of your country call it?"

Achmed hung his head.

Alan didn't wait for Achmed to come up with an answer. His mind was fixed on Agnes. Where was she? Where was Drummond? From what Achmed had told them, it appeared Agnes had said or done something which made Drummond realise she was onto him. This was probably why he had told Achmed to drop something into her drink.

Luckily, Agnes had come around and escaped before Drummond had time to get up there.

Drummond had been very clever in not giving himself away later that evening when she had appeared unscathed from her ordeal. Even she had accepted he had nothing to do with her being drugged and hauled up to the attic. The only person she had seen in her room after the manager left was Achmed. Therefore, what was Drummond up to now? What would be his next move?

Obviously he would want to keep a close eye on Agnes. He would need to know what she was thinking. He might even have considered contacting her in an effort to keep up with what she thought was going on. Was that why he had met up with her today?

Agnes had told him about their meeting at the café when she called to tell him her thoughts on Hargreaves. Had he bumped into her 'accidentally' to find out what she knew or even what she might come up with if given a few hints?

Andrews opened his mouth to say something, but Alan held up his hand and sank into a chair opposite Achmed. He was still thinking everything through.

Was it possible Drummond was lurking around outside the hotel today when he and Andrews took Hargreaves into custody? Had he seen Agnes indicating to where George and James were talking? If she had foiled his plans to get to Hargreaves first, then might he be now taking his vengeance out on her? He closed his eyes. One thing was certain in his mind. He had to find her before it was too late.

"Take Achmed back to the station." Alan said, leaping to his feet. "I have got to find Mrs Lockwood, before anything happens to her."

Andrews grabbed Alan's arm and dragged him away from Achmed. "Think about it, sir. Where are you going to start?" He released Alan's arm. "I know you're worried, but you need to stay calm and focused. You can't do this alone. You need me with you, but we must have some other detectives scouring the quayside for both Mrs Lockwood and Drummond. Get another officer here to escort Achmed to the station and activate a search. But don't try to do this alone."

Alan knew his sergeant was right. He was thinking with his heart rather than his head. "Get onto the station and organize it. Tell them to get here as soon as possible."

Once everything was in place, Alan, and his Sergeant hurried out of the hotel in search of Mrs Lockwood. But where would they start looking?

Chapter Thirty-Four

High up in one of the four towers supporting the Tyne Bridge, Peter Noble, the young man whose job it was to do periodical inspections of the massive supports, was carrying out his duties. But today was different. Today he wasn't alone; he was accompanied by two men. One was a journalist from a local newspaper, while the other was the manager of a large restaurant close by.

The council had welcomed the local newspaper being involved in anything to do with the Tyne Bridge. It was the pride of Tyneside and any article about the bridge was welcome. However, they had voiced their surprise that a restaurant manager should be quite so interested in gaining an insight in the towers.

But Gordon Peterson had explained how his customers often asked questions about the bridge. "I simply thought it would be good idea to learn a little more. "Especially as my restaurant is so close to the base of one of the towers," he had told them. The idea had originally come from the recent course he had attended. 'Always try to give the customers what they want, even if it is simply a piece of information about the area.'

Peter Noble had been delighted to have the two men with him that day. It made a nice change to have someone to talk to other than the birds. Though, having already inspected two other towers, he was running out of things to tell them. "Is there anything you would like to ask me? I haven't said much since we came up here."

"I don't think so. I guess they are all the same," the journalist said. He yawned. "Once you have seen one, you have seen them all."

"Quiet, listen," said Peterson. "I can hear voices downstairs."

"I thought I had locked the door once they were all inside," Peter said. He tried to look down the stairs by hanging over the steel girders. "I can't see anyone."

The voices downstairs grew louder.

"Well there's certainly someone there," said the journalist. "I can hear them now." He turned to Peter. "Maybe you should tell those people to leave. If they are injured the council will no doubt be blamed."

"Quiet," Gordon hissed. For a moment he thought he recognised one of the voices as that of his cousin. But on reflection, why on earth would David be down there? He shrugged. Obviously he was mistaken. "Sorry," he said. "I thought I heard the voice of someone I knew."

Peter was about to call out to the intruders, but one of them spoke again.

"Open your eyes; don't you want to see how it is done?"

Now Gordon knew he was right, it was his cousin. What was David up to? Was this part of the case he was working on?

But when a woman's voice drifted up the stairwell, all three men gasped in shock.

"So you really mean it. You are going to kill me." Agnes desperately hoped she had been right earlier, when she thought she heard the sound of footsteps higher up the tower. She prayed they would hear her now and call the police.

"I would like my sons to know that I love them." She continued." I would also like Chief Inspector Alan Johnson to know that it was great meeting up with him again after all these years." She knew she was waffling now, but she was trying to buy some time.

Nevertheless, even standing there with a gun pointing at her head, she suddenly realised she had enjoyed meeting Alan. It had been fun and exciting. Being mixed up in a murder enquiry – even if it meant she would be the next victim – had given her something to remember. At least for whatever time she had left.

"Are you done?" Drummond asked. He held the gun at her forehead. "Can I kill you now?"

"No!" Agnes called out.

"For goodness sake, woman!" Drummond lowered the gun. "What more is there for you to say? Are you planning to re-write the history of the world in your dying hour?"

Upstairs, Gordon couldn't believe his ears. His cousin was down there threatening to kill a woman.

He looked at the two men standing next to him. Peter seemed rooted to the spot with a horrified stare fixed on his face. Who could blame him? However Lowry had managed to gather his wits together. He was already punching the emergency number into his mobile phone.

Gordon turned back to look down the stairs. He still couldn't see who David was talking to; though he had a distinct feeling he had heard that voice recently. However, there wasn't time to think about it. If he was going to be able to do anything to stop the killing, he had to get down there – and quickly. He carefully made his way down the stone steps, hoping the grit crunching beneath his feet wouldn't give him away.

Drummond twirled the gun around in the air. "So what do you want to know now?" He was getting bored; this had gone on long enough.

"You didn't tell me why you killed your brother and sister."

"They got in the way," David replied calmly.

Gordon was stunned. He stumbled and would have fallen if he hadn't caught hold of the hand rail in time. He would never have believed his cousin was capable of killing his family. But he had just heard him admit to it. He held his breath, hoping David hadn't heard him stumble.

"What was that?" David stopped swinging the gun around and turned it towards the stairs.

"Probably the birds," said Agnes. "I understand the place is filled with them.

"Damn birds!"

Gordon breathed a sigh of relief. It seemed he was safe, for the moment. He wanted to get as close to David as possible before he was discovered. He didn't have a plan; actually, he had no idea what to do when he got down there. But he knew he had to try to stop David from killing the woman.

He heard a slight sound behind him. He turned his head to see the journalist creeping down the stairs.

"The police are on their way," Lowry whispered. "DCI Johnson is already somewhere on the quayside; they're getting in touch with him."

The mention of the chief inspector took Gordon back to the day the detective came to the restaurant. He had a woman with him… He recalled she had found his cousin's body in the river. It was then that he realised that the voice downstairs was that of her – Mrs Lockwood.

"Good," Gordon whispered. "Now you should get back upstairs…"

"Are you kidding me? This story could make me bigtime. I am in this, whatever!"

Gordon realised that it was no good arguing. A journalist always put a good story first and there wasn't time to discuss the issue.

The two men crept slowly down the stairs. It seemed to be taking forever. Neither of them recalled it having taken so long to get to the top.

Gordon had thought about leaving the small group after seeing the first two towers. What more could there be to learn? He felt he could have won first prize in a competition about anything referring to the towers of the Tyne Bridge. Nevertheless, he had decided to stay with the tour. Now he was relieved he had made that decision. Though, on second thoughts, it could get him killed.

He stopped and turned his head when he felt Lowry tap him on the shoulder.

"What's the plan?" Lowry whispered.

"What plan? I haven't got a plan. How could you plan for something like this?"

"Okay," Lowry grinned. "Just kidding."

Gordon took a deep breath as he continued down the stairs. This reporter was either a brave man or an idiot. But then couldn't he say the same thing about himself? Drummond had killed his brother and sister, why would he hesitate at killing him? Shouldn't he be leaving this to the police?

"Enough!" Drummond's voice echoed up the stairwell. "I am tired of listening to you."

Agnes closed her eyes again. This was it. She was about to die. But she didn't want to see him pull the trigger. She wanted to see the faces of her boys and her husband, Jim… and Alan… But then she heard an explosion and felt something whiz past her head. It came from somewhere behind where she was standing.

Agnes opened her eyes hardly daring to believe she was still alive. She found Drummond lying on the floor in front of her. Blood was already beginning to pour from the gunshot wound between his eyes. A few feet away from his outstretch hand, lay his gun.

Still in shock, she slowly turned around and saw four men standing on the stairs behind her. One she recognised as Gordon Peterson, the restaurant manager she and Alan had interviewed earlier in the week. The other three men she didn't know. One was taking countless pictures of her and the man lying dead at her feet. The third, a young man in jeans and a high viz jacket looked like he was in shock. But lurking in the background was a man she knew she owed her life to. He was holding a gun. He had fired the shot which had stopped Drummond from killing her.

Chapter Thirty-Five

A few minutes later, the door to the tower burst open and DCI Johnson was the first to appear. He was quickly followed by his sergeant and several armed officers.

Alan was relieved to see Agnes standing there alive and well. Having heard a gunshot as he was approaching the tower, he had feared the worst. He had been worried when he received the call telling him there was someone in the tower who was threatening to kill a woman. No one knew who the people were, but he knew they had to be Agnes and Drummond. His concern had changed to anger, as they drove along the quayside to the tower. What the hell was she doing there? Hadn't he warned her about going anywhere near Drummond? Did the woman ever listen to anyone?

However all that was forgotten when he saw Agnes standing there with tears flowing down her cheeks.

"I thought I was going to die," she uttered. "He saved my life." She turned and pointed towards the staircase, but the man had gone. "Where did he go?" she asked. "I didn't even thank him."

Gordon and John turned to see Peter a short way behind them, but there was no sign of a man with the gun.

"Take a look upstairs." Alan said to one of the officers. Though he guessed the man was well away from the tower by now.

Gordon Peterson hadn't said a word. His eyes were still fixed on the body. Slowly, he began to make his way down the remaining stairs and would have stepped towards the body, if the chief inspector hadn't stopped him.

"I'm sorry, but you can't touch anything. Our scene of crime officers will be here very soon."

Sergeant Andrews had put in the call the moment they had smashed through the door and found the body.

Gordon nodded. "I understand."

"Did any of you see the man who fired the gun?" Alan asked the three men.

They all shook their heads.

"It all happened so quickly," Peter said. "I was the last one to come down the stairs. He must have been somewhere behind me. But where the hell did he come from – and how did he get in?"

"Okay, Alan continued. "The officers will escort you to the station and take your statements. Don't leave anything out and be sure to tell the officers where you can be contacted; it's likely we'll need to speak to you again."

"I need to stay here. It's my job to make sure the doors are locked when I leave."

"We will see to it today," said Alan.

One of the officers led the men out of the tower.

"Alan, do I have to go to the station?" Agnes asked quietly, as they stepped out of the tower and into the sunshine. All she wanted to do was to go back to the hotel.

By now crowds had gathered and were being held back by police officers. Cameras flashed as the witnesses strode towards the police cars. John Lowry nodded towards some rival journalists. They might have photographs of the aftermath, but he had caught the action.

"You will have to make a statement," Alan replied. But then he saw that she was shaking. "But I can send a WPC to the hotel if you would rather."

She nodded. "Yes please."

Alan called over to one of the officers and told him to take Mrs Lockwood to her hotel. "I'll come to the hotel as soon as I can," he told her, as she stepped into the car.

* * *

Back at the hotel, Agnes sank into a hot, scented bath. She had always found it a good way to relax and today was no exception. She had received a call from Alan to say a woman police officer would be with her in about an hour. Just enough time to pull herself together after her ordeal.

She had been foolish. No, it was more than that; she had been damn stupid to follow Drummond. He was trained to pick up when someone was following him. She was lucky to be alive. If it hadn't been for that man... She didn't even want to think about what might have happened. Yet she was going to have to go through the whole thing again when the police woman arrived.

As it turned out, the police officer was very nice; she sat back and allowed Agnes to tell her story at her own pace. She had obviously been trained in how to deal with people who had been stressed for some reason.

Agnes had thought she would break down during the interview, but she found herself totally at ease with the woman constable. Instead of it being a nightmare trying to go over what had happened in the tower, she discovered it was actually a relief to talk openly about her terrifying ordeal.

It was while she was explaining what she had gone through in the tower that she recalled those terrifying seconds when David was about to pull the trigger. It was then that the faces of her husband, Jim and their two sons had flashed through her mind. But then she had seen Alan standing someway behind them.

Why had he appeared in that fleeting moment? Could it be that he meant more to her than she realised? However, she didn't mention any of that to the police woman. When the officer left, Agnes thought about it for a while before deciding to go downstairs.

In the Drawing Room she ordered coffee. At first, she was concerned about bumping into Achmed. But she got chatting to the waitress, who brought her coffee. During the conversation, Agnes learned that one of the bar waiters, called Achmed had been arrested that morning.

Agnes tried to look surprised. "Oh my goodness, why was that?"

"I don't know," she replied. "He seemed like a nice man; always willing to help out. But, I suppose you never can tell what a person is really up to."

"That's true."

When the waitress was called away, Agnes sat back on the sofa and sipped her coffee. At least she felt safe now. Achmed was in police custody and David Drummond was dead. For a moment she felt sorry for Gordon Peterson. It was bad enough having two cousins murdered, but to find out that they were killed by their own brother was something else. She wondered what was going on at the police station. Maybe she should have gone there after all. She hated missing out on seeing all the pieces being put together. But thinking it through, perhaps she was better off where she was and no doubt Alan would fill her in with all the details later that day.

Chapter Thirty-Six

At the police station the three men gave their statements and left the building.

John Lowry couldn't wait to get back to his editor. His photographs would show that what had been going to be a simple story about the maintenance of the four towers supporting the Tyne Bridge had actually turned out to be an exclusive. No other journalist had been there and watched David Drummond being shot in the head just as he was about to kill someone else. Some officer had let Drummond's name slip in the interview room. It was a shame he hadn't managed to get the woman's name, though he did have photos of her standing there with Drummond's body crumpled at her feet.

* * *

Gordon just wanted to get back to his restaurant and have a stiff drink. Once Television News started broadcasting the incident, he would be receiving calls from other members of the family. What could he tell them? He had no idea that David was responsible for the deaths of Mary and Dennis.

Nor had he known that David was involved in the theft of a priceless necklace. He had only learned about that while at the police station. No, they hadn't said used the word 'involved'. That would have simply made him a part of a gang of thieves. They had told him David had been the thief. As far as they were aware, there were only three other people involved, but David was the top man. It was his plan; he carried it out. The others were there merely to help make the plan work.

It had been Detective Chief Inspector Johnson himself, who had informed him of this news.

At first, he thought the police might believe he had helped his cousin in the robbery, especially as he had been in London for a few days. However, the DCI assured him he wasn't a suspect. He had merely taken him aside to inform him ahead of the news broadcasts.

He took a large gulp of brandy and looked around the empty restaurant. Maybe it should remain closed tonight.

* * *

Peter Noble wasn't in a hurry to get back to the council offices. If he hadn't forgotten to lock the door to the tower, none of this would have happened. It could cost him his job. He could have sworn he had locked the door once he and the two men were inside. Was it possible that the lock was so old it hadn't clicked into place when he turned the key? That was one of the reasons he hadn't wanted to leave the tower earlier. He had wanted to place the key in the lock and turn it a few times to see whether it worked or not.

How was he going to explain it to his boss in the office? He could deny it all he liked, but they would probably see it as the two other men had – he had forgotten to lock the damn door. Then there was the other man. The man, who came from nowhere, killed the man who was going to kill the woman and then disappeared. His head was starting to hurt. All he wanted to do was to go home, but he couldn't do that. He had to go to the office and face the music, even if they weren't playing his tune.

* * *

Alan walked into the interrogation room and sat down. On his right was Sergeant Andrews and sitting opposite him was Achmed. A solicitor was sitting alongside Achmed.

"Drummond is dead," said the DCI

"You killed him?" Achmed asked.

"No. He was shot dead just before we arrived."

"How very convenient."

"We would have preferred to have spoken to him," said Alan, trying to stay calm. "But someone shot him before he was able to kill someone else."

"So you say," Achmed grunted.

Alan slammed his fist on the table. "Stop messing me around. This is not a cover-up. There were three witnesses who saw the whole thing as it happened. They were trying to get down the stairs to stop him; one was a journalist, he even took photographs. You are in a whole lot of trouble already – by your own admission you assisted in a theft, not to mention you were an accessory to murder. For goodness sake, we have been through all this. Why are you being so hostile now?"

Achmed looked down at the table, as though he was considering his options.

"What do you want to know?" he asked.

"For a start, how did Drummond steal the necklace?"

"He didn't tell me everything," said Achmed, quietly. "David didn't trust anyone. He only told me what he thought I needed to know."

"But you helped him steal the necklace. What part did you play?"

"There were two guards on duty outside the room where the necklace was displayed in a glass case."

"You mean the necklace wasn't stored in a vault?" Sergeant Andrews interrupted.

"No. Not at the time David stole it." Achmed replied. "There was a special viewing that day; important people from Europe were coming to see the necklace before it went on display to the public. He chose to steal it after the viewing, but before the necklace was moved back to the safe. Once in there he would find it much more difficult. Though not impossible," Achmed smiled.

The sergeant gestured for him to carry on.

"His plan was simple. He went into the room with the officials, but he didn't come out at the end of the viewing."

"But weren't the people checked as they went in and again as they came out?" Alan asked. He sounded exasperated.

"Yes, they were, but David made two identity cards. One was for me one was for him. Both had the same name and details, but each showed a different photo of the named person. I have to admit he did a great job. They looked like the real thing." He paused expecting one of the detectives to say something, but they remained silent. "Anyway, David hung around until a group of people were waiting to be admitted. He acted as though he was part of the group. The guards hardly looked at his identity card. They just ushered everyone through the door." He looked at the chief inspector. "Can I have a glass of water?"

Alan turned around and nodded at the guard at the door.

"So what happened next?" Alan asked, turning back to Achmed.

"At two o'clock the doors were closed and at half past two, the guards went off duty and two new men took their place. That's where I came in. I ran up to the men and showed them my card. I told them that I was late for the viewing due to a traffic problem and that I need to get in as soon as possible or I would miss the whole thing."

"And they let you in – just like that?" asked Andrews.

Achmed threw his hands in the air. "Why wouldn't they? I was smartly dressed, I had an identity card and I had a foreign accent. There was no reason why they shouldn't believe me."

"Someone down there needs to overhaul the security system." Sergeant Andrews was disgusted that they had got into the room so easily.

"So, you are both in the room when the display was brought into sight?" Alan asked. This was taking too long. "What happened next? Did Drummond pull a gun and threaten to kill everyone if the necklace wasn't handed over to him?" He knew that wasn't the way it had gone down. It would have been all over the papers. There would have been no way they could have kept that quiet. He just wanted this guy to get to point.

"It was simple," Achmed continued. "When it was time to leave, I made sure I was the last to leave the room. I showed my card to the guys on the door and they ticked off my name on their chart. Meanwhile, David placed himself behind a small screen near the door. Once everyone was clear, the doors were locked with David still inside. All he had to do was to open the glass case and take the necklace – simple as that." He clicked his fingers. "But that's ridiculous," Andrews exclaimed. "He couldn't have simply walked up to the bullet-proof glass case and opened the door. I understand there was a coded lock on it – and what about CCTV? They must have had a camera in the room."

Achmed nodded. "Yes, there were two coded locks on the case and both had different codes." He laughed. "Much good they did! As for the camera, David was prepared for that. He had something with him, which he was going to insert into the camera to fool the men watching the TV's." He shrugged. "David tried to explain it to me, but I didn't understand."

"I don't believe it. It's not possible." Andrews looked at the chief inspector. "You haven't said anything. What are your thoughts on all this?"

Alan was thinking back to when he and Agnes were talking to Gordon Peterson. He had said something about his cousin David being a wizard with locks and codes and computers. He hadn't taken a lot of notice at the time. But now it was beginning to make sense.

"It is possible." Alan said, slowly.

"But even if he did get the necklace out of the case, how the hell did he get out of the locked room," Andrews was beginning to lose his temper. "Surely there were guards at the door day and night?"

"There were. Or at least that was the plan." Alan looked at Achmed. "That's when you made your second entrance, isn't it?"

Achmed glanced at Andrews and grinned. "Your boss has it." He looked back at the chief inspector. "Shall I tell him or would you like to carry on?"

Alan gestured for him to carry on. "It's your story."

Achmed shrugged. "The necklace wasn't due to be moved until later in the day. Therefore I was to stay in the building. I had afternoon tea. Then I looked at all the portraits, trophies and rare books until it was time for the guards to change again. Once the new guards were in place, I ran back through to where they were standing. I started shouting that someone was trying to steal a painting from the wall in the gallery and the security man was being attacked. I told them they needed to hurry. They didn't hesitate. They followed me down the corridor and into the gallery. That's all the time David needed to break the code on the door and get out of the room. Once out, he set the code again and he was home and free."

"You're telling us it was as simple as that?" Andrews stood up and paced around the room. "I am in the wrong job! Even an idiot would know that if you have a priceless antiquity in your care, you need better security than a glass case and two men standing guard on the door."

"You are admitting that you acted with David Drummond while he stole the necklace from the museum?" The chief inspector said calmly.

Achmed nodded.

"One more thing," said Alan. "How could Drummond know there would be a two hour gap between the viewing and the necklace being moved back to the vault? Surely once the viewing was over, the safest thing would have been to remove it from the room."

"There was the possibility of another viewing," Achmed replied.

"What other viewing? All the people expected at the event were there. You said so yourself." Andrews had had enough of all this.

"There was no one else, Sergeant," said Alan. He was watching Achmed closely. "It was Drummond, wasn't it? It was he who rang the museum and informed them another person or persons of importance were interested in seeing the necklace privately."

Achmed nodded. "We needed time. If they thought someone of importance was coming to view the necklace, then they would leave it in the viewing room. As far as they were concerned, there were guards outside a locked door."

"Who was the important person?" Andrews asked.

Alan looked at Andrews. "Who do you think?"

"You don't mean?"

Alan nodded. "I think that just about wraps it up. I'll leave you to finish off here while I go and check out how the other team got on."

* * *

Earlier, another group of detectives had been out trying to catch up with the man who had bought the jewellery from Hargreaves. It was important they caught him before he had the chance to pass on the priceless necklace to anyone else. They knew that once he heard Drummond was dead and Hargreaves was in custody, he would realise that it wouldn't be long before the police were onto him. It was likely he would panic and try to get rid of the antiquity as soon as possible.

So far, the news wasn't good. The police had persuaded Hargreaves to get in touch with this man and tell him he had another necklace to sell. Unfortunately, so far, the man hadn't answered his phone.

"Keep me informed. And keep trying that damn number." Alan yelled as he strode out into the corridor. "We haven't got much time. The news could break any time now. Once that happens we will never find him." He knew all the loose ends were never tied up on the day of an arrest. But a great deal of money was at stake here. Yet more than that, the reputation of the United Kingdom was at stake. Once it became known that the necklace had been stolen days after it had arrived in the country, not to mention how easily it had been taken, the security of the nation would be the laughing stock of the world. If it was the last thing he ever did, he had to find that damn necklace.

He looked at his watch. Did he have time to ring Agnes? He needed to know that she was alright after her ordeal. Damn it! He wasn't going to ring. He was going to go to the hotel and see for himself.

"I won't be long," he called out to Sergeant Andrews as he passed the office door. "I've got my phone."

Andrews was about to ask where he was going, but stopped before he had uttered a word; he knew exactly where his boss was going.

* * *

At the hotel, Alan found Agnes in the Drawing Room.

"How are you?" He took off his coat and sat down next to her.

"Better than I expected," she replied. "The officer you sent to take my statement was very kind and understanding. I felt at ease talking to her." She paused. "Have you learned the identity of the mysterious man who saved my life?"

"No and I doubt we ever will." Alan was thoughtful for a moment. "But I would hazard a guess that he's the agent London sent up here to watch Drummond."

He was still puzzled how the guy knew where Drummond was at the time – unless he had been listening in to police radio calls. Or could he have managed to place a bug on Drummond. Who could have got that close to him...?

At that moment a thought entered his mind. Terry, the new waiter in the bar; was it possible he was really an agent? Alan recalled a moment when Terry had brushed against Drummond very briefly when he stepped back to admire the table he had cleaned with such gusto. Drummond had mocked the man, but it could turn out that the waiter was far cleverer than he was. It would be interesting to see whether or not Terry turned up at the hotel ever again.

"Okay!" said Agnes. "I realise that there are some things we will never know. But I find it very frustrating."

"What things?"

"Things like, why was David Drummond running away from the murder scene," said Agnes. "If he had shot his brother where we found the blood and then bundled him into the van to dispose of the body, why didn't he get into the van there and then? Why run away? Where was he going?"

Alan sighed heavily. She was right. Why was Drummond running away? Achmed had said he was in the van with him. It would take two at least to throw the bodies in the river. Had he been running towards the crime scene and not away from it? Could Alice Thurgood have made a mistake about which way she was facing when she took the photo?

"Anything else you think needs an answer?"

"I was under the impression Drummond knew the people on the yacht; the one that moored on the quay the morning he was following me. If so, where do they fit into all this?" Agnes shrugged. "Maybe I got it wrong and he was just interested in the boat. I have to say it really was quite something."

"Like you say, there are somethings we will never know for certain," said Alan. He would speak to Andrews about Agnes's thought later. But for the time being, he wanted her to believe the whole thing was over and done with.

She smiled. "I was thinking it might be nice to take a walk. I feel the need to get some fresh air. Do you have time to come with me?"

At that moment Alan's phone rang.

"I guess not," she said.

Alan answered the phone and listened patiently, while Andrews told him that at long last the man, who was buying the jewellery from Hargreaves, had answered his call.

"Hargreaves has arranged to meet him in their usual place," Andrews continued. "I gather it took a bit of persuading on George's part as the stolen items are usually dropped from the hotel windows. They only meet when money is being paid out." He went on to tell the chief inspector where the meeting was to take place.

"I have to go," said Alan.

"I know," Agnes replied slowly. She glanced down towards the floor. But then she looked up sharply. "Take me with you."

"What?" Alan gasped. "Haven't you had enough? You could have been murdered this morning."

"Take me with you," she repeated. "I'll stand across the street. I'll stay out of your way, I promise. But I need to come with you. I want see this through to the end. Please Alan."

Alan shook his head. There wasn't time for this. "Okay; get your coat. But be quick."

About ten minutes later she arrived in the reception area of the hotel.

"What kept you? Alan looked at the large handbag on her shoulder. What do you need that for? I thought you were only going to get your coat."

"I thought I might need some money afterwards and then I wondered whether I might need some credit cards..."

"We haven't got time, Agnes. Come on!" Alan ushered her towards the hotel entrance.

"George meets up with this man near The Millennium Bridge," Alan told her.

"What do you want me to do?" she asked.

"What do you mean? We agreed that you would stay well clear of the action." Alan replied. He knew from the beginning this was a bad idea. Yet he had the feeling she would have followed him anyway if he hadn't allowed to her to come with him. "Don't you understand? If George sees someone he recognizes his reaction could give the game away. It could blow the whole thing. We have one chance to get the necklace back, Agnes. We can't let it slip away."

Agnes nodded.

Outside the hotel, Agnes stayed on the same side of the street, while Alan crossed the road and sat on a seat near the bridge. There were still a few minutes to go before the meeting was to take place.

Alan pretended to look at a newspaper he had picked up in the hotel shop while he was waiting for Agnes. Out of the corner of his eye, he saw a couple of his detectives strolling along the pavement. Someway behind was George Hargreaves and behind him were another two detectives. So far, it looked good. All the detectives looked like tourists or men discussing business. No doubt there would be another two or three men or women on the other side of the road. However, looking around to check it out might only result in him drawing attention to himself.

Keeping his head buried in the newspaper, Alan continued to watch Hargreaves as he walked to where the meeting was to take place. His detectives were doing a good job of being discreet. If he hadn't known who they were, he would never have guessed they were police officers tailing a suspect. Now everything was in place. All they needed now was for the dealer to show.

* * *

The minutes ticked by. Hargreaves had reached the point where he was due to meet the dealer. George had told the detectives that he sometimes had to wait a couple of minutes before the man appeared; most likely due to the guy being over cautious.

Hargreaves stood by the railings and looked down into the water just as he did every time he waited for the dealer to show up. He knew this had to go down well. His wife had been to see him at the police station. Tears had flowed down her cheeks when he explained why he had done it. She was so sympathetic. If only he had explained it all to her, he – no, they, wouldn't be in this mess now. She had promised to stand by him, but she had also told him he must help the police.

* * *

Alan continued to watch as a man walked towards Hargreaves. The man paused and leaned over the railing and looked down at the river. This could be it. This could be the man who would lead them to the valuable necklace; a coup that would put the Newcastle Police Force at the forefront.

Then it happened. But not at all what the chief inspector had been expecting.

There was a traffic accident. A car pulled out just as a lorry was passing. Didn't the driver of the car see the huge lorry? How could he have missed it? Nevertheless, it happened. And the traffic was brought to a standstill.

Even though the officers across the road were supposed to be undercover, they abandoned their posts and hurried across to speak to the driver of the car.

Alan turned his head for one second to see what the commotion was about, but when he swung back, he found the suspect had gone. Hargreaves was alone. Where the hell had the suspect gone?

The detectives, who had been trailing Hargreaves, rushed up and placed handcuffs on his wrists. Andrews was one of them. Once Hargreaves was secured, the sergeant hurried across to his boss.

Alan stood up and threw the newspaper in the bin in disgust. "What the hell is going on? Those people are supposed to be undercover detectives, yet they give up on a case for a minor traffic incident!" he roared. "The man has got away. We've lost him!"

Suddenly they heard a loud cheer from across the road.

"I don't think we have," Andrews grinned. "Look." He pointed across towards where Agnes was standing. At her feet lay the man Hargreaves had been meeting. She raised her handbag and waved at Alan.

"I don't believe it," said Alan. "I sent her over there so she wouldn't get caught up in the action."

"It seems the action seeks out Mrs Lockwood," Sergeant Andrews replied as they both hurried over the road to get their man.

Once the detectives had the dealer safely in custody, Alan turned to face Agnes. "I told you to stay away."

"I did stay away," Agnes said. "I stayed over here just like you said. But I wasn't going to let him run past me and get lost in the crowds after all the trouble he's caused."

Alan didn't reply. She was safe and that was all that mattered. But he would give the officers who had deserted their posts a stern talking to when he got back to the station.

"I'll finish off here," said Andrews. "Why don't you both go for a coffee somewhere?"

Alan was more than happy to do that. He told Sergeant Andrews he wouldn't be long as both he and Agnes strode across towards the café by the Millennium Bridge.

"It's over," said Alan. "We have the killer and with a bit of luck we will get the valuable necklace back, together with all the other jewellery taken from the hotel." He paused. "Or at least we will have an idea where to start looking for it." He looked down at his coffee. "What are you going to do now?" He was dreading the answer. He knew she would be going back home at some point, but he hoped that it wasn't going to be too soon.

She smiled. "I'm going to stay on at the hotel for a little while longer. There are still some places I would like to visit. "I don't seem to have had the time this last week."

"Would you like to tell me more about your plans over dinner?" he asked.

"I would be delighted," she replied.

Shortly afterwards, Alan escorted Agnes back to the hotel and told her he would pick her up at seven o'clock sharp.

* * *

Later that evening, as Alan and Agnes strolled past Bessie Surtees House, he suddenly remembered the person she had seen at the window.

"You know, we never did find out who was at the window the night we found the body," he said, glancing upwards. "All the key holders still swear they had the keys in their possession the whole time and were nowhere near the building."

Agnes thought about it for a moment. Suddenly she stopped in her tracks. Turning around, she stared up at the window.

"Oh my goodness!"

"What is it?" Alan turned his attention to the window expecting to see someone looking down at them. But the window was shut tight and the whole place was in darkness. "Did you see someone?"

"No." Agnes grew very excited. "But I've just had a thought."

"What is it?"

"On the night of the murder," she continued. "I know I saw someone closing the window. Yet, the staff says no one was there."

"So?" Alan looked puzzled. "Where is all this leading?"

"Don't you understand?" Agnes said. "It can only mean one thing. What I saw at the window that night must have been a ghost!" she cried. She looked back up at the window and clasped her hands together. "Alan, this is so exciting. We could do a ghost hunt or something. We could..."

"Oh no... Agnes, I think..." Alan began.

However, whatever Alan thought was left unsaid when Agnes linked her arm in his and began to lay out her plan...

The End

About the Author

Since finishing a comprehensive writing course with The Writers Bureau on September 27th 2001 (a Certificate of Competence proudly hangs on the wall of my study to prove it), my writing took off. Many of my articles and short stories were accepted and published in several magazines here in the UK. These magazines include *The People's Friend*, *The Lady* and *Scottish Life*. A couple of my short stories also appeared in *Anthologies*.

Firstly, I concentrated on writing articles. Here I enjoyed researching and writing about the towns, cities and historical buildings around the area where I live: Jedburgh, Lindisfarne and Newcastle on Tyne, to name but a few. My husband, being a keen photographer, accompanied me and took photographs of the various places of interest to go with my writing. But after a while, I decided to change my stance and set my imagination to work on writing short stories.

Strange as this may seem, I always began my short stories at the end. By that I mean, I thought of a last line, which would also become the title of the story. Only then did I begin to work on the story itself, making sure the last line ended the whole thing perfectly.

Then, for some reason, I decided I needed to move on and to write a full blown novel. My first published novel was The Trojan Project, a suspenseful conspiracy thriller. The sort of story readers can get their teeth into. Writing for magazines can be restricting. Therefore writing a novel meant I was able to really let my imagination run away with me. And it did. I let my hair down and brought all the horror and terror I could think of into the story. There were times when I couldn't believe it was me who had written it.

From there, I went on to write a fun romance, Divorcees.Biz. A novel where I was able to show there really is a lighter, more fun side to me. Here I created four divorced ladies who, when out for a few drinks together one evening, decide to set up their own dating agency in order to find new men for themselves.

Only Twelve Days was my next novel. This is a love story set back in the late 70's; a time before computers and mobile phones took over. The outline of this story had been mulling around in my head for some time before I actually got around to writing it. I really enjoyed writing it and I am so delighted I did, because of all of my three novels, this is my favourite.

Lastly, I put together a collection of twelve stories previously published in UK magazines. These are all light-hearted and so easy to read. Some are quite uplifting, if you happen to be feeling a little down.

Before I go, I should add that I am a member of the Society of Authors and have been for several years. I am also a member of the Society of Women Writers and Journalists, as well as being an Associate Member of NAWG (National Association of Writers Groups).

I have a website (http://www.eileenthornton.com/) which I hope you will visit, and also a blog at http://www.lifeshardwinehelps.blogspot.co.uk, where you will find I let my hair down and talk about everything and nothing.

Also by the Author

- A Surprise for Christine
- Divorcees.biz
- Only Twelve Days
- The Trojan Project